Dream Chasers

*The final instalment in the
Victorian Meryen Saga series*

Matthew Faraday, squire of the mining village
of Meryen, decides to hold a May Day festival. But the day is spoiled for him when he
argues with spirited Clemency Kivell, the girl
he loves. Meanwhile, trouble is brewing in
the village for more than one family. Matthew
struggles to cope without Clemency's support
– but when Clemency realizes her feelings for
him, has she left it too late?

Recent Titles by Gloria Cook
from Severn House Large Print

The Meryen Series

KEEPING ECHOES
OUT OF SHADOWS
ALL IN A DAY
HOLDING THE LIGHT
DREAM CHASERS

The Harvey Family Series

A STRANGER LIGHT
A WHISPER OF LIFE

Dream Chasers

A Meryen Saga
Gloria Cook

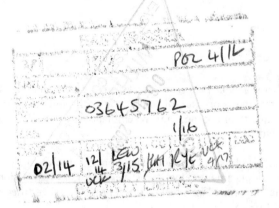

Severn House Large Print
London & New York

This first large print edition published 2011
in Great Britain and the USA by
SEVERN HOUSE PUBLISHERS LTD of
9-15 High Street, Sutton, Surrey, SM1 1DF.
First world regular print edition published 2009 by
Severn House Publishers Ltd., London and New York.

British Library Cataloguing in Publication Data

Cook, Gloria.
  Dream chasers.
  1. Cornwall (England : County)--Social life and customs--
  19th century--Fiction. 2. Cornwall (England : County)--
  Social conditions--19th century--Fiction. 3. Large type
  books.
  I. Title
  823.9'14-dc22

ISBN-13: 978-0-7278-7927-1

Severn House Publishers support The Forest Stewardship Council
[FSC], the leading international forest certification organisation. All
our titles that are printed on Greenpeace-approved FSC-certified paper
carry the FSC logo.

Printed and bound in Great Britain by the
MPG Books Group, Bodmin, Cornwall.

To Bernice and Tina

One.

It was an amazing sight and so out of the ordinary for Meryen. The predominantly copper mining village was having its traditional day off for May Day but it was about to experience a whole new festival. This year, added to the usual garlands of greenery adorning the porches, and the window boxes bursting with daffodils, crocuses and white hyacinths, all indicating the fresh, hopeful colours of spring, there were reams of crisp green, white and yellow bunting festooning the cottages and shops, the inns and the hotel. The ornate lamp posts in the High Street were linked with bunting and spun round with flora.

On the doorstep of her music shop, her arms folded snugly, breathing in the mouth-watering smells wafting up the street from the bakery, Clemency Kivell was imprinting on her mind the cheerful bustle of the villagers, from the urchins to the well-to-do. There was a particularly infectious buzz of excited expectation among the mining fraternity, replacing the usual weary solemnity of setting off for a day's hard and dirty, sometimes perilous, labour. There were no carts laden with mine props or

7

ironmongery rumbling down the street, heading for the Carn Croft Mine and the Wheal Verity, a few miles away on the heath and scrubland of Nansmere Downs. Instead, small home-made conveyances were being trundled along in the opposite direction by a merry force of willing arms, heading for Church Field with things needed for the festival; trestles, crockery and cutlery, table linen, foodstuffs and, for the non-Methodists and Bible Christians, the all-important barrels of ale.

Many of the arrangements for today had evolved from Clemency's ideas and suggestions, solicited from her by Meryen's young squire, Matthew Faraday. A Londoner, he had held the position of squire on the Poltraze estate for just three years, following centuries of rule by an old Cornish family. A former military man, partially blinded in an act of courageous rescue from long years ago, Matthew Faraday had spent his first months at Poltraze as a committed recluse, offending the hard-working, poor but proud miners, the traders and the genteel people alike by shunning them.

Meeting Clemency had led to a dramatic change of heart and, after his first tentative steps to acquaint himself with Meryen and gain its respect by discreet acts of charity, some scant public appearances and a little perseverance, Matthew had put forward the idea of holding a much larger May Day celebration to fully bring in a new era.

With the village more or less won over, anticipation had risen. New entertainments and prizes for competitions had been announced. The poor, out of hope and gratitude to escape life's drudgery and deprivations awhile, and the rich, hoping to get on good terms with the area's principal man, had both drifted into calling the new festivities Squire's Day. So Squire's Day it was to be, and long may it continue, was the hope of both Clemency and Matthew.

'You waitin' for something, miss? I'll run an errand for'ee, for the right price, of course.'

Glancing sideways, Clemency set disdainful eyes on the young scruff who had crept up to her. 'Go away, Sammy Juleff.'

'Why should I?' As always, in the miner's son's avid expression there was cheek and challenge.

'Because I told you to.' Clemency did not have regard for the undersized shoeless brat dressed in filthy clothes, his skin blotchy and his long hair greasy and ratty. His upper lip was plastered with days' worth of grimy nose effluence and he smelled like a drain.

He shifted directly in front of her, his dirt-ingrained hands on his ripped shirt front to display bloodied knuckles, his way of boasting he'd won a recent scuffle, either with one of his warring siblings or another village boy; someone he had deliberately provoked, no doubt. 'There's no need to be like that, miss. Why you being like that? I was only being civil to'ee.'

Ignoring him still, although keeping wary,

9

Clemency returned, 'You've never known a civil moment in your life, Sammy Juleff, and you can't be trusted one jot. There's no point in you lingering here. You don't bother me at all, and you've got as much chance of stealing something from me as you'll have of not getting your ears boxed if you don't disappear this very instant.'

'Stuck-up mare!' Sammy gagged up a huge ball of spit and projected it expertly on the ground below the granite step, inches from the hem of Clemency's bell-shaped skirt. It was just one of his alarming varieties of disgusting habits, which included relieving himself in public. He peppered his next words with vulgarities. 'Owning a shop don't make you no lady, nor none of your finery. You aren't much, only think you are 'cus the squire's got the heat for 'ee. Might have been some bluish blood in your lot back-along but it's got mixed with thieves, gyps and madmen. There was an old woman of yours who saw into minds and the future. Witchery, my father calls it. And your father was a rotten murdering whoremonger. You Kivells should all be sent off on the convict ships. You should...'

Clemency let the boy spew out his spite. The reference to her late father was true and it was hurtful but she was strong enough not to let it bother her publicly. People across the narrow street from her, all neat and reputable sorts, some carrying stuff to take to Church Field, where the festival was being held from eleven o'clock, paused and listened, while shaking their heads and tutting. The Juleffs – this boy, his oft-drunken father, his trollop banshee of a mother and the rest of the obnoxious brood – were a blight on Meryen. Clemency's shop adjoined the New Oak Hotel, owned by Logan, who was one of her brothers. If Logan heard the boy's increasingly vile abuse he would thrash him soundly.

'Hello, Abe!' Clemency waved to a young man pushing a handcart her way.

'Clear off, Sammy!' Abe Deveril yelled with grim meaning. A Juleff only understood threats. 'Or I'll tan your rotten little hide.'

'Can't make me go and you couldn't catch me anyhow, you bleddy cripple!' As suddenly as the boy had appeared he shot off. Sammy was sharp and clever. Abe Deveril had been a miner until he was badly injured in an underground accident, but he was still strong and a Cornish wrestling champion, perfectly able to mete out a little just punishment where he saw fit. From a safe distance, Sammy turned round and used both his hands in an insulting gesture to Abe.

Clemency decided to give Sammy Juleff no more thought. She came from a powerful protective family and, although the Juleffs harassed and sometimes terrorized others, they knew better than to repeatedly offend a Kivell. She hoped the Juleffs would keep in line at the festival.

Abe now made his living doing odd jobs. An only surviving child, he was much admired for

11

his good humour and his dedicated support to his elderly feeble parents. Three years ago, Abe had saved the lives of two local girls, one about to be married to Logan Kivell, when Clemency and Logan's crazed father had tried to murder them in a cruel act of arson. Abe had declined Logan's offer of financial support, preferring to go his way, but he allowed Logan and Clemency and their large extended family to give him regular work.

One of his legs weakened from being badly twisted, and the other from loss of muscle, Abe shuffled up to Clemency. 'That damned little heathen. Good morning, Clemency. I've lined the cart with straw and a horse blanket. Your instruments will be quite safe. Ready to go?'

'I am,' she smiled. Although from different backgrounds, the pair had a valued friendship three years strong, bonded on Poltraze land when Clemency had come across Abe – who was there to poach – in the act of aiding young Hattie Faraday, the squire's sister, after a riding accident. All three had become friends, but terrible circumstances – another crime perpetrated by Clemency's father – had soon changed that for Hattie.

Clemency and Abe made a striking contrast. She was fashionably dressed, although just for the occasion, preferring easy-to-wear clothes. Her dark-amber hair hung in loose ringlets under a fine bonnet trimmed with white, green and yellow ribbons. He was dark-haired and unfussy in his best white shirt and waistcoat.

While Clemency radiated a dazzling superiority to the world, Abe showed a quieter self-confidence.

Clemency opened the shop door, its overhead bell ringing melodiously. 'Mr Keast, if you please?'

'At once, Miss Kivell.' Her shop manager, who lived with his wife above the premises, signalled promptly to his youthful assistant, then barked orders at him.

Clemency stood aside, humouring Mr Keast's disdain for a young lady lifting anything heavier than a teacup. She and Abe passed grins. It was well known that Clemency had the strength of will and the toughness characteristic of all the Kivells.

Mr Keast was tallish and straight-limbed but carried the swollen waistline and podgy features of the well-fed middle aged. His bristling eyebrows rose in a look of horror when he realized that the dozen finely crafted string and woodwind instruments under his care, to be put on display at the festival – albeit carefully wrapped in their cases – were to be loaded into a common handcart, along with the painted wooden sign echoing the words above the shop: *C. A. Kivell's Music Emporium. Instruments of the Finest Quality*. With the Kivell family now scattered world wide, Clemency's acquisitions were eagerly sought after by the best homes and many other esteemed outlets.

'Miss Kivell, I really think it would have been wiser to have allowed Mr Faraday to organize the conveyance of the instruments to Church Field, as he had offered.'

'So you keep saying, Mr Keast,' Clemency replied, not keeping the haughtiness out of her voice. 'Mr Deveril has my total confidence. Now let us get on. I want the instruments set up securely in my allotted tent. Men from Poltraze will watch over them, but you are not to leave the tent. You are responsible for taking any orders, and ensuring that the instruments are returned in mint condition. I have many other things to see to in Church Field. The festival has attracted a lot of interest and people will be coming from Gwenap, Redruth, Camborne and even Truro.'

'Indeed, Miss Kivell,' Mr Keast said, evidently a little flustered. He closed the shop door gently, yet the bell clanged, as if to mock him. He glanced through the window, past the range of wares set on stands, in the direction of Mrs Keast. She was now stationed in her portly manner, her starched cap tied neatly under her sharp chin. She was to take charge of the shop until ten thirty, although little in the way of custom could be expected on Squire's Day, when the village would more or less shut down.

Mr Keast then turned to glare at Abe and sniffed derisively, then set on his pale-faced assistant, a weedy looking but eager individual. 'Boy! Boy! Get yourself round on the other side of this contraption. Ensure nothing gets bumped about or receives the slightest scratch or dent.'

* * *

When they set off, Clemency led the procession, Abe trundling the cart along with care. High Street was an undeserving title for the rough main thoroughfare of the village. In many places it afforded one-way traffic only. It reared up slightly this way and was quite bendy, but it gave little difficulty to Abe, despite his injured legs.

Mr Keast stuck out his chin, embarrassed by the indignity of travelling beside a labourer in this lowly manner. Mr Keast held a good position in the shop, which was newly built nearly three years ago. His rooms were well furnished and comfortable, with the prized convenience of indoor plumbing. His wage was the best he had ever earned. It was his misfortune, however, to be employed by a woman; one who was high minded, stubborn and outspoken to a bullish degree, and not yet twenty years of age! Only the Kivells would allow such an outrageous thing. In his opinion, Miss Clemency Kivell's only saving graces were that she still lived in the once self-contained community from where the Kivells had originated – Burnt Oak, a hamlet a mile and a half outside Meryen, which was sandwiched between Poltraze's sprawling lands – and was an obedient daughter to her widowed mother.

Mr Keast smirked at Abe, although he did so without turning his head. If the odd job man had designs on the young lady they were absolutely hopeless. She was shockingly independent and

15

never seemed to swoon over the eligible men, as normal young females did. God help the man she did finally marry; he would discover no obedience in her.

Church Field was tucked away behind the churchyard's high back wall. The tower of St Meryen, the grey-stone Norman church, seemed to float along against the virtually cloudless bright blue sky. The church had been much updated by the former squire. It now had Victorian stained glass windows and brass fittings, wide gravelled paths, and boasted pews impressively carved by Kivell craftsmen. Clemency was proud of the abundance of her family's stamp in and about Meryen, including the introduction of the Miners Institute and the Kivell Charity Fund – both set up between squires, when Poltraze had lain abandoned for two years – though there were some who resented the Kivells' ever widening grip on respectability and local affairs.

The shorn and well-raked field was accommodatingly flat and was awash with people, including servants and workmen from Poltraze who were setting up for the day's delights, all under the direction of the estate steward. The sideshows, tents and tarpaulins had been put in place the day before; the important ones, like Clemency's, and the grand dais for the squire's opening speech, backed on to the shelter of the church wall. Traders' stalls, those for home produce, and craft stations, were all being set up

16

with their particular wares. In a straw-strewn pen was a greased piglet from Poltraze Farm, which would be released inside a long run of straw bales, the prize for the first person who could catch and hold on to its little, squealing, pink body for a full three minutes. Jugglers, country dancers, fair entertainers and animal acts, tinkers and gypsies were drifting in. The ancient maypole was set in the middle of the field and was resplendent with bright new ribbons.

It was fast becoming a highly successful scene, and nature wasn't to be left out. With the sky set fair, the breeze was soft and refreshing, and the hedgerows that sheltered the rest of the huge field had bursts of wild daffodils and creamy primroses, some pink and red, and purple dog violets. Shiny yellow celandines glowed further down near the ditches. New leaves were springing out on the trees and the budding hawthorn bushes showed a little of their delicate, lacy, white may flowers. Clemency was pleased to feel a growing sense of an almost childlike thrill from the people. Even though Meryen was a large rambling village – virtually a small town – of good repute and some local importance, the lives of the poorest inhabitants were all too often ones of debilitating drudgery, and for those further up the social scale life could be dull and repetitive. This new Squire's Day, thrown by a man who was closed and enigmatic to all but those nearest to him, held promise for something to look forward to year upon year. Squire Faraday, who so far had done little speaking for his self, had pledged, through his steward and the vicar, that if anything proved a failure today he would see it was improved on next time.

When they had arrived at Clemency's music tent at Church Field and the cart had been unpacked, Clemency walked beside Abe while he pushed his cart off out of the way. Most villagers were used to their friendship, but one or two frowned on it. Some didn't approve of any villager mixing with a Kivell, due to their colourful God-shunning history.

'Have you heard lately how Miss Hattie, I mean Lady Stapleton, is?' Abe said, referring to their former mutual friend. She had left Poltraze for Devon shortly after her ordeal, and had married a year ago.

'Her husband, Sir Julian, informed the Faradays that she has delivered a healthy son; that would be three weeks ago. I sent Hattie a letter of congratulation and a small gift for her son. I've received a short reply of thanks from her personal maid.' The shame of what her father had done to Hattie – abducting her and planning to murder her, along with Logan – would always burn deep in Clemency, although it was soothed a little by the fact that it was her actions that had led to Hattie and Logan being saved. They had both paid a heavy price, however. Hattie had been scarred on the face while trying to escape. Seth Kivell's brutality had cost Logan an arm. Seth Kivell had died the same

18

day from a heart attack, although it was whispered in the family that one among them had cleverly poisoned him. 'I feel sad that Hattie doesn't want to keep in contact with me, but I understand. She suffered a lot of trauma.'

'You've got nothing to blame yourself for, Clemmie, remember that.' Abe rubbed her arm. He was never shy in giving her little affectionate gestures. 'Well, Miss Hattie's got the rich titled husband she'd always wanted, and now a son,' Abe mused.

'I don't suppose Hattie will ever come down to Poltraze again. Her parents miss her dreadfully.'

'Are those quaint old dears coming this afternoon? I've heard a lot about them; would be fascinating to see them at last.' Like all the villagers, Abe was evidently curious about the squire and his strange sounding family. Eccentric, spaniel breeding parents, and a cold-hearted widowed sister who, until apparently forced to stop by Squire Faraday, had morbidly mourned her Army officer husband's tragic death for a great many years. 'What about the woebegone Mrs Hartley?'

'I don't know about Jane Hartley. She's a snobbish misery. I'm glad she's moved out to the former dower house on the property. I rarely catch sight of her nowadays. But Mr Faraday senior and Mrs Faraday will be putting in an appearance. I think the people will like them. They're jolly and sweet. I adore them.'

Abe looked at Clemency. 'I bet they adore

you.'

Clemency liked the way Abe's ready smile reached all the way to his bright eyes. 'They treat me like a little girl at times. Mr Faraday says I'm like a third daughter to him.'

Abe put his head close to hers in a confidential way. 'He'd probably like you as a daughter-in-law. The squire's in love with you, after all.'

'Abe, why do you say that?' Clemency acted as if she were horrified; as if Matthew Faraday had never declared his love for her soon after she had discovered his presence at Poltraze, when they had shared a passionate kiss. Matthew's constant warm attention to her while she was at Poltraze had led to inevitable rumours in the village. She liked Matthew very much, but back then, at such a young age, she had told him she wasn't ready for a commitment. She still felt the same way. She enjoyed the sort of freedom that men took for granted and she wasn't about to give it up. She was making her own way in life. Love and marriage could wait. It would shock her mother and women in general if she admitted she did not greatly desire to have children. She was quite determined that unless she met the man who was her absolute soul mate she would always remain single.

'Wouldn't you like to be mistress of Poltraze?'

'Heavens, no.'

'Because it's a dark, old place with an unfortunate history?'

'That doesn't bother me at all. And I'd sooner marry you,' she laughed.

Abe rolled his eyes and laughed with her. 'Heaven forbid, I'd never cope a single day with you.'

'That said, I'd better get on. I need to check all is happening in the right places and everyone is sure of their part in today's activities.' She glanced round. 'Oh...'

'What?'

'That man over there, now striding away. He's a stranger to me but from the glimpse I caught of him I'd say he had the unmistakable look of a Kivell.'

'Well, that's not unusual. Members of your family have come back from far away to pay a visit on several occasions.'

'On the other hand, he could be anyone, but if he is family I hope he comes to the festival. I'd be interested to meet him.'

Two

The man who Clemency had spied leaving Church Field made his way to the New Oak Hotel, where he had stayed the night before. Harry Bonython received a few nosy stares on the way, but people were evidently too busy preparing for the day's fun ahead to linger and try to strike up a conversation with him. He wasn't bothered if his Kivell likeness had been noted; people would soon learn exactly who he was. The doorman ushered him inside the square-built hotel, which took up the corners of two roads, and seemed grandly out of place in the rustic simplicity and roughness of the industrial village. The spacious foyer was milling with guests, but there were no staff in sight. With a playful hand, Harry zinged the bell on the long, curving reception desk.

The duty clerk sprang up from behind the desk – he had been picking up fallen papers. He was thin and bony, his cheekbones and teeth sharply prominent, and Harry wondered, as he had on arrival here last evening, why kin of his should employ such a gruesome sight at the point of welcome in their fine new establishment. The clerk had a spray of yellow crocus

22

and green leaves in his buttonhole. Daffodils and white camellias and masses of greenery filled large vases and urns everywhere.

'Please accept my humble apologies, Mr Bonython, sir. What may I have the honour of doing for you this fine morning? I trust everything is satisfactory with your room? I do hope you and Miss Bonython enjoyed your breakfast.'

'Rest assured, Mr...?' Harry said, speaking quietly.

'Clench. Oswald Clench, sir, always at your service.' The clerk bowed sombrely, the crown of his head revealing a few strands of greying hair springing up from his shiny, bald scalp.

'I enjoyed breakfast in the grand dining room. Miss Bonython was happy with the room service. Is Mr Logan Kivell on the premises? He is expecting to receive me. I sent him a note last night.'

'Indeed he is, Mr Bonython. He informed me before he entered his office just ten minutes ago. I'll show you there myself.' Mr Clench slammed his palm down three times on the desk bell. A younger man came hurrying. He was dressed in the uniform of the hotel – dark and light brown, with gold cord trimming – which blended in discreetly with the handsome entirely oak furnishings. He was of a good build; an attractive soul, unlike the simpering clerk. 'Take over the reception desk, Scobel, and keep sharp. I will be but five minutes.'

Scobel sprang to the post with an easy

expression. 'Good morning, Mr Bonython.'

'Good morning to you, Scobel,' Harry replied, impressed by the prompt, polite service.

Mr Clench led him past the wide staircase, then turned down a short corridor. Its walls, like everywhere in the hotel, were half panelled and then wallpapered above to the picture rail. Elaborate mirrors, paintings and tapestries, many bearing the signatures of Kivell crafters, covered nearly every space. In lighted niches were statues, busts and colourful vases. A handsome Grandfather clock stood beside the office door. Logan Kivell was obviously proudly displaying the various fine crafts of his vastly creative extended family.

Harry was delighted he shared the same blood, through his maternal grandmother. She had left Burnt Oak with her Falmouth-born husband, moving to Yorkshire, where Reuben Bonython had quickly established a number of carpet factories. Four years ago, Harry, an only child of an only child, had inherited the company. His grandmother had always kept in touch with her family and had proudly told Harry how much he reminded her of the warrior-like breed she had sadly left behind at Burnt Oak and Meryen. She had made him promise to look them up one day. He was doing so now, leaving his business in trusted managerial hands.

Harry had been fascinated by his grandmother's tales of Cornwall, hemmed in by cliff and sea, its wealth elicited from the sea, and the minerals lying down in its depths, playing a rather cruel game of 'come and get me, if you dare', but producing a highly skilled workforce and some of the world's most ingenuous inventors and engineers. Harry would often take a look at the sea: the rugged north coast – Portreath was short miles away, where the copper ore was shipped out – and the milder south coast, where his grandfather had hailed from. Sadly Harry's last Bonython relative, a cranky nonagenarian spinster, had died some years ago.

Harry liked to be away from the huge cities and their churning populations. He found Cornwall had much simple beauty, and the haunting loneliness of the moors touched his soul. There was something captivating about the indigenous people. Some of their thick burrs made their words as indistinguishable to him as a foreign language yet he seemed to grasp their meaning; something in his blood, he was happy to suppose. The people had a way of gazing at 'furreigners' – summing them up – and were both wary and welcoming. Harry's grandmother had been deeply superstitious, a Cornish trait harking back to their Celtic roots, and Harry had seen evidence of that in the village. There was a lot of natural greenery decorating Meryen, but no one was wearing green clothes. 'Wear green, wear black,' his grandmother had fearfully warned. He had heard the word 'rabbits' a lot this morning – 'rabbits' was said first during a greeting on the first day of a month to bring good luck.

Harry had intended, after seeing Logan, to go straight to Burnt Oak, but on hearing about Squire's Day, he had decided the ideal place to meet many of his distant relations, uncles and aunts and cousins aplenty, all at the same time, was at the festival. After an early breakfast, he had wandered about the village and ended up in the field behind the church. He would return there after his meeting to take in the sights of Squire's Day properly.

'There's no need to announce me, Mr Clench.' Harry eased the skinny clerk aside. 'Mr Kivell won't mind me going straight in. I'm part of his family.'

'If I may say so, I thought as much.' Mr Clench was probing for details, but Harry waved him away. He tapped on the solid oak door and went in. 'Logan, good morning. May I come in? I'm Harry Bonython.'

All smiles and interest, Logan Kivell sprang up from the stately kneehole desk. 'Harry. I'm so pleased to meet you. So, we are kin. If I'd known beforehand that you and Miss Bonython were on your way to Meryen, I would have been here with my wife to greet you. I wish you a belated welcome to the New Oak. You have come at a very good time. There's a new festival starting today, and family from Burnt Oak and much further away, like yourself, will be here.' Logan proffered his right hand. The left sleeve of his bespoke coat was almost empty, the cuff neatly stowed in the pocket. His button-

26

hole was filled lavishly with maidenhead fern and white and yellow flowers. 'Do sit, Harry. It's not too early for you to take sherry? I trust the hotel is providing splendidly for all your and Miss Bonython's needs.'

'We've never received better service and the surroundings are excellent and comfortable, Logan.' Parting his tails, Harry eased himself down on a red leather button-back sofa. Logan offered him hand-rolled Turkish cigarettes from a carved box and passed him the sherry. Logan sipped his own drink, leaning against the side of his massive desk. The men were roughly the same age, in their late twenties, and of the broad, dark build, with a hint of the common man, and the certain toughness and arrogance that typified a Kivell. Harry's clear-cut, sound features, like Logan's, showed a certain generosity. Both of them had neat black side-burns.

'I noticed from the shop names there are many family businesses hereabouts,' Harry said. 'I've heard about Chy-Henver, the carpentry and cabinet making works on the outskirts. It was one of the first to be taken over by a Kivell, wasn't it?'

'Jowan Kivell owns Chy-Henver. He had it jointly with another cousin until a year ago, when Thad took his high-born wife to live near Truro to start up on his own. If you can hold your liquor and enjoy a party, Harry, you'll find Jowan a riot.'

'Oh, I'm definitely game for that and a lot

27

more,' Harry said with an outrageous gleam in his smooth brown eyes. Lounging comfortably, he finished his sherry. Logan refilled both glasses. 'I strolled to the field where this Squire's Day is to be held. It seems to be very well organized.'

'A lot of recommendation can go to my sister, Clemency, for that. She's on good terms with the squire and his doddery old parents. Matthew Faraday would like to make her his wife; to become the mistress of Poltraze. Jowan also has her in his sights. The men have absolutely nothing in common but neither will do for her, so Clemency says. She can be quite a force to be reckoned with.'

'She was probably in the field. It's a pity I didn't see her. She sounds fascinating. I have no brothers, as you do, but I have brought my adopted sister, Georgette, down with me. She's another headstrong young lady. She could have married a hundred times over by now if she wasn't so particular. I fully expected this baronet's son to ask for her hand in marriage but suddenly she would have none of him. It was a pity. He was a thoroughly decent sort. Meryen, and Cornwall, in fact, won't suit her tastes at all, but because she has no family of her own she is interested to see the origins of the one she was adopted into. I know only a few details of the family down here. You are married, you say?'

'I have a very wonderful wife, Serenity. We have an infant son and a newly born daughter. I

28

also have a ward, Jenny Clymo, a sweet, quiet girl, whom I took under my wing the same day I bought my house. I allowed the former owner, a dear, elderly lady who had nowhere else to go, to stay on. Serenity and Jenny were formerly bal-maidens – that is, mine workers. We are an unusual mix at Wingfield House, but it works really well and we are all content.'

'I'm glad for you. I have noticed that some of the ordinary, local young women are very attractive.'

'Have you a special someone, Harry?'

'I did have until a month ago. She jilted me for a scrawny weakling who has seventy-five thousand a year. So there was no contest.' Harry shrugged philosophically. 'I had a lucky escape – she was of little substance – but it has made me wary of the intentions of women. Well, I had better go up and rouse Georgette. She always takes mountains of time to get ready. I don't want us to be late for the festival. I'm so glad to be in Meryen, Logan.'

The men shook hands. 'You will not receive a bill for your stay here. Family never charges family,' Logan said.

'As you wish, I thank you. Perhaps Georgette and I can accompany you and your household to the festival?'

'We'd be happy to have you with us. We'll meet in the foyer at ten forty-five.'

'Georgie, can I come in?'

'Of course you can, Harry.'

29

Harry entered one of the hotel's best single rooms; its theme lavish oriental. The curtains were pulled back and gentle sunlight streamed in, highlighting the sumptuous reds and gold in the gilt wood frames, cranberry glassware, and the velvets and sateens, and adding a healthy glow to his sister's perfect, pale complexion. 'Good heavens! You're up and dressed and your hair has even been done.'

Georgette Bonython swung round from the long wardrobe mirror where she was appraising her superb, fair reflection. She put her white-lace mittened fingers together and chuckled. 'Oh, Harry, you should see your face. You look utterly silly with your mouth sagging open and your eyes seemingly about to pop out.'

'Well, I've never seen you completely turned out this early before. You look utterly gorgeous, as usual.' His compliment contained reams of proud admiration. Harry had been spellbound by Georgette from the first time he'd seen her, he then at seven years, and she a three-year-old orphan who had been snatched from the flames of her razed home; the fire in which her coal-mine owning parents had perished. She was devoted to him in return. Georgette reminded Harry of a porcelain figurine, but she was not a fragile little thing. She had a fierce will to survive, created out of the hard discovery – suffered at such a young age – that her security and all she cherished could suddenly be wrenched away. She found all things academic boring but otherwise excelled in the attributes expected of a young lady. At home she was Society's darling. To Harry, she was his treasure. Even though he had considered the young and presentable Rupert Goring an excellent match for Georgette, he was pleased she had so far turned down all her marriage proposals, although she had left a string of broken hearts behind her. Goring had turned up at the house on the day of her and Harry's departure for Cornwall and pleaded, or rather demanded, to see her, necessitating Harry to get harsh with him and have him escorted out. A relieved Georgette had declared Goring a nuisance, and had refused to talk about him after that. Harry was sure he would find it difficult to adjust when his sister finally moved out and had her own household, and was glad to be able to put off that day for a while longer.

Harry held out eager hands to Georgette.

She glided to him in her satin-topped buttoned boots. 'It's easy to look good with the way you spoil me. Have you met your relation Logan yet?'

'Yes, he's a very good fellow. I'm sure we'll love meeting all the family.'

'I can't wait. Perhaps I'll find a suitable husband among them.'

'I hope not, Georgie.' Harry frowned. 'I don't want to leave you down here. I want you to settle very close to me.'

'I was only joking.' Sliding her hands from his, Georgette closed in for a hug. They wound their arms round each other. She hid from him

31

an expression of desperation that would have surprised and alarmed him.

He tenderly kissed her brow. 'But husbands and wives have a tendency of ending up barely tolerating each other. This way we will always have each other.'

Releasing herself from his arms she returned to the mirror and teased at her tight ringlets. 'Harry after we've left Meryen, please, please could we travel overseas? I'd so love to see something of the world before I settle down. I don't want to recommence all the social rounds yet. Say yes, Harry. I really, really don't want to...' Georgette realized he was not listening to her. He seemed to be in a trance and his eyes were staring into nothingness.

'What is it? What's wrong?' She ran to him and clutched his coat lapels. 'Are you feeling ill? Don't be ill, Harry, I couldn't bear it.'

Harry blinked and came to with a shudder. 'Oh, Georgie, I—'

'What happened to you? It scared me.'

'I'm sorry, my darling. It was nothing really. It was a little strange and silly. I got this feeling there was something bad looming.' Georgette's panicky expression made him regret his last words. He had been foolish. Georgette relied on him, she needed him and she only really trusted him. It was no wonder she scorned love and marriage as of yet. Hopefully, when she grew older and wiser, she would find her perfect partner. 'As I said, Georgie, it was nothing. Let us go downstairs. You will enjoy meeting Logan.'

32

'No! Tell me what you felt just then and don't lie to me.' Georgette was wringing her hands. *Please God don't let it have anything to do with my predicament.*

He took her gently by the shoulders and smiled his most reassuring smile into her frightened eyes. 'Georgie, you mustn't worry, trust me. It was merely some business matter that popped into my mind. It doesn't affect you at all. And I've absolutely no need to worry about the business; all is in the most excellent and trustworthy hands.' He kissed her furrowed brow. 'Now, let us enjoy the day. I've been out in the village and I know you'll find it a quaint and distracting little place. Shortly, we will be able to experience the rural delights of this new festival.' The festival – he got that strange ominous feeling again.

'Very well.' Taking a deep breath, Georgette smoothed out her marble-toned complexion. Then she put herself into Harry's arms and sought his comforting, strong embrace. 'Promise me you'll always take good care of yourself, Harry. I couldn't go on without you. I'd rather be dead.'

Three

Clemency angled her head as she appraised the three-foot high dais, which had been built for the opening festival speech. It was of polished wood, and two wide steps were placed on one side. At each corner was a hefty pillar and these were topped with a flat, crisscrossed frame – the support for the jade-green, scalloped-edged canopy. The drapes of the canopy were tied to the front pillars by gold coloured cords and trimmed with extravagant tassels. It was tasteful and opulent and was provoking a lot of overawed gazes.

'Do you like it, Clemmie?' Jowan Kivell asked. He was studying Clemency with the same intensity she was using on the dais. He had drawn up the plans for the dais and his six-man workforce, all family members, had fashioned and erected it.

'Meryen has seen nothing like it. You've surpassed yourself, Jowan.' Clemency's gemstone eyes expressed her pleasure and approval. 'It's fit for a king.'

'It's certainly good enough for the squire and his party,' Jowan said, closing his eyes at the thought of the man he held in low opinion.

Matthew Faraday had chosen Poltraze, a gloomy, lumbering old house, to deliberately hide away in. The partial loss of his sight – while unsuccessfully trying to save his brother-in-law, a fellow officer in the Life Guards, from dying in a fire – was not good reason enough, in Jowan's view, to shun all contact outside his family. The Faradays were a rum lot, each living in their own peculiar closed world. Why did Clemency, with her vibrancy, intelligence and keenness of will, continue to seek their company? 'Our Uncle Cary and Uncle Henry, as two prominent members of the whole community, will be up there too. Meryen should have a mayor, and one of our uncles should hold the position.'

'I agree.' Clemency viewed Jowan wryly. He was in his habitual stance, his mighty shoulders squared, and chest out and his chin thrust up to the heavens. A man proud of his background and achievements, he had no time for those he considered weak and a failure, hence his swipe at Matthew Faraday. His big, sinuous hands, which honed perfect pieces from all woods, were also quick to defend the family honour and had been bloodied in the odd brawl. He was a freewheeling man and a dedicated woman-izer. Women of all ages, and from all classes, vied for his attention and a great many dreamt of becoming his wife at Chy-Henver, where his workshops and huge rambling cottage were, just outside the village. Clemency always brushed aside Jowan's regular hints of him

35

wanting to form something closer with her. She believed he would not be ready to settle down until well into middle age, and then he would make some fortunate woman a good husband, for he had a good heart and a level temper.

Clemency's ears picked up a squabble some distance away at the Punch and Judy puppet theatre. Sammy Juleff and four of his scraggy siblings – the youngest two, infant boys with poor limbs, were nauseatingly soiled – were being chased away by the angry puppeteers, who were being jeered at by the little rabble. No doubt the Juleff litter had been creeping in under the booth curtains and grabbing at the puppets. 'Those obnoxious brats,' Clemency seethed. 'I've a good mind to ask the constable and the Poltraze men to gather them up and lock them in a cellar for the rest of the day.'

'Never mind them.' Jowan slid an arm round her waist. 'Come with me, Clemmie. I want to talk to you somewhere quietly.'

She stiffened, sure that she knew what was on his mind. 'I'm busy. I've still got lots of things to do here.'

'Running the whole of this event is not your responsibility.' Holding her tightly, Jowan propelled her away quickly, denying her the choice to stay put. He stopped when they were behind the dais and near the church wall, totally out of sight. He went on, sounding frustrated, 'Matthew Faraday has put people in place to see things run smoothly today. He didn't intend for you to run yourself ragged. Damn it, Clemmie!

He doesn't own you, although every fool knows he wants to. And that would be ludicrous; you're not in the least bit suited.'

'And you and I are, I suppose you think? So, it's this again, another of your silly hints about us getting married.' She struggled and shrugged him away. 'Why do you persist in this, Jowan? To prove to yourself you can have any woman you want? This is too much. When will you get it into your stubborn head that I don't want to marry you, not now, not ever?'

His dark eyes flashing with intent, Jowan grabbed her by the arms and held her fast. 'Listen to me seriously for once, hothead. You've got to get married one day. You want children, don't you? Logan will be here soon and he'll be full of talk about his young family. I want that too. I've had enough of going from woman to woman. I want a lifetime partner. You have my word as a Kivell that I'd be true to you. Think about it, Clemmie, think hard. We've got so much in common. We put the family first in all things. You're proud of the Kivell name, so you wouldn't have to change yours. Neither of us would be happy with some-one from a different background. We both had vengeful murderous fathers; we know how traumatic that was. We both like our freedom. Marrying me wouldn't change that for you, I promise. I wouldn't tie you down or interfere with your music business or anything else that you'd want to do. We'd complement each other, I'm sure of it. I'm not asking you to give me an answer now. Think about it, talk to your mother, I'm sure Aunt Verena would be happy to see us together. I'm sorry to be forceful, Clemmie, but it can be so hard to get through to you.'

All through his declaration, Clemency had stared at him unblinking. Feeling the pressure where his hands had been, she rubbed her palms there. She dropped her eyes a moment. That had been a long, passionate speech for Jowan. She admitted to having some respect for his persistence. It seemed she had presumed things about him wrongly. 'Jowan, I've listened to you and now I beg you to listen to me. I will never marry you. There are three good reasons why I will not. I'm not in love with you and you are not in love with me, and very importantly, I can only ever think of you as a cousin. You're like a brother to me. Anything closer between us would be inappropriate and very wrong.'

He grew as still as the graves beyond the church wall. He had not seen things in that way before – that to Clemency a union with him would be paramount to incest. It hurt like hell. Cold fingers of disgust twisted up his insides for even alluding to marriage with her. He knew he could never look at her in the same way again. Clemency was right. He wasn't in love with her and never would be. She was strikingly beautiful and admirable in many ways, but she could be mulish and even contemptible at times. They would have inevitably vied for supremacy, and perhaps even ended up loathing each other. Squire Faraday, with his withdrawn and poetic ways, would never fit the bill for her either. Would any man? She was ardently a Kivell, happy to live at home at Burnt Oak Farm with her immediate family, but otherwise she was a nonconformist. He nodded his full understanding and then he walked away.

'Jowan, I'm sorry...'

He did not turn round, and strode away at the back of the stalls.

'Damn you, Jowan!' Clemency pressed her fists against her hot, humiliated face. He had made her feel she was a faithless lover. And there had seemed to be more in that simple nod of acceptance. Scorn? Or had it been pity for her she had seen, reflected through his hurt and sorrow? She didn't deserve to be deserted as if she had done something wrong, and he'd had no right to take offence. 'Why did you have to spoil this day?'

She hurried into the churchyard via the nearby arched wooden gate. Then she ran until she was sure she was obscured among the oldest graves, which were overhung with beech trees, laurel and holly bushes.

Until Jowan's plea – in which he had sounded at first as if he had the right to her, despite his fine sentiments – she had felt that the uncommon freedom she enjoyed, her music business, and the security of living at home with her beloved mother, was enough to satisfy her for a long time yet. But now, for the first time ever, she felt lonely and empty. It scared her. She put her hands to her heart only to be chilled through with a sense of debilitating panic and despair. Beneath her clutching fingers it was as if there was nothing there, just a void like an empty grave.

Four

The instant he had scurried out of Church Field, Sammy Juleff shook off his four younger siblings and slunk off alone, the way he preferred to be. He hated being ordered to watch out for Joe, Jacka, Eddie and Becky, aged from two to nine years. They were a crabby, whining lot. He hated being in his dump of a home, where hunger and cold were the norm and fleas, lice and even rats reigned free.

Zack Juleff, a simian-looking hulk, his brain long dulled by overkills of grog, had brought his family to Meryen when Sammy and his older sister Nora were babies, after absconding from Chacewater, owing rent on his miner's cottage and other debts. He had taken over a long-disused hut, once well built but now falling to bits, at the back of the village close to a thicket of hazel trees. Zack had allowed the trees to grow over the hut and hazel saplings had sprung up around it, and the family had to wend their way through them, often bowing their heads, to reach home. It suited the Juleffs and the villagers that their unsanitary, stinking home was hidden from view, but the nearest neighbours, several hundred yards away in a row of miners' cottages, complained to no avail about the constant vicious quarrels, shouting, screaming and foul language that was carried to their ears every day. It was Sammy and Nora's job to haul water home from the stream that divided the village from the downs; water that was never used for washing Juleff bodies, clothes or dishes. Zack and his slovenly wife Ruthie eased their thirst only with beer and grog. The Juleffs lived upstream and the villagers were disgusted and berated the family for using the stream as a midden; again to no avail.

Sammy, Eddie and Becky worked at the Wheal Verity as riddlers, sieving the spalled ore that had been hammered down by boys, older girls and old women. They would set aside the largest pieces to be spalled again. The only protection against the burning sun, the wind, the rain and the hail was a sort of three-sided shed with a canvas roof. The children walked the mile or so to the mine barefoot. Then, for a little protection against the rough stony ground, they pulled on 'shoes' that Nora had fashioned out of rags, canvas and animal skins; anything she could beg from the villagers, traders and workshops. Thirteen-year-old, waifish Nora tried her best to be a mother to Sammy and the others. Becky did not have a bonnet with long protective flaps, a gook, like the other balmaidens, but every morning at dawn, when Nora woke the children to send them out, invariably without breakfast, for the seven o'clock start of the shift, she tied a voluminous scarf around pocket-sized Becky's head, pulling it forward as a little safeguard for Becky's reddened, sore eyes.

Sammy's arms were strong enough to cope with the big oak, iron and mesh sieve, and the weight of the ore he shook in it, although at the end of every shift he had a badly aching back, neck and shoulders, but Eddie and Becky, their noses running with grime-laden snot, struggled with much smaller loads on their sieves. They cried and snivelled, coughed all day long, making the Mine Captains and managers fear they would peg out and die on the spot. If the pair was dismissed, even out of genuine concern, all three children would be thrashed by Zack for 'letting him down', so all three pleaded that Eddie and Becky be allowed to stay on.

All the children were usually given a little something to eat – a piece of hevva cake and hunk of bread to share – every day in the crib shed. ''Tes from Jesus,' the chapel-goers would say. 'He always provides, so you can thank Him for that.' Sammy always grabbed the offering and never said thanks to anyone. He'd decided he would never thank Jesus until He provided him with a better life. He'd scrabble away with Eddie and Becky, who would snatch at his arms for their share of the food. Sammy would break the food in half. One half was for him, the second half he split in two for his brother and sister. The women and girls drinking tea and eating and chatting, and the other children, would scoff or tut-tut over the manner in which

Sammy, Eddie and Becky gobbled down their food, making sure they never missed a crumb. After that, Sammy and his brother and sister would annoy the workforce by staring at every bite they brought to their own mouths. 'Ungrateful imps, no manners at all,' people would mutter. They'll all end the same way as their father, mother and their sister at home.'

Nora was not sent to the mine to toil. When her mother Ruthie could be bothered to drag herself off her straw mattress she would abandon the infants Jacka and Joe, and go out and earn pennies by lifting her skirts to any man who'd have her, and poor Nora was forced to sell herself too. The severe beatings Nora received had taught her not to object, but she cried for hours afterwards each time. Sammy couldn't stand to hear her suffering. He hated his parents, really, really hated them. When they were slumped in a drunken stupor he got revenge by kicking them and throwing things, even filth, at them. He would happily smother them both to death, but he feared not escaping in time, and being dragged off to the workhouse, more than the hangman's noose or transportation to the Colonies.

Once, Sammy had made a bid for total independence and had set up home for two nights in a hideout in an abandoned fox's lair. He'd made it comfortable with stuff he'd stolen: a rush mat, a small horsehair blanket, and a bucket which, set upside down, served as a seat. One of his rotten siblings had squealed to his father that he was missing and Zack had some-how tracked him down.

Zack had meted out justice on Sammy with his fists in a prolonged attack. 'Run out on me again, you treacherous little runt, and I'll throt-tle the ruddy breath out of you. You're my son and that means you're my property and you got no rights at all.' Limping home behind Zack, Sammy, bruised and swollen all over, and some of his ribs cracked, did not doubt his father's threat. Last year his mother had given birth to a deformed girl, the mite undersized as all her babies were. 'We're not rearing that useless piece of scrag end,' his father had snarled. The baby had probably been too feeble to survive for long, but Sammy had been sickened to his soul to witness the brute suffocating the mewl-ing baby with the flat of his hand. Laughing, Ruthie had said, 'Thank God for that,' then had lied that the baby had been stillborn. The Church had deemed that the baby had never had a soul and she was denied burial in consecrated ground, and had merely been holed up some-where in the churchyard hedge. Sammy was used to concentrated neglect and physical pain, but the fact that his baby sister had not even been given a name had ripped his heart wide open. Now Nora had a suspiciously jutting stomach. Sammy felt sick at the thought that his father, who could even have sired Nora's baby, would likely kill it the instant it was birthed.

Sammy was planning one day soon to walk away from everything and go to sea to become a pirate, as he'd long fancied. He wished that Zack would die in an accident down the mine; plummet down the black depths so deep his body could never be recovered, denying him his eventual fate, a pauper's funeral. No one would mourn him. All his children loathed and feared him. Ruthie would do as she'd often threatened, give her younger children over to the workhouse and leave Sammy and Nora to fend for themselves. Ruthie would exist on whoring until drink or disease ravaged her. Sammy hoped someone would murder her horribly.

Now that he'd had some fun in Church Field, Sammy was about the serious business of gaining some money, on orders from Zack, who had, as usual, drunk away all his monthly wage. If Sammy went home empty-handed, leaving Zack nothing to spend at the festival, Sammy would feel his father's belt buckle gouging at his back.

Outside the village, along the turnpike road, hedgerows bordering Poltraze property and banks of golden gorse, heather and briars at the edge of the downs verged to form a crossroads. With people, both rich and poor, drifting into Meryen from farms and other villages and hamlets, for Squire's Day, it was a good spot for Sammy to lean on a makeshift crutch and pretend to be lame and hold out his raggedy cap and beg. He'd chosen a pretty place where rogue trees and bushes had been cut down to widen the road. Sunlight could now bathe the ground, allowing early purple orchids and primroses and bluebells to grow. In the cracks and crevices of the stonework of the Cornish hedge, pennywort grew in abundance, the dimples in the fleshy green round leaves echoing the dimples just obvious in Sammy's thin cheeks. He looked much like a dirty earth sprite. So far he'd been tossed a few farthings, two halfpennies and a penny. A pitying farmer's wife, up beside her husband on their creaking cart, had handed down two fat brown eggs. Sammy decided that that was enough to satisfy his father's greed, although he would eat the eggs raw to satisfy his grumbling belly. Any more offerings would be his.

The next passer by, a hard-faced, gaudily dressed, female pedlar on foot, knowing Sammy's game, scowled at him. 'Bitch!' Sammy shook his fist at her stooped back.

Minutes passed. A portly merchant-type, up on a clumpy, dappled horse, leaned down to Sammy. 'I'll give you a nice shiny shilling, boy, to go to some secluded place with me,' he leered throatily.

Howling with fury, Sammy picked up a large stone and threatened to throw it at the man with a profane oath. Sammy would never go down that particular road, even though his beastly, rotten parents would be angry if they knew he had refused to earn that shilling. In a blistering rage, he hurled the stone after the galloping merchant.

'Hell to this shitty life!' he yelled at the top of

his voice. He'd had enough. He would leave Meryen tonight; smuggle himself into one of the carts or wagons leaving the village. He would find his way to Falmouth and run away to sea.

Sammy calmed himself and decided to stay a bit longer to continue begging. Soon he heard the snorting of horses, and heavy wheels crunching over the toll road. He was right in thinking it was the squire's carriage on its way. The open-top affair bounced along on its springs and filled the breadth of the road. Where the dust hadn't reached the coachwork, it gleamed with polish and much elbow grease. The lamps for safer passage after dark impressed Sammy and he wondered how easily they could be prized off and how much he could sell them for. A simpler carriage travelled behind, carrying the personal servants. Sammy worked up his best angelic mournful look, even producing a tear to dribble down his grimy, sunken cheek.

The Poltraze driver and groom ignored him. Sammy scowled but then was hopeful at seeing the old lady in the carriage bend forward and speak to the man across from her. He was a young man, wearing a shiny, tall hat and dark-lensed spectacles, who could be none other than the squire himself.

The squire called, 'Stop!'

In some surprise, the driver pulled up the matching four, the hooves of the horses and the wheels of the carriage dragging and spitting up stones.

Sammy didn't wait. He hobbled up to the carriage door, making his cap tremble in a hesitant hand. He performed his best humble bow. 'Thanks for stopping, m'lord,' he murmured in fake, watery despair. It wouldn't hurt to elevate the squire's position. To anyone else Sammy would have dropped his head respectfully, but the squire had rarely been seen abroad so Sammy took the chance to have a good look at him. Mr Matthew Faraday was lean in the body and his appearance was as smart as new silver. His suit was dark and precision cut. His shirt was snow-white, his necktie bold, and his waistcoat of silver brocade. As always when encountering a gentleman, Sammy surreptitiously eyed his watch chain. Gold of dignified size and weight gleamed back at Sammy. The squire had class and taste. He didn't favour much in the way of facial whiskers and his jaw was square and firm. Sammy fancied that women would find him good looking, and his shaded eyes and the scarring on the right side of his face made him seem heroically mysterious.

So what exactly was strange about this so-called strange gentleman? Nothing in particular that Sammy could make out. There were rumours about the squire's spoiled eyes; they were exquisitely beautiful or really weird, or missing altogether. Outlandish and silly tales had done the rounds. A single look from his burning orbs could turn people to stone; he was blinded and scarred because he'd done something really bad; he was active in the occult. All this and more accounted for why he'd come all the way down from the capital and had kept himself aloof for so long. He had brought his own servants down from London, and it rankled among the lower ranks in Meryen that so far he'd employed no one from the village in his house.

Ophelia Faraday had told Matthew there was 'a poor, desperate beggar boy' on the side of the road, and 'something must be done for him'. While both Matthew's elderly, simple-thinking parents believed all adults, even in the direst misfortune, must be responsible for the own miseries, they had a soft heart for ragamuffins.

From behind his tinted protection from light glare, it took Matthew some seconds for his tunnel vision to focus on the little beggar. 'Are you from the village, boy?'

Sammy was impressed by the squire's strong low voice; there was no hint of loftiness in it. This gentleman, who was not readily approachable, was not so high-minded that he'd refuse to halt on what was an important occasion to address a lowly unfortunate. 'I'm a miner's son, m'lord.'

'I'm to be addressed as either Mr Faraday or sir.' Matthew, a former colonel in the Life Guards, knew the wiles of men, and recognized the lie of lameness in this boy. No doubt he had been forced to grow up beyond his years and to live on his wits. 'Tell me your name.'

'Juleff, sir. Sammy Juleff.'

'Why are you begging, Sammy Juleff?'

50

'For my fam'ly, sir. For my sick mother and poor starving brothers and sisters.'

'Why does your father not support his family?'

''Fraid my father spends all his wages on grog, sir, and my mother's worn out with child-bearing,' Sammy said quickly, fearing the conversation might be turning away from his advantage. The squire might not be able to see him properly but Sammy sensed he could see right 'into' him.

Matthew nodded gravely. This was not an uncommon tale among the godless in the labouring classes. He already had a florin in his fingertips. He dropped it into the boy's hat, but before Sammy could snatch the hat away and mutter ingratiating thanks, Matthew grasped the tatty cloth. 'I don't doubt your parents are irresponsible, Sammy Juleff, but I can tell that you're a little rogue and will probably follow your father's wickedness. You're welcome to the money. I'll leave it to your conscience to decide how you spend it. Good day to you. Now, step back safely from the carriage.'

Sammy leapt back out of instinct, worried that the bounty, so willingly given, might suddenly be taken back. He bowed to all the high company, while hiding a smirk. If the squire thought to shame him he was out of luck. Life was too hard and too uncertain to share the two shillings with his ragtag siblings. Their hungry bellies were his father and mother's fault. What did his conscience matter, anyway?

'That boy'll not change, but I believe he'll make his way in life,' Matthew informed his parents, making out their images fondly as the carriage swayed on its way. Clarence and Ophelia Faraday were rather theatrical in nature and apt to wear mismatching, garish outfits of no particular fashion. Matthew had ensured a dressmaker and tailor had rigged them out for today. The joint effect was pleasingly elegant, with clean lines. Matthew had persuaded his mother to keep her pearls to the minimum. The usual long staffs they went about with had been exchanged for an ivory-topped walking stick and a parasol. Matthew took great pains to protect the ageing couple from ridicule and hurt. Clarry and Phee, as they liked to be called, were both edging towards happy senility. They were childlike, and existed mainly in a world of themselves and their many spaniels. They had been disappointed not to be able to bring their dogs, but Matthew had counselled it was unwise to let their temperate and healthy dogs mix with the local curs. The couple had driven only once through Meryen before today and were as excited about the festival as two young people about to attend their first ball.

'Good works do not change everyone, Matthew,' said Phee, who usually spoke before Clarry did. 'One can only try and do one's best.'

'Indeed, Mama.' Matthew had a brother and two sisters but he was the only one who knew the Faradays had adopted them all. None of them shared the same blood and all had come from distressed gentlefolk. Not unexpectedly, each of them had different characters. Kingsley had married his mistress, the mother of his two children, and it was Kingsley who had taken Hattie to live with him in Devon. To Matthew's joy, despite Hattie's anxiety that her scarred face would deny her a well-placed husband, she had met and married the older, doting, Sir Julian Stapleton, and now had a son. Matthew had tried to persuade his widowed sister, Jane Hartley, who lived in the former dower house not far from the big house, to attend the festival, hoping it might be a way to root her out of her self-indulgent depression – before that, Jane had gloried in an unhealthy manner in her widowhood. He was, however, secretly relieved that she had flatly refused. Jane was a washed-out shadow; scornful and selfish to an irritating degree. He was pleased she had moved out of Poltraze with her mealy, old-maid companion, to Wellspring House. The world was better off with Jane shut away from it.

Matthew was very much a closed tome himself. Clemency was the only one he had ever confided in. She knew about the adoptions, and he trusted her in everything. A prolific poet, Matthew's work sold well and was a welcome monetary addition to the dues he received for leasing the mineral rights of his land to the mining shareholders. He had penned reams of poetry about Clemency, all kept private and hidden. He loved Clemency with his whole being and dreamed of her one day soon returning his love. His most feared rival was Jowan Kivell, who had much more in common with Clemency. Matthew sighed inwardly. He was expecting to have to ward off the carpentry owner from Clemency's side all the way through the festival.

Five

Jowan had lost heart for a lot more than the festival. He'd spent an hour cradling a couple of drinks in a public house, and was now on the way to get his horse from the New Oak stables. He would ride hard the mile and a half to Chy-Henver, pack a bag, and leave a note stating his absence for an indeterminate length of time. He would go far from home, far from Meryen. Clemency's blunt rebuff had left him feeling awkward and lost. Clemency had put him in his place and it didn't sit easily on his proud shoulders. He needed to reassess his life. His six-bedroom cottage was lonely without his cousin Thad and his wife. He had a live-in housekeeper, but he needed closer company. New experiences should set him right and put him on a worthwhile new course. He'd seek excitement and exhilaration and adventure beyond his imagination.

Mining folk and others were passing him by as he walked. A farm labourer, up on a rough cart pulled by a lumbering ox, trudged up the High Street, and a stray dog sniffed at his heels, but he was unaware of all of it, so deep was he in his thoughts. People paused and puzzled over him. It was unknown for Jowan Kivell to stride along with his head down.

Jowan reached the hotel's forecourt. A small cry, of something between surprise and alarm, brought his head up. Across the street, Sammy Juleff was harassing a dainty young woman. Jenny Clymo, Logan's ward and companion to the sedate, elderly Mrs Alice Brookson, was raising her arm to prevent Sammy from tugging a shawl away from her. 'I don't need your help, Sammy,' she protested. 'I can carry it myself. Please go away.'

'But miss, I need to earn some money for the festival. Be mis'rable else. Give me some pennies then. Come on, you know what it's like to be poor.'

'Eh, you boy! Get away from the lady.' In a few long strides Jowan was over the road to them and had hooked Sammy up off his feet by his tattered shirt. 'This is what you'll get, you little brat.' Plonking Sammy down, he boxed his ears until they were red.

Jenny winced at each slap, but Sammy, like a stubborn sapling in a gale, took the punishment without a sound. Then, with a river of obscenities, he kicked out at Jowan and spat at him, while darting out of reach. 'You bleddy, stinking bastard! I'll get you. I won't forget, just wait and see. I curse you to hell.' He jettisoned another huge blob of spit. Jowan dodged to avoid it. 'I curse you and all your devil family.' Sammy ran off shrieking, 'I hope Chy-Henver burns down with you inside it!'

'You'll end up dangling from a noose, Sammy Juleff. Be careful not to cross my path again or I'll string you up myself,' Jowan called after him.

Jenny was shocked by the aggression between the man and the boy. Mr Jowan, as she called him, looked as if he wanted to obliterate Sammy. Her hands worriedly straightened the shawl over her arm, a large tasselled silk affair, embroidered with exotic birds and flowers.

Jowan took in her pinched, hot cheeks. Jenny was like a tender female deer, doe-eyed and long-lashed, cautiously curious but shy and eager to slip away. From each side of her simple beribboned straw bonnet, two pretty ginger ringlets swayed gently as she looked down bashfully. A former mine girl, who had met with inestimable tragedy – her entire family had died from cholera – she had been the first to soften Logan's once cold heart. 'Did he alarm you? Where are you going, Jenny?'

Jenny looked up politely. She had fine clothes, money in her drawstring purse, and a secure future, but she was always keen to show she knew her place. 'No, Mr Jowan, Sammy's a little nuisance, that's all. I went back to the house to fetch this shawl for Mrs Brookson in case it gets chilly. She's with Mr and Mrs Logan in the hotel. Sammy was hoping I'd let him carry the shawl to earn a penny or two, but his hands were too dirty to allow that.'

'You're feeling sorry for him, aren't you?' Jowan didn't really have to ask. Jenny's whole regretful demeanour sang it out. 'It's good and honourable of you to work so diligently for the poor but it's a waste of time and effort to help that brat and his ilk. They only take advantage of kindness, Jenny. They don't have any gratitude and never will.'

'I can't help feeling a little sorry for Sammy. He's just a child. He stands no chance in life with parents like his. He's never known a settled life. It's no wonder he's learned no manners and is hardened to life.'

Jowan shrugged and then nodded.

Jenny gazed at him. His anger had gone but there seemed to be something else gnawing away at him. She was too inexperienced in life to guess what it might be.

'I'll escort you to the hotel.' He hadn't intended to do so. The words just slipped out of his mouth. Jenny only had to cross the road and she'd be there. She wasn't distressed by her encounter with Sammy. She had been born and bred in poverty and primitive conditions, she knew how hard life could be, but her meekness and absolute honesty brought out the protective side in others.

Jowan offered to carry the shawl for Jenny. He liked the shy way she thanked him. Jenny never took anything for granted. She made a man feel strong and whole. Jowan understood why Logan had literally lifted her up off the street in her despair and sworn to be her champion. Jenny was sweet and lovely. She made a man proud to escort her. She did not want to be a man's equal, or to enjoy the same freedoms, or as Clemency seemed to, be even more powerful. 'Are you looking forward to the festival, Jenny?'

'Oh, yes, Mr Jowan, especially the theatre show. Meryen's had visiting acting troupes pass through before but never anything like this, on a proper stage, with changes of costumes. The Kernack Players,' Jenny said dreamily. 'It sounds very important and grand.'

Jowan was sure she was as quietly enthusiastic about all the delights ahead. He pictured her tonight, all ready for bed, writing it all down in a journal. Bless her. It was what everyone said when speaking about Jenny.

'Did you know you've got visiting family staying at the hotel, Mr Jowan?' Jenny asked.

'That doesn't surprise me. Family members often arrive in the village.'

'Would you excuse me for a moment, please?' Jenny came to a halt in order to address a bent old woman, who was just appearing on her tiny, uneven granite doorstep. 'Good morning, Miss Tamblyn. Are you going to the festival? Is there someone to take you?'

'Bless you, Miss Jenny,' replied Miss Tamblyn, in gummy tones that Jowan barely understood. He could smell the musty scent of her and the same intense whiff emanated from her tiny, pitiable home. 'I can't stand all the noise, and my poor old feet wouldn't bear it. Mrs Treneer promised to bring me in the free pasty the Squire's handing out to all, and a nice bit of saffron for me tea, and t'tell me all about it. Well, I've had me breath of air. I'm going back in, if you'll excuse me. God bless you, my handsome girl. Good morning to 'ee, Mr Kivell.'

'Dear of her.' Jenny smiled when the make-shift little door had been dragged shut. 'She's never had a thing in all her life but she never grumbles.'

Jowan saw the door, made of scraps of thin wood that had been badly nailed together, was full of gaps and splinters. In poor weather it must let in fearfully cold draughts. Jenny, no doubt, knew all about old Miss Tamblyn's sorrowful life story. As they walked on, he asked, 'Did she work at one of the mines?'

'Until she was sixty-one. Then she got too weak.'

'And now she lives on charity?'

'She's not too proud to accept it. She says if the Lord wants her to have something she wouldn't offend Him, nor the kind giver, by refusing it.'

Jowan gave regular donations of money to the Kivell Charity Fund, but he had never thought much about the ordinary working folk of the village. 'How old is she now?'

'Sixty-three.'

'But she looks so much older.'

'It happens.' Jenny's face was partially concealed by her bonnet, but he detected no bitterness in her. Jenny would no doubt have accepted a similar fate for herself if she were still a

60

bal-maiden.

'Jenny, would you ask Miss Tamblyn if she would like her door fixed? I'll do it myself with strong, new timber.' Another statement had just tumbled out of his mouth; not that he minded helping the unfortunate old dear. So much for him hurrying off somewhere new and afar. Well, he had never run away from anything before. Why start because his feelings had been trampled on, and, he acknowledged, because of bitterness about the way Clemency had rejected him? The hurt had lingered in him like a sore headache, but just a few moments in Jenny's company and his resentment was gone. Her compassion had not allowed self-pity to get a stranglehold on him. It was frighteningly easy to subscribe to self-destruction.

Jenny turned to him with wide, shining eyes, her well-shaped, freckled cheeks pink with excitement. 'Would you really do that for her? Miss Tamblyn would benefit so much and she'd believe she'd been blessed by heaven.'

'Blessed by you, not me. Being with you, Jenny, gave me the idea. You're an angel.' Jowan could hardly believe he had confessed this so lyrically. Usually he'd have shrugged and said something like, 'Consider it done'. He had obviously embarrassed Jenny, because she blushed the deepest red and her smile grew ragged on her lips. Sweet lips so smooth and pink and unkissed. What had got into him? Clemency's rejection had catapulted him from a determined adventurer to a would-be seducer of the innocent. It was bewildering and a little scary. Thank God the New Oak Hotel was just across the street.

He guided Jenny over to the forecourt. 'Here you are, safely arrived.' He thought to scarper, but it would be rude to let Jenny walk in unescorted after bringing her this far. The porter opened the doors for them and Jowan led Jenny through the lobby into the foyer.

'Thank you Mr Jowan,' Jenny said. 'When may I tell Miss Tamblyn to expect you?' She felt shy at asking, but she was eager to extract a firm promise on the old lady's behalf. Jenny had been born an underdog. Her sick and frail parents and all her suffering little brothers and sisters had never known a moment's relief from poverty. She was resolute in her attempts to ease the miseries of those still existing in dire circumstances.

Jowan considered the question. His craftsmen enabled him to do exactly as he willed, but he relished the feel of wood under his expert hands and creating fine pieces from start to finish. He found himself looking forward to fashioning Miss Tamblyn's new door. 'Would you kindly enquire if Tuesday morning would be convenient for her, Jenny?'

'I shall be pleased to, Mr Jowan.'

Logan was waiting for Jenny with his wife Serenity, Mrs Brookson, and Harry and Georgette Bonython, on the plush sofas, and he beckoned to Jenny and Jowan to join his group. 'The carriages will be brought round shortly.

We're going to arrive at Church Field in style. Let me introduce you to two of our distant relatives, Jowan. Are you joining us for the day?'

Apart from not wanting to see Clemency again today, Jowan had no other reason to shun Squire's Day. He replied, in his usual easy manner, 'I suppose I might as well.'

Six

The front doorbell of Poltraze House jangled urgently sending the Faraday spaniels into a barking frenzy. The butler, Rumford, was grateful the dogs were shut in the morning room as he hurried towards the carved double doors, which were now being fiercely knocked upon. The squire and Mr and Mrs Faraday had left for the festival twenty minutes ago. Had something gone wrong? Had the master or one of the old couple fallen ill? Otherwise, who had the affront to rouse the house so fiercely?

Mrs Secombe, the housekeeper, had hurried after Rumford and dashed to a hall window. 'It's Miss Hattie! I mean Lady Stapleton,' she informed the butler, who had only been three months at Poltraze. 'It's the squire's dear youngest sister and she's being carried up the steps by the coach driver. It looks like she's fainted. There's also a gentleman; Sir Julian Stapleton, I should think. Open the door to them, Mr Rumford.'

'Ring for more servants, Mrs Secombe.' Rumford was sharp with the order, offended that the bespectacled housekeeper, of long-time service to the Faradays, should act his superior.

Some time later Mrs Secombe was sobbing to the cook in the servants' hall. 'I couldn't believe it was her, our dear Miss Hattie. The same dear girl we both watched to grow up from the cradle, Mrs Cooper. She's so thin, just a shadow of the bright, bouncy girl she was. She was perfectly fine until she met that Kivell girl; that wretched Clemency.' The house-keeper's well-rounded, thread-veined cheeks became suffused with the dark pink of angry indignation. 'When that girl's brute of a father abducted Miss Hattie and told her he was going to burn her alive, and she was badly scarred trying to escape, Miss Hattie lost all her confidence. She thought she was doomed to spinster-hood. When she married Sir Julian I hoped – well, we both did, didn't we? – it would bring her back to how she used to be. The letters she so graciously sent us both at Christmas seemed really quite cheerful. But now I've never seen her look so ill.'

Mrs Cooper nodded, listening patiently.

'Sir Julian said Lady Stapleton insisted on bringing young Master Freddie down here to present him to his grandparents and the squire. He didn't mention Mrs Hartley, but why should he? She wouldn't be at all interested in her new nephew. It's obvious the journey was too soon after the birth. It's taken its toll on poor Lady Stapleton. Sir Julian is worried, but then he should have had more sense, bringing her back here where she has such terrible memories.'

Mrs Cooper, who shared middle age with Mrs

Secombe, had vinegary features, yet had a tendency towards optimism. 'P'raps he shouldn't have, but don't forget Miss Hattie was always a stubborn soul and couldn't be easily refused. Hopefully, she'll rally soon, 'specially when she sees her mama and papa. I'll make her a sturdy chicken and vegetable broth; that'll build her up. The master and Mr and Mrs Faraday will be so delighted to see their surprise visitors. As for the Kivell girl, I agree with you, Mrs Secombe. It's a pity the squire still entertains her, but then he's hopelessly smitten with her, so there we are. Has someone been sent to tell the squire of Lady Stapleton and Sir Julian's arrival?'

'Sir Julian said not to. Said he was sorry but he'd quite forgotten about the letter informing them about Squire's Day, and that he doesn't want to precipitate the master and Mr and Mrs Faraday into feeling they must leave the festival early or to worry about Lady Stapleton.'

'He sounds a very fine gentleman indeed. I'm sure we'll all see a good end to the day.' Mrs Cooper checked her sleeves were rolled up, and ordered a kitchen maid to fetch plenty of fresh vegetables.

'Where am I?' murmured Hattie Stapleton. She was laid on her parents' bed, in the chamber nearest the stairs, which more ably accommodated the old couple's ancient legs. The room was stuffed with the miscellany of their lifetime, including a number of old wax dolls,

66

bisque dolls and mechanical toys, and it smelled thickly of dogs. Hattie's skin was as grey as stale dough, highlighting the dark-pink, ragged scar on her left cheek.

'You're resting in your old home, my darling Hattie, at Poltraze,' Sir Julian said with pure tenderness, stroking her hand and gazing down at her anxiously. 'The servants are preparing a room for us – the principal bedroom, which was your old room. Is there anything you'd like, my precious? Your maid and I managed to get you to take a few sips of brandy. Would you like some more brandy, or a drink of water, or a refreshing cup of tea?'

'Don't fuss me, Julian,' Hattie got out in a faraway voice. To her it sounded as if it was down a long tunnel, which reflected how she had felt since the birth of her son. Her limbs seemed watery, as if they weren't actually hers, and her head was strangely light, as if she were about to float away. She feared becoming totally out of control and had the most terrifying episodes of panic. Her physician had diagnosed post-natal anxiety after a long and traumatic confinement. He had prescribed tonics, and after the lying-in period, short afternoon carriage rides in the parklands of Sir Julian's estate, to be immediately followed by complete rest. But Hattie knew she was stricken with more than that. Julian and the physician had done a lot of whispering together just beyond her bedroom door. 'Help me to sit up.'

'Of course, my darling.' Julian carefully slip-

67

ped his arms around her back and gently eased her up, as if she was made of thistledown and might disintegrate at any moment.

'Do not be so rough with me,' Hattie complained hoarsely. 'I'm not a sack of coal.' No one treated her well nowadays, she thought. It was because she was a nuisance to everyone. No one said so, but she wasn't fooled. She was treated with sighs and the turning of backs from her husband and the servants. It was the way she saw things.

'I'm sorry, my darling,' Julian said in soft and loving tones. Nothing Hattie accused him of, no amount of her protests, and sometimes even her hostility, could make him love her any less. It wasn't her fault she interpreted everything mistakenly.

He had adored Hattie from the first, when he'd chanced upon her out riding in a country lane. He had been unable to understand why the lovely young lady, with hair the colour of buttercups, was not out on the social scene. She had muttered only a brief response to his polite salutation and ridden off at a gallop. At the time, the reason for her curtness, her scar, had been hidden by the thick, black net of her hat. Undeterred, Julian, a childless widower, had tracked down the fascinating stranger to her brother's house. He had called there unannounced, and spotting his quarry alone in the gardens, had crept up on her and declared his presence. Hattie had been mortified and angry, but Julian had found her flawed cheek completely unimportant. He had instantly loved everything about her, although it had taken long patient months to convince Hattie of this. She had finally accepted his constant proposals, on one condition: that socializing was kept to her brother, sister-in-law and the few select people she trusted. Julian was happy with that; all he wanted was for Hattie to be happy. Hattie proved an affectionate interested wife, she ran his household perfectly, and she had given him a son and heir. They were the meaning of his life.

But the happy event of the birth he had so looked forward to had been plagued all the way through by fear and anxiety. He had pleaded with Hattie against coming down to Cornwall to the place of her scarring – the ordeal she had never come to terms with – fearing the return of her depression of the early days of their meeting and that the travel would overtax her fragile mind and body. But she had gone into sulks and rages and he'd had no choice but to relent. Now, he was praying that time in this dull, quiet place with her squire brother and treasured parents would somehow bring his beloved wife back to normality.

Hattie suddenly giggled, sounding like the playful girl that her brother Kingsley had told Julian she had formerly been. 'I'm in Mama and Papa's room, with all their preposterous things. I told you, didn't I, about Mama's enormous doll's house, and Papa keeping a real cannon in their room? But where are the dogs?'

Julian was pleased that a little pinkness was

flushing her cheeks. She was no longer slumped on the pillows and a touch of life was returning to her. 'I believe the dogs are downstairs. I'm afraid there's none of your family here to greet us; they're attending the Squire's Day.'

'Squire's Day? What's that? It will be good to see the spaniels again. Did you know they've all been given names from nursery rhymes? Miss Muffet is my favourite. Julian, be a dear and send someone to fetch her. She can keep me company.'

'Straight away, my love.' Julian went to the bell pull. 'Would you like to see Freddie? I could get Nurse to bring him in here for a few minutes.'

'Freddie?' Hattie whispered, her eyes growing vacant. 'Is there a new puppy? I don't recall one called Freddie.'

Julian went back to the bed, hiding his dismay that Hattie's lucidity had gone so soon. 'Freddie is our son, our little baby remember, Hattie, darling. Try to remember him.'

'Oh, the baby.' She nodded, lifting her head up and down rapidly.

Julian bracketed her face in his hands fearing she would give herself a painful wry neck.

Hattie's whispers sunk to almost inaudible. 'Our little boy ... Yes, yes, I had a baby, didn't I? He's somewhere. I'm so tired.'

'Freddie's here, darling. We brought him down with us. He's safe and well with Nurse. Now, you must lie down and sleep again. I'll stay at your side.'

Julian laid Hattie down as gently as he'd lifted her up minutes ago. She fell into a deep sleep, breathing heavily, and he held her hand, so small and soft and cold in his own. He wanted to cry. He couldn't bear seeing the woman he loved so completely suffering in even the smallest way. He had secretly vowed there would be no more children. When Hattie recovered – please God, make it soon – he would not risk her going through all this torment again. He would sacrifice his husband's rights and be content only to hold her in his arms for the rest of their lives.

'My poor darling.' Julian kissed her hand and caressed her face. 'This is so unfair to you, to us.'

Hattie had been weak but otherwise quite well for the first few days after the birth, but then the rapid mood swings had started. One minute she had been silent and depressed and the next she would snap over the slightest thing, throw things and make unreasonable demands. She'd sob hysterically for hours, then suddenly became bright and animated and laugh wickedly. She would fear for the baby's safety and then forget he existed, or scream for him to be taken away from her, either because she believed she was a useless mother, or because she couldn't stand him near her. She had to be strictly supervised with Freddie. She had once put him out on a window ledge in the rain. Fortunately, the nurse had been there to snatch him back inside.

Hattie also had terrible nightmares. She swore

there were things in the room that were impossible to be there: a tiger, a pack of wolves, and she even said that the mantel clock actually talked to her. Sometimes she was lucid and quite normal; other times in dreadful panics or the direst terror, cringing up to the bedstead or cowering in corners. She had to be watched at every moment. The physician had grimly confirmed that Hattie had puerperal psychosis; a quite rare condition that a very few unfortunate new mothers suffered after a traumatic birth. In the worst cases the mother had to be placed in an institution for the mentally ill for her own, or her baby's, protection. Julian had vowed he would never allow that to happen. One reason he had undertaken this ill-advised journey was to avoid the physician, and his own unfeeling family, insisting on it. With medication and rest, and by being back with the family so dear to her, he was hoping desperately that Hattie would come through it without any lasting effect.

Hattie's eyes flew open. Julian flinched at her glazed expression, which could only be described as crazed. 'They're coming,' she intoned, as if with an old woman's croak. Her head whipped from side to side. Julian reached out to soothe her but she sat bolt upright and wailed as one in abject terror. 'Don't let them in! Too late! They're here!'

Seven

Word spread quickly round Church Field that the squire had nearly reached the village. Clemency stationed herself outside her music tent to wait for the Faradays' grand entrance. Her mother was beside her.

'I should think the squire is probably feeling quite nervous,' Verena Kivell said, catching the crowd's heightened sense of excitement. 'He will be delighted, I'm sure, at the great number of people who have turned up.'

'It's a big step for him,' Clemency replied quietly, picking out her family in the mass of people and acknowledging them with a small wave. Although she was trying hard to leave behind her moroseness after the confrontation with Jowan, she was still offended at how he had made her feel. He had made her examine her commitment to staying unmarried until it pleased her to change her status. Her choice would seem odd in all quarters. Most saw marriage as the only way for a woman to be truly successful. It was her mother's view, and Clemency knew that Verena's dearest wish was for her daughter to be settled and to raise a large family. But Clemency knew she could never be like Verena, whose youthful poise and calm personality were testament to her acceptance of past bad times, including the heartbreak of her husband nearly tearing her family apart and forsaking her for a whorish kitchen maid.

Clemency tightened her lips at spotting Jowan strolling nonchalantly along with Logan and his party. He was escorting the elderly Mrs Brookson and Jenny Clymo. He seemed full of verve, the opposite of how she had last seen him, and he was being very attentive towards Jenny. He was actually gazing into Jenny's innocent face as if she was the only thing to hold his interest. Strange behaviour for a man who'd just had his fervent marriage proposal turned down. *If he's flirting with Jenny to make her jealous he's out of luck*, Clemency thought. Also with the party was the stranger from earlier that morning. This better view of him announced he clearly was Kivell kin. Clemency was always fascinated to meet family members. Looped possessively to his arm was an exquisitely turned out young lady; probably his wife. Clemency noticed that, between conversation and broad smiles, the man's eyes were darting hither and thither.

'Look there with Logan, Mama, we surely have more kin among us.' She decided she would not allow Jowan another instant's room inside her mind.

'Oh yes,' Verena said.

Clemency and Verena both looked around. After the day was over, a huge gathering was planned at Burnt Oak – a party that would go on all through the night. The full details of the newcomers would be learned then. They took in the mining and labouring fraternity decked out in their church and chapel best. The bonnets of the younger, unattached bal-maidens tended to be rather bright and gaudily trimmed; an indulgence to compensate for the usual tough cloth of their work dresses and petticoats. The better off paraded in crisp newness and had flashes of jewellery. Everywhere, faces were beaming like miniatures suns.

While fiddles, pipes, accordions and regional drums played joyful country music there was a sense of fun in the great many voices and activities. The choice of fares, from lace-crafted items to pottery, plants, preserves, carvings and paintings, were being called out with gusto. There were the inevitable cheap jacks and fortune tellers, and flower and heather sellers. The animal acts, the jugglers and the strong man act were practising, and the actors and actresses of the Kernack Players were bobbing about in medieval costume. The young Queen of the May, a local butcher's daughter, was suitably pretty and sweet in white muslin and with flowers in her hair. She would have the honour of being crowned by Mrs Faraday.

'There is so much going on and everything is so colourful, Clemmie. I'm so proud of you,' Verena enthused. 'The squire will be simply amazed.'

Clemency muttered, 'It's getting cold.' She glared up at the sky. From being obligingly bright a few moments ago, it was quickly becoming covered by a blanket of grey cloud. Far from remaining in the promise of a still day, a blustery wind was now buffeting the ladies' parasols and the canvas bottoms of the tents were beginning to flap quite noisily. The painstaking arrangement of the drapes on the squire's dais lost its faultlessness. Clemency gritted her teeth. This was another dampener on the event.

Clemency winced at her self-pity and sourness. What was happening to her? Where had this bitterness come from? It was getting harder to paint on a bright face for her mother's sake. People were clamouring about the dais for a good place to watch the squire's speech. She heard a familiar laugh. It was Abe and with him was a village girl. They were flirting with each other. Clemency wanted to demand from Abe who this girl was, but then, of course, it was none of her business; a thought she found chilling but why? Her new inner loneliness had got a frightening grip on her.

'Excuse me, Mama.' Overcome by shivers, Clemency slipped into her tent to fetch her shawl.

Verena frowned at Clemency's slumped shoulders when she reappeared from her music tent arranging the shawl to its fullest, the long fringes nearly touching the ground, almost as if she was hiding herself away. Her daughter had seemed to have lost interest in the festival, and that was sad after all the effort she had put into helping to arrange it. It was perplexing. Clemency was full of life and energy. She was unlikely to have got anxious about her part in the festival. Clemency got angry easily and she met life's challenges head on, but she had never once before become despondent.

'Yes, it has gone a little chilly,' Verena agreed, and fastened the buttons of her capelet, as Logan brought the Bonythons over to them for a brief introduction. Before he moved on with them, Verena noticed that he looked hard at Clemency and said, 'You're in a strange mood today. Stir yourself or you'll not make good company for anyone.'

'Do try to cheer up, darling,' Verena said when they had left. 'You hardly endeared yourself to Harry and Georgette. I don't understand why you've got so down. Come along, smile and make the most of the day. We'll have a good long talk later.'

People were lining up all the way from the dais to the field entrance for the squire's carriages. A roar of cheers went up and the crowd burst out into spontaneous applause when the first carriage appeared.

'It's time for you to take your place up on the dais with the dignitaries, Clemmie,' Verena exclaimed with pride in her voice.

Her daughter remained frozen. 'I can see well enough from here.'

'But you've the right to be there. Besides, the squire will expect you.'

That was exactly so, Clemency brooded. *Like Jowan, Matthew Faraday, another man she wanted only as a good friend, expected too much from her.* Clemency kept coolly quiet.

As his carriage bounced over the field, Matthew waved and smiled down at both sides of the crowd. He was thrilled at his rapturous reception. Everything was a blur to him but his mother compensated by giving an account of all there was to be seen. Phee made much of the excellence of the dais. Matthew was pleased his money had been spent well, but most of all he was filled with gratitude to Clemency. He wished he could thank her in his speech but she had warned him not to embarrass her in this way.

His heart leapt when Phee announced she could see Clemency standing beside her tent next to the dais. He set his eyes in the direction Phee gave him, eager to make out the woman he loved so. Matthew kept hoping she would allow a deepening of their relationship. She had been enthusiastic about this festival from his very first mention of it. She cared about it being a resounding success for his sake.

When the carriage stopped the welcome committee headed by the vicar greeted Matthew and his parents and showed them to the dais. Matthew used his long walking stick to guide him up the steps. He could see the drapes of the dais now and he looked all around the structure for Clemency. He had expected her to join in the welcome.

As Matthew approached the dais, Verena nudged her daughter sternly. 'Go to Mr Faraday, Clemmie. He's looking for you. You know he's not comfortable with crowds. Don't let him struggle. Don't ruin the day for him.'

Knowing it would be petty to hang back and leave all three Faradays wondering why she was snubbing them, Clemency went forward reluctantly. It was the correct thing to be formal in public. 'Good morning, Mr Faraday, and to you both also, Mr and Mrs Faraday.'

'Good morning, Miss Kivell,' Matthew said, smiling widely. 'I can't thank you enough for all you've done today. Shall we get the festival under way? I can feel the people champing at the bit.'

'Of course.' She stepped back quickly behind Matthew, her expression one of faint disinterest. People had made a lot of her being so highly involved in Squire's Day. She regretted it now. It had reinforced the view that she was the squire's romantic interest.

Matthew appeared to believe that Clemency's reserve was her being circumspect. He delivered a long and well-thought-out speech. He promised to be out and about more in Meryen and added that the villagers were welcome to apply for employment on the estate when any new vacancy occurred. He bid all to enjoy the day and to avail themselves of the free food and tea, and he declared Squire's Day formally open. His speech was received with enough decibels of favour to topple the church's ancient bell tower.

Immediately, he turned round to Clemency. 'Would you do me the honour of showing me round, Miss Kivell, and introducing me to some of the people?'

'It's not my place to,' she stressed, taking no pains to disguise her sudden horror. It would be seen as tantamount to an announcement of their engagement. The honour of that should fall to the vicar. Matthew had gone too far. How dare he take her for granted?

'But everyone knows you're mainly responsible for the planning and success of the wonderful layout in the field, Clemency.' Matthew sounded both hurt and embarrassed by her appalled refusal. He whispered to her, 'I don't understand your objection.'

'That's just it, Matthew,' she hissed for his ears alone. 'You don't understand me at all.' Why did the men in her life have to complicate things? Why couldn't they be content to allow her to live her life her way? She was still very young, just twenty-one years, not some lovestruck girl or desperate old maid.

Wishing she could leave the field and festival, she stepped down off the dais with the intention of going to her tent and staying in it for some time. Verena waylaid her and pulled her out of earshot of others. 'What has got into you, Clemency?' she demanded crossly. 'You were unforgivably rude to Mr Faraday. People will have noticed. Was it your intention to shame him?'

'No, of course not,' Clemency replied. She hated herself for her rudeness, but she wasn't repentant about her declaration to Matthew.

'Then tell me what is wrong with you? Has someone offended you?'

'It's nothing,' Clemency replied sharply. Verena's disapproval and questions had made her feel uncomfortably guilty. Her nerves were on edge. She didn't want to explain right now how Jowan and Matthew's intentions for her had made her feel trapped. She didn't understand herself why she was so offended by them, why she was experiencing an unidentifiable emptiness in her soul. It was like a tiny jagged black hole deep inside her. Never, not even in the past when her father had dragged his immediate family out of Burnt Oak Farm and, with his cruel, belligerent manner, had set the whole Kivell community against him, had she been daunted. What was so different now? It wasn't a life or death situation. It was crazy to be so bewildered. 'It's just that, oh, why must people presume? Mama, please, don't go on about it.' At once she regretted the way her weary words came out in a snarl.

'Well, if that's your attitude I'll leave you on your own. It's obviously how you want to be.' With a dark look at her daughter, Verena walked away.

Clemency stayed rooted to the spot. She watched her mother leaving her to join Logan and his party by the maypole, where the children were lifting the ribbons for the first dance.

Clemency had never been insolent to her mother before. She must find her feet and run after her and apologize. Then she saw Matthew was being taken towards her mother, and Jowan was also there, still hanging about little Jenny Clymo. Neither Verena, nor Matthew, nor Jowan, looked back in Clemency's direction. She had excluded herself from the company she should be closest to.

As if she was invisible and not actually there, Clemency stared about the cheerful, hectic scene. Phee and Clarry, with their servants attending them, were taking joyful delight in the animal acts. The heavily bearded, greasy-haired Zack Juleff was at a stall demanding a free pasty for himself and each of his four youngest scrappy brats. The children were dirty, shoeless, clad in bits of rag, and snotty-nosed. When they turned round one at a time, biting into small pasties – something they had probably rarely tasted before – their eyes bulging in bliss over this rare treat, something snagged at Clemency's heart. Compassion for these poor, neglected tiny ones, who would experience little joy in their lives, made her ashamed. She shouldn't have thought of them disparagingly. They were innocents and they suffered in so many ways every day of their wretched lives. Their parents' lax and brutal lifestyle offered them no future at all. The absent Sammy, probably up to no good somewhere, would likely end up like his father or in gaol. The elder girl, Nora, wasn't with Zack either, nor her mother.

The foul-mouthed, gin-soaked Ruthie Juleff had doubtless dragged the poor girl off to some lonely place and was making Nora sell herself, as Ruthie did, to supplement Ruthie and Zack's heavy drinking.

Zack suddenly cuffed one of the children on the head – a tiny, nearly naked boy – making him squeal and drop his pasty on the grass. As the boy scrabbled to pick up his precious food, Zack bawled, 'Now get away from me for the rest of the day, the lot of you!'

Clemency could stand it no more and stormed off towards the Juleffs. Her fighting edge was back in full force. 'How could you hurt your own child like that, Zack Juleff?' she shouted in anger. 'He's just an infant. Their mother should be here looking after them. I suppose you're off to the ale tent. Rather, you should act like a man and be responsible for your family, all of them, including poor Nora, instead of exploiting her. You should buy some proper clothes for your children and see they're fed every day. I've never seen such badly neglected children.'

'Mind your own damned business, you uppity bitch,' Zack roared, lifting his meaty fist at Clemency. The children backed away, obviously fearing that their father's wrath would also be meted out on them. 'I can do what I bleddy like with my own family. And you've never cared about my young'uns before, ya bleddy hypocrite.'

'Lower your arm and move away from the lady,' a strong male voice forcefully threatened.

It was Harry Bonython, and Clemency had never been so glad to see anyone before in her life.

Harry Bonython had been circling the field. A horrible sensation of impending doom had been crowding down on him, and he was looking for the trouble that his earlier premonition had foretold.

He saw his distant, glum cousin taking a brute of a man to task and Harry knew that the trouble, the disaster, or whatever he had sensed, had something to do with Clemency Kivell. His every nerve was on alert. The danger was imminent and he being here meant he should be just in time to prevent it.

As the last word of Harry's command to Zack Juleff left his mouth, a terrible screaming came from beyond the churchyard wall. There was a confusion of shrieking and shouting of three or four voices.

'That's my Nora and Ruthie!' Zack yelled.

'Help! Help us!'

Clemency was horrified to recognize Sammy as the one making the terrified pleas. The missing Juleffs were either being attacked or there had been a catastrophic accident. She started to run for the churchyard, but Harry pushed her behind him.

'Stay here!' Harry yelled at her.

Harry beat Zack through the gate in the wall, and Clemency went through after them. The men bounded among the graves looking about wildly for sign of the distressed victims. No one was in sight. Clemency feared that they could have been carried off. Her eyes travelled along the ivy-covered wall, where tall nettles and brambles grew to a trampled down space, and her hands flew to her mouth. This couldn't be real. Shock and revulsion slammed, slammed, slammed into her. She fought back the force making her want to be sick. 'Oh my God! They're here! They're here!'

The men ran back to her. Shuddering violently, Clemency pointed.

'No!' Zack bawled as if from his bowels. Blood was splashed up the ivy-covered wall and was pooling on the ground. Ruthie had her back to a tree, holding her arms out rigid, and blood was dripping off her hands from deep cuts, her eyes bulging with horror. Nora was in a heap on the ground. The sight of her was indescribable. Sammy was slumped against the wall shivering, twitching and holding his chest, blood spilling over his hands.

Harry and Zack crashed through the heavy growth. Somehow Clemency mobilized herself and went after them. She suspected that Harry would have told her to stay put, but she had already seen the carnage and he probably knew that she was unlikely to obey a second order. Harry took off his coat and laid it over the girl, and Clemency swallowed hard on the bitter bile building up in her throat.

Zack went up to Ruthie. 'What happened?' His voice was a small squeak – then he was raging again. 'Speak woman!'

'I–I tried,' Ruthie whimpered. 'I tried to st–stop him.'

'Who?' Zack thundered. 'Who did this?'

'I–I don't kn–know his name. He was a stranger.' Ruthie's eyes fastened on her daughter's covered corpse. 'Sammy tried to s–save her.'

'It'll be all right Sammy. We're here to help you.' Clemency pulled off her shawl, eased Sammy gently forward and wrapped it round him. Squeezing half in behind him she cradled him in one arm and using her free hand, pressed on his hands, to try to stop the flow of blood. He was gagging, and clearly both in tremendous pain and terrified. 'N–Nora,' he got out in a gurgle of blood.

'Don't speak, Sammy,' Clemency said, unable to stop tears spilling from her eyes.

Harry knelt beside her. 'Others are coming. It will be all right, boy. We'll get you to a doctor.'

Clemency glanced at him. Harry shook his head. As she feared, there was no hope for Sammy.

Sammy centred his sight on Clemency, and obviously called up his last ounce of strength and determination. 'Nora didn't w–want to go with the man. Mother m–made her. He was hurting her. I tr–tried to stop him. He had a knife and went mad.' Sammy winced and drew up his knees in pain.

'You were very brave, Sammy.' Clemency tenderly caressed his brow, wondering if he had ever known care and affection before. 'I'm

86

sorry Sammy.' Sorry that she had been hostile towards him early this morning.

'Is Nora d–dead, Miss?' Sammy murmured, his strength fading fast.

'Nora's at peace, Sammy,' she answered softly, kissing his cheek.

'I'm so cold. I want th–that peace.'

'Then go to it, Sammy.'

'Nora will take me, she will, w–won't she?' Sammy groaned in pain and fear.

'Nora will do that, Sammy, I promise.' Clemency cradled him in closer, her tears mingled with the dirt on his face. 'I promise.'

'No–ra...'

Sammy died with a glimmer of a smile on his ragged little lips.

Eight

'Is this a good place for you to be, Clemency?'

'Harry.' It was all Clemency could say. She was in Burnt Oak's private burial ground, which was laid out as a peaceful memorial garden. She was sitting on a carved wooden bench amid the graves and beautifully inscribed stone tablets, her head down and arms wrapped about her slumped body. Most of the family now chose to be buried in St Meryen's churchyard, but those of no religious belief, and the few Kivells still uninterested in life outside the community, continued to be buried here.

'Do you mind if I stay here with you?' Harry said, hoping she would not ask him to leave. From the moment of his first time here, with Georgette, to lay flowers on his great-grandparents' joint grave, he had felt the sense of continuity of being where his forebears, dating back centuries, rested in the ground. He found it reassuring, and right now he needed to be with Clemency.

'You're welcome to join me, Harry.' Clemency understood his necessity to be with her. She needed his company too and had intended to seek him out on leaving here. She and Harry shared a bond of more than kinship – the terrible, gruesome discovery in the churchyard, and the comforting of poor, tragic Sammy Juleff as he'd died. Verena had invited Harry and Georgette to stay at Burnt Oak Farm for the remainder of their stay in Meryen. It was comforting for Clemency to have Harry in her home. She had taken instantly to Georgette, who had endeared the whole family to her. Immediately after the tragedy, while distressed and terribly anxious about Harry and his involvement in it, she had gone to lengths to console Clemency also. She had wept for the dead children. She had not complained about the smallness of her room, which her maid had to share, or the lack of refinements in comparison to what she was used to. Understandably, she was clingy to Harry, but the family sensed she always had been. She wanted to know where he was every minute – even going often to his room, despite knowing he was sharing with Clemency's widowed brother, Adam. Clemency's eldest brother Tobias owned the farm and he and his wife and his children had the other rooms. Clemency expected Georgette to join her and Harry in the burial ground at any moment.

With the horror so often in Clemency's mind also was Matthew. He had arrived in the churchyard moments after Sammy's death. Matthew's manservant had guided him through the tangled growth and had related to him the full brutality of the murders.

'Dear God, this is the boy I spoke to on the road,' Matthew had gasped, the husky cadence in his voice thick with sickened disbelief. 'He was a bright boy. This shouldn't have happened to him. I was hoping to meet him again. Given the chance, he could have had a bright future. That poor girl ... Clemency, may I suggest you come away from there?' Matthew had said so kindly, so full of concern for her, and Clemency had been needled by guilt for having shrugged him off so unfeelingly.

Harry had taken Sammy away from Clemency and laid his little limp body carefully on the ground, folding Clemency's shawl over his face. Lifting Clemency to her feet, Harry had held on to her. Their hands and clothes bloodied, they had clung together in shock, trembling.

Matthew had said gravely, 'I'll allow the festival to continue for those who desire to stay. I'm sure people will wish to respect the tragedy in a quiet way, and some will need to keep company after this terrible affair. I'll return to them. My parents and I will speak to as many people as we can. This will be the first and last Squire's Day.

'Mr Bonython, may I suggest you take Clemency to the vicarage? The vicar is here to take you both there. The constable will follow in due course to take your statements. He and some of my men are searching for the murderer. He will undoubtedly bear the marks of his appalling crime and therefore I have hopes he will be quickly apprehended. Clemency, I am sorry you should have been a part of this. If you should have need of me...'

'Of course, Matthew,' Clemency had whispered to his final soft words, hoping to convey her contrition and her hope of continued friendship with him. How could she have been so beastly to Matthew? She might not want to become his wife, but outside of her family he was the closest man to her. She valued him tremendously. He was a man of great depths and warmth, who was clever and always intriguing.

'What about us?' Zack Juleff had bawled at Matthew as Matthew had made his departure. 'We're the boy's parents and my wife's been badly cut up. Don't we get an invite to the vicar's parlour?'

Matthew had whirled round and pointed accurately in the direction of the miner's rasping voice. 'What you can do, Juleff, is to gather up your remaining children and take them and your wife home. Tend to your wife's injuries. In your greed, cruelty and flagrant immorality you're both responsible for the deaths of your poor children. Keep your faces indoors. I fancy the mood of the people will be running high against you this day.'

Matthew had not been mistaken about that. Clemency had heard about the second speech Matthew had given up on the dais. He had implored the crowd, in their justifiable anger, to do nothing that would lead to Zack and Ruthie

Juleff venting more cruelty on their surviving children. Cries of shame had been hurled outside the Juleff's shabby home, although many would have liked to do a lot more. Much weeping, screaming and swearing had been heard echoing inside the pathetic place for the rest of the day.

Clemency had planned to go to Poltraze the following day to talk to Matthew, and to see Clarry and Phee. Then she had learned that Hattie had turned up unexpectedly at the big house and was unwell. Feeling it inappropriate to go, in view of her loss of Hattie's friendship, Clemency had written to Matthew instead. She had apologized for snapping at him – it sounded very feeble on paper. She had added that she would explain her rudeness when next she saw him. It all felt selfish and pathetic in light of the tragedy.

She was sure Matthew would readily forgive her, but she fretted over how badly she might have hurt him. He was so undeserving of her marring the day he had set great hopes on right from the beginning. How he must be suffering at having the entire festival so appallingly ruined. Yesterday would go down as one of the worst in Meryen's history. At least for Clarry and Phee the introduction of their healthy little grandson should provide a wonderful distraction. Thankfully, the brutal murderer, a drunken member of the acting troupe, had soon been discovered running across the downs looking for a hiding place. He would soon intimately know the hangman's rope.

Harry sat down beside Clemency. They stared silently ahead. Then Harry took her hand and Clemency leaned against him. The horror of the slayings hit them yet again and they shuddered. Harry put his arms around her and Clemency did the same to him.

Clemency rested her head against Harry's chest. Tears glittered on her eyelashes. 'It's Sammy and Nora's funerals tomorrow. The poor mites are being buried together in a pauper's grave. Their wretched father refused the offers from both our family and from Matthew Faraday to give them a proper funeral. Zack Juleff is a beastly, rotten brute. He cared nothing for his dead children and he cares nothing for his living ones. People were so moved over the tragedy that there were offers to sponsor schooling for the little ones, as Zack refuses to send them to lessons at the village school or Sunday school. He's refused those too. I'm sure he would think differently if money were also to be had so he could toss more beer down his throat. Now his wife's hands are shredded, making her a cripple, I'm afraid he'll force his younger daughter to prostitute herself. He'll certainly make his son Eddie take poor Sammy's place and steal to fund his drinking habits. Something should be done to save the rest of the Juleff children from coming to a terrible end. I'm trying to think of a way to get them away from Zack and Ruthie for good.'

'I'll support you in any way that I can, Clemency,' Harry promised. A shiver ran down the length of his body and his hold on Clemency tightened.

Clemency got the impression – no, it was more than that, she *knew* Harry was in greater need of solace than she was. 'Harry, what's the matter?'

'I'll tell you, Clemmie.' It felt natural for him to slip into using her pet name. 'I trust you to understand and not believe I'm crazy. You see, I knew something terrible was going to happen at the festival. I *felt* it. I had a premonition. I didn't know exactly what was going to happen, and I spent the entire time looking for a hint of some coming disaster. Then I saw you confront Zack Juleff and I knew it would involve both of you. When I reached you both we all heard the screams.' Clemency felt the tremors racking his body. He was burning hot against her. 'Clemmie, am I a freak? I felt weak and helpless because I couldn't prevent what happened.'

Clemency lifted her head. 'Of course you're not a freak, Harry. Please don't believe that. Many years ago, Tempest Kivell – she's laid to rest just over there – had the gift of second sight. She was a remarkable woman. I was a little girl when she was murdered inside Poltraze House. She sacrificed her life to protect her grandson and to save the previous squire and his family from being slaughtered by one of our own kinsmen. Laketon Kivell was so evil that he isn't buried here. The men took his body

94

off to some secret place. It was probably thrown down an old mine shaft. What I am saying, Harry, is that psychic powers are in our blood.'

Harry was thoughtful. 'Is it possible I was drawn here for a reason, other than sensing tragedy at the festival? I suppose time will tell. Apart from the dreadfulness of what happened, Georgette and I have loved meeting all the family. We've no relatives in Yorkshire, and many of our acquaintances are a rather prim lot. I'm so very glad to have met you, Clemmie. Shall we take a walk or a ride perhaps? It would do us good to use up some of this awful energy surging through our veins. I, and you, I fancy, weren't born to stay idle for long.'

Clemency got up. 'That's a good idea. A long ride will help us, I'm sure. Georgette will want to come with us. Does she enjoy riding?' She regarded him. His dark eyes were completely open to her. She could trust Harry entirely. 'You understand me, Harry.'

He stood facing her. 'And you already seemed to know me, Clemmie, to really know me. And no, Georgie is not keen on the saddle. She prefers to get about on four wheels.'

'Would she mind if we go on our own?'

'I'll promise to take her shopping at Truro tomorrow.'

'Let's go then. I'll show you some of my favourite places.'

'I shall love that.'

They left the burial ground holding hands.

* * *

Dressed in black, as he had done since being tragically widowed three years ago, Adam Kivell was on his way to the stable yard. He walked in a shuffle, his head hung and arms listless, the embodiment of a man who did not care if he lived another second and wished, preferably, to die on the spot. He barely ate – a constant worry to Clemency and Verena, his sister and mother – and he was thin as a tooth-pick. His once black hair was flecked with pure white and his skin was nearly as pale. Three times a week he went to the churchyard to take flowers to and tend the secluded grave of his dead wife, Feena, who had died suddenly of heart failure with his full-term baby inside her. Inconsolable then, and intending never to banish his grief, he was now drifting out of the world of the living, waiting only for the moment he and Feena and their baby would be reunited. His family did not know that he had already planned his funeral and the inscription to be added to Feena's headstone. He prayed every night that God would send Feena to fetch him to join her. He would have killed himself but he couldn't bring himself to hurt his family in this way, and he felt it would be a dishonour to Feena.

Adam's heartache was even more intense today. Yesterday, two children had been slaughtered in the churchyard, the act of malicious evil tainting the sacred resting place. The vicar, assisted by the curate, was going to walk the boundaries and sprinkle holy water on them and over the graves in some sort of service of re-sanctification and to combat the powers of evil. While welcoming that, Adam had decided he would keep out of their way. He wanted to 'reassure' Feena all was well and that his own love, as well as the Almighty's, protected her and their baby's souls.

Not knowing if his child had been a boy or girl was another great sorrow to Adam. When he talked to Feena he spoke of their baby as 'our precious pearl'. He was a good artist and he had drawn many pictures of Feena cradling the baby with her gentle-faced, kitten-eyed likeness. He kept these pictures in all his pockets, looking at them at regular intervals and kissing them with tenderness. 'I'll soon be with you my angels. Not much longer now.' The truth of this kept him going, because every drop of his future had run, in the instant Feena had perished, into his past. His death was coming. It was inevitable. Nothing could deny him that.

He reached the stable block and a stable boy had his mount ready, a plodding old mare, for Adam was no longer up to controlling a fleet or spirited horse. The boy, a typical freckle-faced, gangling sort, doffed his cap. Adam nodded his thanks. He spoke not a word to anyone if he could avoid it. Speaking meant thinking what to say and he did not want the bother of that.

'Mister Adam, look behind 'ee,' the boy said in his husky local accent. 'The lady what's staying here is coming after 'ee.'

Adam begrudged the energy he had to use to turn his body round. He did not have the mental strength to sigh inwardly at the coming sight. The stable boy turned his head to smirk.

'Mr Kivell, do wait,' Georgette simpered urgently as she tried, but failed, to pick her way daintily over the cobbles in a pair of high boots borrowed from Adam's mother. The silk parasol she was holding in a lace-gloved hand veered above her from side to side, as if being used by a circus artiste in a balancing act. Her maid was trailing behind her holding up the hems of her skirts. 'Please be kind enough to allow me a few moments of your time.'

Adam was not discourteous but he did not spare the young lady's indignity by advancing on her instead. From the first instant he had summed up Miss Georgette Bonython differently to the rest of his family. Harry he liked, but he didn't care for his sister. She wasn't all sweet forbearance, there was something false about her, but because she didn't matter to Adam he kept this to himself. She looked so out of place in a dress made for gracing a morning room in a desirable residence, not a rough workplace; a handkerchief up to her delicate nose to combat the farmyard smells. Good-hearted, honest and down-to-earth, Feena had never complained about the whiffs of dung, fowl or beast. And how different this woman was to Clemency who wore her simple dresses several times over, with dust invariably riding up the hems. Clemency shunned gloves and let her dark-amber hair tumble free. Georgette Bonython would probably faint, Adam thought, if she *saw* a lamb being born, let alone help a ewe to birth one, as Clemency had done from girlhood.

'How may I help you, Miss Bonython?' Adam said, not caring that his toneless, quiet voice would force Georgette to listen hard to catch his words.

'I was wondering if you've happened to have seen my brother, Mr Kivell? I've been looking for him, you will understand.'

That goes without saying, Adam thought, rising to impatience despite wanting to remain without feeling. *You never let the poor man have a minute's peace.*

'He's not in the house and he doesn't seem to be in the front or back gardens,' Georgette continued, taking a deep breath inside her handkerchief in fear her cheeks would become unbecomingly flushed over this man's, although civil, difficult manner. When introduced to her, he, without word or manner, had somehow made it plain he did not like her. This had peeved and infuriated Georgette. 'Have you seen him, Mr Kivell?'

'I have. He was on his way to the resting ground. My sister had gone there earlier. After their ordeal yesterday, I think they may be seeking peace and reflection.' With cool directness Adam made his meaning plain to Georgette – leave my sister alone with your brother, do not pester them. Adam was protective of Clemency and his entire family, ruthlessly so. They were all he had since losing Feena and, during those first agonizing months without her, he had killed two people – one his own father, one the kitchen slut bearing his father's child – to save his mother and Clemency from unbearable suffering. Clemency should not be interrupted by this selfish piece of fluffiness.

Georgette would not meet his piercing colourless eyes. Insufferable prig. 'In that case I'll content myself with some other matter. Good morning to you, Mr Kivell.'

Adam bowed his head to her then immediately looked to the saddle, preparing to swing up into it. From the corner of his eye he saw Georgette tripping back across the cobbles, her maid trailing after her. A ridiculous procession.

'I knew I'd find you here, in one of your favourite places.'

Matthew was astonished to be joined on the veranda of the summer house by his youngest sister. 'Hattie! You sound so bright and you're positively radiant.' He rose from the cane chair on which he'd been lounging, trying not to dwell on the wrecked Squire's Day, and even more so on Clemency. He usually came here to write his award-winning poetry, published under the pseudonym MR Dayton. He had perfected a way of writing in fairly straight lines in little light. With him was his constant companion: Sandy, a golden retriever, trained to help guide him about the gardens and in the house.

He stood up and made to give Hattie a hug, but she threw herself into his arms and laughingly peppered kisses all over his face and squeezed him tight until he thought his ribs would break. Hattie had not only recovered from the journey, and the episode of hysteria the servants had overheard, but she was pulsating with an amazing strength. At length Matthew had to push her off him. 'Sit with me, Hattie. You'll wear yourself out.'

'No, I'll stand, thank you,' she trilled, and she twirled in a full circle, sending her skirts smacking against Matthew's legs.

He blinked under his dark glasses. 'Hattie, please be still. It's unnerving for me when I'm not prepared for what you're about to do.' *Unnerving*? Why should he use that word just because his sister seemed wonderfully happy?

He tried to follow his sister's face and gain a long look at her. In the days before her abduction ordeal and subsequent scarring, she had been sweet, excitable, a little dizzy and enthusiastic in all things. Her ambition had been only to have a fairy-tale romance and wedding and live a happy life as an important man's wife. Hattie had never been a realist like Clemency.

'Have you seen my little baby, Matthew? My beautiful little boy?' Hattie put her hands together and swayed from side to side, rather like a child, in utter delight. 'Wasn't I clever to have him, so very, very clever? He's the sweetest, most adorable son in the whole world. Julian is so proud of me. He's promised to buy me

101

diamonds, as many as I like, in any setting I choose. Mama says she's never seen such a gorgeous child. And Papa is so proud of me too. When Freddie's a little older, Papa is going to breed a puppy especially for him. Won't that be a wondrous thing, Matthew, a darling little boy growing up side by side with a delightful, faithful spaniel dog? It will be brown and white and have curly ears and Freddie will call him Jakes. Jakes! Yes, it will be perfect. You know what it's like to have a faithful doggy companion. Matthew, you really must come up to us and see darling Freddie playing with Jakes. Can't you see it already? Oh, I can't wait.'

The more Hattie rambled on, the more troubled Matthew became. Hattie was in the grip of a different kind of hysteria to that she had suffered on her arrival at Poltraze. She was ill. He needed to talk to Julian. Matthew had noticed how his brother-in-law watched Hattie every second. It was not overindulgence or jealousy – Julian was anxious for her. He was at present likely to be searching for her. 'Hattie darling, I think we should go inside.'

Hattie swiftly sidestepped his hand reaching for her arm. 'No, no, I want to stay out here.' Her voice rose and there was desperation in it. 'I love the outdoors. I feel I'm about to suffocate inside. What's that you've got there in your pocket, Matthew?' She giggled, as she had done when she was a little girl, playing tricks.

Matthew was not quick enough. She swiped the folded sheet of paper peeping out of his coat

102

pocket and she pattered down the veranda steps waving it above her head. 'Hattie, please give it back. It's private to me.'

Matthew followed her but Hattie kept backing away from him. Sandy kept to his master's side, unsettled about what was happening.

'Let me see it,' Hattie sang, dancing about the lawn.

'Hattie!' Matthew shouted in frustration and nagging anxiety. His sister seemed to have gone quite mad. 'Please be still and give me the letter!'

Hattie could not be pacified or brought to order. Turning her back on Matthew she began to read the letter. 'Oh! It's from Clemency Kivell. Very big, bold writing, I see, so you're able to read it. Why do you still bother with her, for God's sake?' She waved the letter furiously then flung it to the ground at her side. Sandy promptly padded forward and picked up the sheet of paper gently in his mouth. He took it to his master, and then stood alert between the couple, ready to defend his master if need be.

'What's got into you, Hattie?' Matthew said quietly, keeping still. It was the only way to deal with her now. To be vexed and impatient would likely send her off into another kind of frenzy, and he was filled with compassion for his dear, young sister. The unsightly, white, slightly puckered scar, resulting from the torn flap of skin on her cheek, was more apparent on her blood-infused face. There was no sweetness, innocence and wittiness left in her, as in

103

his sister of old. It was a terrible thing for a young lady such as Hattie, who had desired to make a good match and fling herself into a high social life, to be scarred on the face. It was this, and childbirth – Matthew had heard about women acting irrationally after the event – that had brought Hattie to this dreadful condition. Hattie needed help. She needed her family. She was uncontrollably swept up in some mental disorder. Matthew wanted to weep for the beloved girl. Hattie needed strength and understanding, and peace and solitude. She had come to the right place for that. He would ensure she received it above all things.

'I loathe that Kivell girl,' Hattie bolted out, her eyes wild and desperate. 'I wish I'd never met her, that she'd not been trespassing in the empty house the day Kingsley first brought me here. Her father ruined my life. Seth Kivell wanted me dead in revenge against all of us at Poltraze and he chose me!' she wailed. She was sobbing uncontrollably, but it was chilling to Matthew as her eyes were waterless, her unnatural energy now all soaked up. She was sagging in the middle, about to crumple to the ground. Matthew would have caught her but Julian had been stealing up to her, and Matthew allowed him to enfold Hattie in his arms.

'He was going to burn me alive, with his own son, Logan,' Hattie went on in a terrible, bewildered child's voice, limp in Julian's arms.

'I'll take you inside and up to rest, darling,' Julian said, obviously fighting not to break down in tears.

'I'm so sorry, Julian. Our poor, dear girl,' Matthew could only whisper. He walked at Julian's side to the house.

'How can a father do that to his own son?' Hattie asked plaintively. 'Torture him and then plan to kill him in the most horrendous manner? Clemency allowed it. She was my friend but she allowed it.'

'But Clemency would never wish you any harm, Hattie. It was her quick thinking that saved you and Logan, don't you remember?' Witnessing Hattie becoming delusional was the worst experience of Matthew's whole life.

'No, it wasn't! She ordered her father to hurt me. She's evil. She mustn't go near my baby. Keep her away from my baby. She'll want to kill my little boy. Promise me both of you, swear it to me! That you won't let Clemency Kivell go near my baby.'

Something dark and flapping caught Matthew's eye. He strained to focus and make it out. It was moving away at speed but he was just able to distinguish the shape of a woman fleeing the scene. He was worried it was Clemency and she had overheard Hattie's ravings. No, Clemency would never retreat. She would face Matthew and ask what ailed his sick and distressed sister.

He pondered the runner's identity; then was quite sure he knew who it was. Once Hattie was settled in her bed he would go to the old dower house, Wellspring House, which was away at some distance and out of sight of the big house. He'd confront his other sister, the uncaring, cloistered Jane Hartley. Through her own selfishness and peculiar ways Jane was, although differently, nearly as disturbed as Hattie.

Matthew's heart sagged under the weight of his needy family. More than anything right now he needed Clemency's strong and good-hearted presence. At the festival it seemed he had offended her somehow, and although she had sent him a hand-delivered letter speaking of her remorse and deep hope to remain his friend, he feared things would never be the same again with her.

He damned his own heart and half-useless eyes for wanting to integrate with Meryen, for thinking up the wretched festival. He should have remained a determined recluse. Then Sammy Juleff and his sister would still be alive. He resolved that he would place the Juleffs under watch until he decided the best way to make atonement to the memory of the scallywag who had delighted him on the road.

Nine

At the Wheal Verity copper mine – the newer and larger of the two mines, on the far reaches of Nansmere Downs – Zack Juleff finished his early-morning shift, and rode up to grass-level with the last set of miners on the man-engine's narrow platform. The other sweat-stained, dirt-smeared men and youths held friendly banter, but no one spoke to Zack. Keeping his thick arms folded across his chest, his pick and shovel in his tight grasp, Zack eyed his fellow workers with hostile derision. He had received endless snide remarks and direct insults over Sammy and Nora's deaths. If any man dared to abuse him today he would push the big-mouthed swine off the platform to plunge to his death down the 150 fathom shaft, without fear of the consequences. Throughout the core – the traditional miners' shift – Zack had not uttered a civil word himself, just growled and sworn at anyone who got in his way. He had eaten his crib alone, kicking at loose rubble on the galley floor to show his seething bile.

Each stinging accusation thrown at him about his failure as a father, as a husband, and as a good neighbour, twisted up his guts, and over the days his fury had grown ever closer to exploding into some violent action. 'Sweet mercy, Zack Juleff, you know no shame,' blast man and lay preacher, Jeb Greep, a peaceful individual, had said, bravely confronting him. 'If you don't repent your ways and take care of your four young'uns, you'll know the wrath of Almighty God, you and your wife will.'

'His trollop of a wife you mean,' someone else sneered. 'He'll no more repent than Farmer Sampson's donkey will take up dancing. Zack Juleff's a heathen. A man who denies his own murdered children a decent Christian funeral is a dyed in the wool Devil's man.'

Zack had let that go, and much more, in case the accusers and mockers were among those who had left charitable handouts for his youngest four – food that had mostly ended up in his belly, blankets that he had put over his own body – but now that was drying up he was ready to lash out. He missed Sammy and Nora's incomes but he didn't miss them. He now had only four children to drag him down and he was glad of it. The brats he had herded home from Church Field might not be his anyway but products of his wife's earnings. Ruthie was already a whore when he had taken up with her, and he had never married her.

The four children had huddled together that night sobbing and whimpering for the big brother and big sister who had shared the rags they slept on, under the single window of the hut. 'Shut up yer bleddy caterwauling or I'll take my belt to the lot of 'ee!' Zack had bawled, snatching up the poker and brandishing it in the air. That always terrified the children. With no hearth and chimney no fire had ever been lit, and the hut was always cold. No sun, and very little daylight, was able to fight its way through the hazel barrier, and the floor was damp, stamped-down earth. The two chamber pots were never emptied until they overflowed, and then the contents were just chucked out of the door. The stench of the place had been likened to a fleapit of rotting corpses. The only furniture was a low table and two stools Zack had nailed together from scraps of wood. Food, when there was some, was eaten from three stolen serving platters: one for Zack, one for Ruthie, and the children were left to share the little bit slopped out on to the last one. There was always a tremendous squabble as they snatched off what crumbs they could.

That tragic day Ruthie had screamed, 'Never mind them bleddy brats, what're *we* going to do, Zack?' The relics of her black teeth poked out of her bloodless gums like toothpicks. She was shaking all over because she was so badly in need of a drink. That, and the loss of blood from her hands, showed in every inch of her rough, raddled features. She never spoke without her voice raised and her words were habitually swathed in complaint and malice. 'Just tell me that, eh. Look what that monster's done to me! My hands are cut to bloody ribbons. I won't be able to do nothing for days. I'm in

109

bleddy agony, I tell ya. All through you wanting more and more money for grog.'

'Shut your clack!' Zack had brought his fist a whisper away from Ruthie's yellowy eyes. 'You drink as much as I do – more, in fact! I bet you're guzzling all bleddy day long when I'm at work. And you've always let any man hump you, so don't blame me.'

'Get away from me.' Ruthie had sworn profanely, kicking out, and Zack had leapt out the way. He and Ruthie got into many a violent fight. It's what they did, and they enjoyed it in a sadistic way, nearly always ending up with fierce sex, sometimes in front of the children. Zack didn't want that now – the sight of his butchered children had turned his innards. Plus, he and Ruthie were so noisy in the throes of passion that the neighbours, now hanging about outside calling out insults, would overhear. They would surely be listening in on his household tonight. He didn't want to be accused of any more bestiality today.

'But that's it!' Ruthie had screeched. 'You drink all your wages away leaving none for anyone else. It's me who feeds you and the brats. Who'll want me now, eh, after what's happened? I'll never be able to use my bleddy hands pro'ply no more. Have you thought about that, eh? There's men round here who pay well for a romp and to keep me quiet so their high 'n' mighty, sanctimonious wives don't find out, but no one'll risk it now. Before, it would have been deemed no more than adultery with a whore. Now, they'd be castigated for going with the woman they claim forced her daughter into prostitution. They blame us for Nora and Sammy's deaths more 'n the murderer. We'll have to move on at the end of the month, after you get your wages. Just don't drink it all away!'

Zack shoved his way first off the platform at the landing place. 'Be careful, you fool,' the lander, outside on the surface, protested.

'Go to hell!' Zack snarled, blinking in the daylight and grimacing as the continuous thunderous clanging, thumping and hammering of the industry hit his ears. It was almost a shock to the system after the claustrophobic, muted silence underground that distorted the noises of digging, shovelling and the blasting that made deeper tunnels.

'You could've caused a bad accident then,' Jeb Greep started then halted, recognizing the simmering darkness marking Zack from top to toe as pure hatred.

The rest of the men stacked up behind Jeb, all as grave as judges, all boring accusing stares at Zack.

Zack yanked off his hard hat and made a fist at each man. 'That's it! Go on then, say what's on your minds, you bunch of manky bastards!'

'You're not wanted here or in Meryen, Zack Juleff,' Jeb said harshly. 'You're scum, Zack Juleff, a black-hearted devil. Take your woman and leave the village today. You can leave your poor children behind. You'll probably be glad to be rid of them. There're families ready and willing to take them in.'

Zack gave Jeb a smile as if spawned from death, then he thundered, 'You can go to hell Greep, you and the whole bleddy lot of you! I'll be off when I'm good and ready and my wife and my brats will come with me. I'd sooner see them in their grave than leave them with any of you bleddy lot. Now, don't none of you dare to speak to me or raise an insult to me again, or I'll take it out on my brats and it'll be your fault, understand? Now, have any of you got anything to say? Thought not. Damn you all to hell!'

Way up on a natural rise of land above the Wheal Verity, Clemency and Harry were on horseback watching the miners changing shifts. Harry had binoculars. 'It's very different to the coal mines in Yorkshire,' he said. 'Out here surrounded by so much land and sky it almost seems to have a touch of romanticism, although I'm sure the death and maiming rate would refute any such notion. The miners here don't emerge quite so black and dusty.'

To Clemency, the great attle heaps scarred the land like hills of oppression, adding to the general sense of gloom. Left as they were in time nature would inevitably reassert itself and grow some sort of rough dressing over them. 'The land has been poisoned by copper residue and will be worthless for wildlife until several generations after the mine has been completely worked out and been "knocked". You must have noticed there're no rabbits and foxes in the vicinity, and no birds because there're no insects to feed on. But they're a proud lot, the men and women down there, proud of their skills. Some of the men work up to be a mine Captain. The best of the boys, if they're very fortunate, go on to Hayle to learn to become engineers.'

She closed her eyes and lifted her chin to thwart a rush of tears. 'Sammy used to work down there. His brother and sister, Eddie and Becky, will be down there now. I've asked their neighbours about them. They're sent off to work no matter how ill and weak they're feeling. All the children are pale with shock and even more fearful since Sammy and Nora were murdered. At least Eddie and Becky are given some food while they're at the mine. Only God knows how little Jacka and Joe – Joe is mentally deficient – are faring at home with their wretched mother.'

Reaching across, Harry smoothed the fabric covering her shoulder. 'I know what you're thinking, Clemmie. I hate what's happened too. If only ... but there's no point in "if onlys".'

'I hate Zack and Ruthie Juleff for what they've done, the way they are. No matter how poor someone is there's no excuse to be cruel to your children. Imagine how those little ones must feel every moment of every day, Harry, abused by the very people who are supposed to love them, do their best for them, comfort them and give them hope. We've got to go from here.

We've got to do something for those poor children.' Resolution and power lifted Clemency up straight in the saddle.

'I understand. To where?'

Clemency felt that Harry had grown so close to her in the last few days he could read her every mood, and she suspected that he already knew what she would say. 'To the Juleffs' place.'

'I thought as much.'

'Zack will find us waiting for him when he arrives home, but first we shall talk to Ruthie. Those four children will not spend another day living a life of purgatory.'

Infants Jacka and Joe Juleff were huddled in a corner of the filthy, rubbish-strewn hut, near the door in case they needed to make a hasty escape from their mother. Most days she literally threw the boys outside on to the hard ground, and would rave and swear at them as they shook with pain and cold. Their lack of nourishment meant they were always cold, their squashed noses continually running with discoloured gunk. 'Don't let me see you pair again this side of daylight or I'll beat you both to a mash of broken bones!' their mother was wont to say.

The scabby, nearly naked brothers were staring at Ruthie who was curled up on the ground beside the table, her head rolling from side to side. She had been vomiting all night and even more since Eddie and Becky had trudged off to the mine and Zack had stamped out in a vicious mood for his shift. It wasn't unusual for Ruthie to throw up after downing too much grog, but now she was groaning and thrashing about.

'Mother? Mother? Can't 'ee git up, Mother?' Jacka did not really want to draw Ruthie's attention for he'd only get kicks and clouts, but he was more afraid she'd peg out and die and that would mean the workhouse for him and Joe. Nora had taught him a few words of prayer that she'd picked up from listening in on chapel, and Jacka prayed them now, asking God over and over again not to let his mother die. The workhouse was the threat used frequently by both parents when one or the other was lay-ing into them or one of the others. Often they were all thrashed at the same time for no reason at all. 'Worse 'n' hell it is in the workhouse,' they'd roar. 'Then you'd see how lucky you were to have lived here and been brung up by yer parents. You'll be made to work day and night in there with no food or sleep. Monsters and spriggans will pour stuff down yer throats to keep 'ee awake. If you stop working as much to scratch yer ass they'll cut the flesh off yer bodies and set dogs on' ee with iron jaws. You'll be made to scrub walls of rusty tin and peel mountains of taatees for rich folk.' The terrifying descriptions of other torments would go on and on and Jacka and Joe would pee themselves as they cowered, and their tiny bodies would lurch with the blows from fist or foot or belt buckle.

'Mother!' Jacka called out in sudden fear, as

loud as his relentlessly sore throat and ragged voice allowed. He'd rather his mother woke up in a violent temper and hurled him and Joe out of the door than have her being dead.

Joe clung to Jacka, sucking his thumb and not comprehending a thing. He was deaf and dumb and incontinent and, like Jacka, rickets bowed his twiggy legs. Joe was constantly menaced by Zack, who threatened to 'aave' him down a mine shift or drown him in the stream for being a 'useless blob of offal'. Nora had done her best to clean up Joe, always struggling to separate him from Jacka long enough to pull away the fetid rag she had previously tied around his waist and between his legs, before cleaning him as best she could and tying on another piece of rag. She had washed out the rags in the stream and dried them on bushes, but they were never hygienic because Ruthie refused to buy a soap ball. Joe's soiling was now days old and together he and Jacka reeked like a steaming midden. Jacka could easily fend Joe off him and give himself freedom of movement, but boss-eyed Joe was everything to him: his company, his sanctuary and his sanity. Jacka was unconcerned by the smell and filth.

Ruthie started to lash out in an even wilder manner. She wailed a fearsome ear-splitting wail, her body suddenly heaved sideways and she puked a stream of vileness. Then she flopped down and groaned and groaned, pulling up her knees as if her insides were in agony.

'She's going to die!' Jacka panicked. 'We'll

116

be blamed. Be worse for us then than the work-house. Gotta get out of here, Joe.'

It was a hard, painful task for Jacka to scrabble to his feet with Joe hanging on to him, hurting his bruised ribs, back and neck. Zack had kicked a huge hole out of the door in a drunken fit last night. Getting scratched and bloodied by the splinters, Jacka climbed out through the ragged space with Joe clinging to his belly like an animal's young.

Holding up Joe's weight as best as he could in his pain and weakness, Jacka slunk off through the trees, throwing his head about warily in fear of seeing another soul. People had sometimes given Jacka food for himself and Joe, but some of those same people had come outside the hut and shouted bad things at his father and mother. Jacka had trusted no one except for Nora. All he knew was that right now he and Joe needed to hide.

Ten

Matthew left the East Wing, his exclusive part of his house. He was turned out for riding, his destination Meryen. Sandy padded along at his side. Sandy knew exactly when his master was leaving the property and not taking him too. Every now and then he licked Matthew's hand, begging not to be left behind.

'Sorry boy, where I'm going is not a suitable place for you. I've got something very important to do today. Don't worry, you'll have company, you're going in with the spaniels,' Matthew said, firm and serious. Barker would accompany Matthew in place of Sandy to ensure his safe passage to and from the village. It irked Matthew that his near blindness necessitated him to always have an escort. It seemed ages since he and Clemency had ridden together. He missed these outings with her. He missed her so much.

It burned in Matthew the need to see her, to know her true thoughts about him. Yet he didn't need to question her, he admitted miserably to himself. Clemency was not in love with him. Her willing absence from his life spoke of that. He was a fool to have lived in the hope, for so long, that his deep and committed love for her would one day be reciprocated. In the usual way of things, the first really serious interest a man showed in a woman soon led to an engagement. Clemency had made it plain, in many ways, that he was no more to her than a close friend, and now it seemed she did not even particularly desire that.

She had used to come to Poltraze as much to see his parents as to see him. Like any love-struck person, to ease his yearning mind he had made excuses to himself for her not seeking something more intimate from him: she was unconventionally independent; the time wasn't right for her yet. She didn't need to explain her uncommon rudeness to him. He realized the reasons for it now. He had been smothering her. She had lost patience at having to fend him off. He had vainly thought that all the work she had put into helping with the arrangements for the festival had been exclusively for his benefit, but Clemency had been pleased to do it for Meryen. He had discomfited her in public by his expectation that she take a prime place close to him during his speech. Something had unsettled her beforehand, angered her – he knew her well enough to be sure of that – but his directness had been too much. He had given her no choice but to disclaim him once and for all.

He wanted so much to see Clemency again, to tell her he wouldn't bother her again in the manner she had come to despise. Could they be friends? It wouldn't be easy. There was an

119

uncomfortable barrier between them now.

'Damn it,' Matthew growled under his breath. He certainly did not want to see Clemency with another man. She was, apparently, spending a lot of time with her distant relative Harry Bonython, a man very different to Matthew. Bonython had the benefit of Kivell blood in him and had perfect sight and stature. He was successful and outgoing, and from the way Matthew had seen Clemency adhere to Bonython at the scene of the tragedy, he was the ideal comforter for her, the perfect companion. The arrival of Bonython and his sister, a young lady Matthew had not taken to for some unaccountable reason, had been to Matthew's disadvantage. If not for Bonython's presence that day, Clemency might have sought comfort from Matthew. It had come to Matthew's ears that she had exchanged angry words with Jowan Kivell earlier that same day, so Jowan wouldn't have counted at the time when she had been most in need of someone. Matthew had lost one rival and gained another. He and Jowan Kivell had been usurped without as much as a backward thought from Clemency.

Picking up his heavy strides, Matthew's face darkened as he sought to bury his pain. He had wasted enough time. He should do the same as he had witnessed Jowan Kivell doing: pass his interest on elsewhere. He should seek a woman of good wife material. He had been a great many years celibate. As a man of restraint and aloneness since he'd been blinded, it had not bothered him unduly. Now, he asked himself, why go on without seeking that pleasure? He would look for some pleasure and take a wife. A refined lady, such as Miss Georgette Bonython, would not fit into the languid life of Poltraze, with its dearth of social life, but a woman of wholesome health, quiet and loyal but firm in nature, would do well to provide him with intimacy and children. A new light glittered in Matthew's grey eyes, his stooped shoulders rose and squared and his step took on some springiness. He did not have to stay in semiseclusion, wasting his prime years. He wanted a family; a wife who would cherish and respect him and fill his house with a brood of contented children. Then, at last, this ancient, creaking house would be purged of the morbid gloom that gripped it, and be transformed into a true home. He would exchange his dream for a solid reality, he decided. After all, nothing usually came out of chasing a dream.

Hence it was with some brightness that he placed Sandy into the care of his parents in the morning room. He found Clarry and Phee had been groomed to perfection and were preparing to receive a visitor.

'It's a pity you won't be here to welcome Miss Bonython, dear boy. Your papa and I are elated that she's accepted our invitation to call on us,' Phee twittered, tying a big, yellow bow around the neck of one of the female spaniels. 'She seemed a dear young lady when we met her on ... um ... on that day. She's very pretty too. Why don't you delay your excursion to the village and stay to greet her? Your Papa and I tried to persuade Jane to join us but as usual she declined. I suppose it was just as well.'

'Jane would not make good company for Miss Bonython. I'm afraid I have something pressing to do, Mama. I am going to confront the copper miner, Zack Juleff.'

'Oh, the um, father of the um ... two um...' Clarry mumbled, looking away. He and Phee did not like to dwell on the tragedy. In the aftermath they had put aside their own distress and shared the grief with some of Meryen's inhabitants, but they had been relieved to get away early and banish the wickedness from their minds. They had ordered their valet and maid to hide the clothes and shoes they had worn and the walking sticks they had used where they would never have to set eyes on them again. Then they had taken their 'precious family' for an extraordinarily long walk in the grounds.

'Indeed. The Juleffs have made no attempt to better the lot of their remaining children and I am determined they will be removed from their home before there are more deaths. I have already secured foster parents for the Juleff children, and I will have their parents out of the village by the day's end.'

'That would be for the best, Matthew. You are very wise. God will bless you for it.' Phee's unease at the subject visibly vanished as she turned her thoughts to something else. 'Miss

Bonython would make an excellent friend for our dear, young Hattie when Hattie is well enough to receive visitors, don't you think?'

'She might do, Mama.' Matthew nodded, hoping his parents would never come to realize that there was more wrong with Hattie than plain exhaustion. They rarely mentioned their son-in-law. Sir Julian spent most of his time watching over Hattie and trying to gauge her moods. He went to the nursery three times a day. While Hattie rested, often under the light sedation prescribed by the Stapleton physician, he wrote to his stewards and relatives, or he read, or took short walks, alone, as he preferred, in the gardens. He ate when Hattie ate. He did not care for dogs so he rarely sought the company of Clarry and Phee. Sometimes of an evening he would ask to be admitted to Matthew's quarters and once there, sipping claret or brandy, he would ask Matthew about every detail of Hattie's life before her disfigurement. Matthew found that Julian's anxiety about Hattie's condition was a cross he gladly bore. 'Is Miss Bonython to stay for luncheon?'

'Oh, yes, she is actually.' Phee tittered and clasped her hands together and beamed with childlike excitement. 'And for afternoon tea also. Will you return in time to join us, Matthew? Do try. You found Miss Bonython agreeable, did you not?'

'I hope to be home for tea, Mama. I shall look forward to it.' Matthew found delight in delighting his parents by saying so. They had also cherished the hope that one day Clemency would become his wife and live here where they could see her every day. As light-brained as they were, they seemed to have realized it would never happen. The thought of their son looking over another prospective bride sent them into a joyful dither of reorganizing the day's program.

Amused, Matthew left them. Georgette Bonython would never do for him. She would find the idea of becoming a provincial wife to a rather insignificant gentleman such as himself, of relatively small means in comparison to her own circle, quite laughable. Every aspect of her character cried out to be yoked to a title and perhaps a statesman. But it would be useful to Matthew to be in her company, to help him recall how to flatter and flirt with a woman. In the old days he had indulged in all the sensuous pleasures. After today he would take more outings, to places well away from Meryen and prying eyes.

He was surprised and annoyed to find Jane in the hall, coolly dismissing Rumford who had shown her in. 'So. Jane.' Matthew regarded her with his most steely manner and without the slightest welcome.

'Do not take that tone, brother. I have come to see Hattie. It's what you wanted, isn't it? I'll go straight up to her.' Jane Hartley, at Matthew's insistence, no longer wore widow's weeds, but her plain, brown attire and severe bonnet, and her thin and stiff form, made her more like a

124

plank of wood than a woman of twenty-eight years. She had a frosty way of tilting her head as she spoke and then clamping her bloodless, thin lips, which Matthew particularly disliked.

'I've changed my mind.' Matthew waved her away. 'Hattie could no more find good use from your presence than she would from a crow in a graveyard.'

'How dare you speak to me like that? You have insulted me, sir.' Jane's bony chin went up and tightened into a deep cleft and her pale-brown eyes blazed.

'My name is Matthew. I hate the manner in which you persist in addressing me either as brother or sir,' Matthew retorted harshly. He had never found affection came to him easily for Jane. She had been a whingeing, resentful child and at times a bully. It had been a mistake to act on his intrigue about why she had fled after witnessing Hattie's delusional episode.

He had walked with Sandy as his aide the quarter mile distance to Wellspring House. Judging from the stones scattered on the path, Jane must have fled all the way home. It seemed her sister's plight had frightened her badly.

Matthew had been astonished to find Jane quaffing sherry straight out of a decanter. Also in the dreary sitting room was her shadowy companion, the grey, ingratiating, Adela Miniver, who was quite the bundle of nerves and squeals. 'Oh Jane, don't. Sit, please sit, and let me send for tea. Shall I get you a calming draught? It would do you better than drink. Oh,

125

Jane, what is it? You are quite sending me out of mind with worry. Shall I send for the doctor?'

Then the women, who both looked old beyond their years, had finally seen Matthew and Sandy standing silently in the doorway.

'Both of you should sit down,' Matthew had said sternly. 'Jane, I am shocked to find you swilling spirit down in the sordid manner of a drunkard. Are you a slave to the habit?'

Adela Miniver squeaked like a mouse caught in a cat's jaws and obediently dropped down in the nearest seat. Jane banged the decanter down on the silver tray. 'How dare you come into my house with that creature,' she'd hissed, her dour features twisted so grotesquely that Matthew saw another sister that day overtaken by some sort of madness. 'I will not have the dirt, hair and fleas that are tolerated in the big house in here. Send it outside at once. And what I choose to do in my house is entirely my affair. Leave if you don't like it.'

'Of course I don't like your wanton behaviour.' Matthew fired his words as if bullets from a gun. 'I will remind you also that it is *my* house and that you live here under my sufferance. Sandy will stay. I wish it, I am the master.'

Jane's hand flew to her chest as if she had been shot there. With jerky movements she got herself down into a chair. 'So I am merely a charity case, am I, and one not willingly given to?'

'Are you not surprised? You give nothing to

126

your family or the world,' Matthew said coldly. 'You can expect no goodwill from anyone. You are a parasite, Jane. Your blood is cold. Your heart is dead. But enough of you; even recounting your faults gives you too much consideration. Why were you near the summer house today? I take it you fled because you wanted nothing of Hattie's predicament, so heartless are you.'

Matthew's head was thundering in pain with the concentration that was necessary to keep Jane in his sight, for she was swaying with indignation. More anger flashed in him as she passed Adela a meaningful look. It was an act of self-preservation. Callous Jane and her simpering companion cared only for their own positions. When Matthew had discovered that he and his brother and sisters had been adopted, he had not felt it necessary to look up all the details of each background. What had occurred to Jane to make her so pitiless?

Jane cleared her throat. 'Well, what is the matter with Hattie? I left the scene because I could not think of a way to help her, and I did not want to embarrass her husband, whom I have not been introduced to.'

'You would not have stayed to help even if you could have. I'm sure Sir Julian would not wish to meet you under any circumstances. I have wasted my time here. I wish you both good day.' Matthew had then turned on his heel and stridden for the door.

Jane was next at his side, dragging at his coat.

It was unlike her to move so fast; what had given her new energy that day? 'What is it you want me to do, Matthew? On the day of Hattie's arrival I heard from the servants she was badly indisposed. I am no good with illness, I confess. I will put aside my own feelings and see Hattie if you think it would be of benefit to her.'

Loathing her beseeching hands on him, Matthew had shrugged her off. 'Do not concern yourself, Jane. I will not throw you out. Do whatever your conscience tells you to do.'

He had walked back slowly to the big house, drawing in clean, fresh air deeply to shake off the sense of decaying humanity abiding in Wellspring House.

Now Jane was in his hall and had brought that dreadful ambience with her. 'I think you should leave at once.'

'Indeed I will!' Jane tossed a small cloth-wrapped package on the credenza. 'This is for my sister's child. I made it myself. She may take it for him if she so wishes or do otherwise. I shall never set foot inside this house again. You have won your way, Squire Faraday. And you can go to hell.' Jane strode out.

Outside on the gravelled court, Jane whirled round to face the house. The uncountable tall windows with their small panes seemed like sneering eyes to her. She wasn't wanted. The house didn't want her any more than the people inside it did. Her parents had never been a mother and father to her, always preferring the handsome, clever and sociable Kingsley and the little princess Hattie. As for Matthew, the quiet, good-natured boy who had become a fine soldier and then a hero, he had ended up in their batty parents' eyes as a fascinating, reclusive figure of folklore. Now they were proud of him setting himself up as the local squire. His compassion over the deaths of a pair of village guttersnipes had earned him respect in the community. He cared about worthless strangers, and the vulgar Kivell girl, but not the sister who had endured the loss of her husband.

She would never forgive Matthew for destroying her fantasy that Hugh Hartley was a sainted warrior, and for the way he had literally torn down her only reason to exist, in front of Kingsley and the servants. She had known exactly what Hugh was like, of course. He had raped her before their wedding day and reviled her throughout their short marriage. 'You are the plainest, most graceless woman I have ever met,' he had taunted her. 'Making love to you is like being with a dead fish.' He had savoured telling her of his numerous affairs and accused her of keeping a poor household. She had secretly rejoiced at learning he had been burned to death in the officer's mess, but that joy had been usurped by the shock and humiliation of learning that Hugh had left her destitute and had run up many debts in her name. Matthew had settled with the creditors but why shouldn't he? He was her brother. She had been forced back to live with her parents, whose childish ways and smelly dogs she hated. Unable to face Society again, and finding men and their base ways disgusting, she had done the only thing she could think of: to form an existence as a grieving widow. It had given her some importance, a reason to be pitied and empathized with. But no one had cared about her at all.

Jane stormed back home from the big house and went straight to the sitting room. She found Adela there with her feet up on a tapestry stool, nibbling from a small, round box of chocolates.

'Jane, you're back already,' Adela tittered nervously, guiltily putting the lid on the box and getting up. To Adela, Jane's steaming dark face told of an imminent rage. She had gone into many, each one getting worse, since the squire's unannounced visit. Then, afraid the squire might cut off part of her generous allowance, she had decided to try to win back some of his favour. It had obviously failed resoundingly. Adela held her breath, dreading what might be to come.

With her hands clenched so tightly her nails dug into her soft flesh, shaking madly, Jane spat out, 'My brother saw fit to order me out of his house. I was denied the opportunity to see my sister. I'm not wanted. My absurd parents have never wanted me. My brothers and sister don't even find me tolerable. I am allotted the worst of maids and no footmen in this house.' She was stamping her feet so hard pictures up on the wall swayed on their hooks. 'And Hugh, my wretched husband, the man who swore he

130

would love me to the ends of the earth, actually despised me from the first. He only married me because of my trust fund and he cleaned that out in weeks. I've got nothing! I've been nothing! And I'll always have nothing!'

Near to tears over Jane's distress and her own torn nerves, Adela whimpered pacifically, 'You'll always have me, Jane. You can always count on me.'

Jane's wrath-filled eyes turned like orbs of splintered glass. She glared at the woman who had proclaimed to be her consolation, as if that would help. Adela Miniver was a toady, greedy nobody who had made herself at home and was getting plump on Jane's food and treats. Since Jane had moved them out of the big house Adela issued orders to the servants here as if she was the mistress. She was getting above herself. Jane had met Adela Miniver at a charity bazaar soon after her marriage. Never one to find social conversation easy, Jane had been finding it hard to mix with the other married ladies, and had resented their confidence. How could they present themselves so cheerfully, to be witty and proud of their femininity, when THAT was happening to them regularly at night? Last night some of these ladies must have succumbed to the ultimate of all humiliations. How could they behave so normally? Some were even boasting of the children they had borne.

As soon as it had been evident Jane had not conceived in the first month, Hugh had branded her barren and deserted their bed. Jane had been relieved to the point of crying with joy, but hurt to her bones when Hugh had jibed, 'I don't want children with you anyway. I'll not tie myself to you for the rest of my life.' Jane knew she would have loathed and feared the process of childbearing, and she had always disliked children anyway.

The only woman at the charity bazaar whom Jane could feel superior to was the wallflower, doomed-to-be-left-on-the-shelf Adela Miniver, so she had made a friend of her. During the few times Adela had met Hugh she had become infatuated with him. Hugh had tormented Jane about her. 'If Miniver wasn't so damned ugly I'd take pleasure in breaking her maidenhead.'

'You think I should be content with only you in my life, do you?' Jane fumed at Adela.

Adela glanced demurely to the floor and then appealed to Jane. 'I am devoted to you, Jane. You gave me a place at your side when I was unfortunately left with nothing.'

'Left with nothing, you say? You are left with nothing?' Jane bawled wildly. 'You're a leech, Adela Miniver. It is I who has been left with nothing and you are not, and never will be, enough to fill the empty places in my heart. Never ever forget it.'

Her senses gone completely, Jane slapped Adela viciously across the face.

Eleven

'There's barely enough space to flutter my fan in this room.' Standing in her petticoats and breath-defying tight corset, Georgette frowned at the adequate, comfortable, but lacking in opulence, furnishings of Burnt Oak Farm's guest room. 'I am not accustomed to being so close to a farmyard and dirty, squealing animals. I dare not ask you to open the windows, Netty, for fear of being overwhelmed by a variety of revolting smells. And those fowls, do they never stop with their honking and squawking?'

Georgette frowned harder at feeling a little ashamed. At first, from a suitable distance, she had found some of the livestock, including the fierce-looking, long-bearded male goat and the batches of fluffy chicks, a little fascinating. Over the meal tables she had questioned Clemency's eldest brother, Tobias, about the gentler side of the farm's husbandry and seasons. She had even watched Tobias's children feed an orphan lamb by hand in the kitchen. Each evening she had filled in the details in her journal and smugly imagined the future amazement of ladies in superior drawing rooms while she impressed them (or, impishly, the contrary) with her unlikely experiences. The few distractions here vanished, however, as soon as she was in the brass-stead bed with its hand-stitched country quilt and Netty had turned off the lanterns. *When* she would be next able to enter Society houses, Assembly Rooms and the theatre depended on the intentions towards her of Rupert Goring, and that – she hoped, she prayed in the darkness – rested on how long she could avoid him, and keep Harry away from him too.

At one time Goring had imprisoned her in his grasp. 'Let me speak to your brother to ask him to announce our engagement before you go down to Cornwall, or I shall tell him everything.'

She could not bring herself to live a lifetime of humiliation, nor to risk having Harry being horrified with her if she confessed to him, so she had fled.

'I grant you that the room is not large, Miss Georgette, but it has done you well enough until now,' Netty replied, lightly smoothing out the day clothes her mistress was to wear to Poltraze. The maid, formerly Georgette's nursery maid, had a down-to-earth, sometimes schoolteacher, manner. Ever grateful to the short, moon-faced, round-bodied woman – whom she affectionately called Netty – for saving her from the conflagration that had destroyed her home and parents, Georgette relied on her much as she did Harry. 'I believe Mr Bonython going out today to ride again with Miss Clemency has quite unsettled you.'

'It has and I am in the right to be piqued,' Georgette muttered, stepping into the skirt Netty was holding out for her. 'Harry should be accompanying me to Poltraze. The invitation was to both of us. He has left it to me to make his excuses and is allowing me to go off on my own to a strange area and to be pitched among virtual strangers. It's very unkind of him.'

'But Mr Bonython had already made his arrangements. He doesn't venture far or often from your side, Miss Georgie,' Netty pointed out, deftly fastening the skirt and reaching for the bodice top. Georgette knew that the outfit of sheer cotton in royal blue, relieved with indigo panels, with a fine lace collar and cap detail on the upper sleeves, would look perfection on her gently curving frame. Netty always saw to that, but was proud of her mistress's appearance in whatever she wore. Netty often said that she could look gorgeous even in rags.

'Really Netty, how can you take his side? An invitation to the squire's house is far more important than taking a ride with Clemency. He might offend the Faradays.' Georgette narrowed her eyes. 'Harry should put me first. He's beginning to dance to Clemency's tune. He spends too much time with her. And she has no sense of shame to seek to be alone with him so often. I don't understand why her mother allows it. It will surely harm Clemency's reputation. She would be considered unfit company

135

in proper circles.'

'We don't have to be concerned with Miss Clemency's reputation or anything else down here, at the end of it. I do understand your point of view, Miss Georgie, but the invitation was from the older Mr Faraday and Mrs Faraday and not the squire. I'm sure Mr Bonython will go to Poltraze with you next time. Please don't keep wrinkling up your face, Miss Georgie. You'll spoil your perfect complexion.'

'I'll see that he does the right thing in future,' Georgette said, feeling distinctly not pacified. 'Do you think there's something going on between Harry and *her*?'

'A romance, you mean? Well, now you've come to mention it I suppose there could be. They are totally at ease together. But I can't see Mr Bonython and Miss Clemency married to each other.'

'Why do you not think so? I have the feeling Harry would think her ideal for him. After the failure with the fickle heiress, I'm sure he would never consider another airhead.'

'I don't know.' Netty pondered. 'I suppose I—'

'Yes?' Georgette was curt.

'Oh, I don't know, Miss Georgie. Even though, in all my years of service, I've witnessed betrothals and nuptials in all the classes, what do I know of falling in love and all that goes with it? I'm pretty sure from what I've seen of Miss Clemency that she'd rather remain unmarried for life than be wedded to someone

136

she wasn't utterly attached to. Don't concern yourself. Mr Harry would never do the wrong thing for himself or for you. One day soon you'll be married to the perfect gentleman and you'll never have another worry in the world, trust me. Now for your shoes: the buckled black leather or the blue with floral details?'

'The blue pair I think. God forbid it that Harry falls for Clemency. With her self-determining ways she would never be a good choice for him. His home is in Yorkshire and hers is here. They are presently enjoying their similarities but they would find their differences would never ever tally.'

'Well said, Miss Georgie. Sit now and I'll dress your hair.'

'But you've also said that love will have its way,' Georgette said, becoming despondent and vexed again.

When Georgette was seated in front of the dressing table mirror, Netty picked up the hairbrush and glanced seriously at Georgette's downcast reflection. 'Mr Bonython will get married one day. He's made it no secret he wants a wife and family. You will have to come to terms with the fact, Miss Georgie. And when you're married you won't be able to run to him on every whim.'

'I know, Netty.' Biting her lip, Georgette reached over her shoulder for Netty's hand. Never far from Georgette's surface was the child in her seeking reassurance. 'I know it's selfish of me but I just want everything to remain the same. I'm frightened of someone coming between Harry and I. Inevitably, a wife will take precedence in his life over me.'

'And your husband's over him. But his love for you will never be less than it is now, Miss Georgie. He's devoted to you. He'd give his own life for you.' The moment was steeped in emotion and time slipped back and Netty embraced Georgette to her bosom.

'I know, bless him so much. It's not been a good time here with those deaths of those unfortunate children. I wish only to leave here now and forget all about it. I've asked Harry if we may travel overseas before we finally return home. He's agreed we may go to Paris and then on to Florence. I want to have our things sent on before us, but Harry says that it would be simpler to return home first and to pack leisurely while he attends to the businesses. I need to convince him to start our travels straight from here. Would you try to persuade him too, Netty? I need the excitement and newness of travel and adventure to lighten my soul. I know I'm a little fusspot but you understand, don't you? You always understand me, Netty.'

'Of course I will speak to him for you if it means so much to you, Miss Georgie, although I think Mr Harry is making the most sense about it. It would be far easier to return to Yorkshire first. Now, I suggest you make the best of your time at Poltraze. Mr and Mrs Faraday are enchanting people, so I've heard from Miss Clemency. You found them agreeable at the festival, did you not? Let them entertain you, and when you get back you can tell me all about it.'

When Georgette was ready to join Tobias Kivell, who was to drive her in a small carriage to Poltraze, Netty sat down to write a letter of the utmost importance to her, to Yorkshire.

Clemency and Harry, and Matthew and Barker, were not the only ones heading for the Juleff home. Jenny was walking in that direction, carrying a basket over her arm, after shopping at the baker's. Zack should be home from the mine by now and the chances were that little Jacka and Joe had been turned out of doors. She was hoping to spot them so she could give them some meat pies and yeast buns. She was going to try to get them to understand to choose a safe hiding place where she could leave something for them regularly. She was concentrating so hard on ways on how she could provide further help for all the Juleff children that she did not see the man approaching her until she was about to collide with him.

'Oh, Mr Jowan.' She bowed her head and pinked from her neck upwards, for it seemed an increasing coincidence she should often suddenly meet up with him, either out and about or at Wingfield House, and she was beginning to look forward to seeing him.

'I see you are on an errand, Miss Jenny.' Jowan swept his hat off. 'May I carry your load for you?'

'That would be very kind. I am on my way to the Juleff place.'

'I thought that might be the case.' Jowan relieved her of the basket and he turned about and fell in step with her. 'Food and stuff for the children, I presume?'

'I do what I can. Mr Logan has said he'd like to tell the children they'd be welcome to call any time at the kitchen, but he won't do so because the parents would be bound to take unfair advantage. I fear greatly for the children. Indeed, I fear they've very little chance of living into adulthood.'

'And if they do, perhaps they will not be unlike their parents. It's a sorry tale.' Jowan reflected on how he knew nothing of what it must be like to live in such dire circumstances. His own father had been good to him, even though Jowan was an illegitimate child of a common-law wife. Except in extreme situations, the Kivells took care of all their offspring. 'Zack Juleff views his children only as a source of income, especially for the day when ill health or infirmity, the inevitable fate of nearly all underground miners, prevents him from employment. His children all fear him now but one day, when they are stronger than he, their feelings will turn to hate and one of them may well kill him.'

'Please don't say such things.' Jenny shuddered. If such an event were probable it would be better if the other children followed poor Sammy and Nora to the churchyard. She could not bear to think of Eddie, and Becky, and little

Jacka and Joe, who would never be fit for work, never living a happy day on earth.

Jowan stopped and faced her, looking up under the unassuming tilt of her straw bonnet. Her sweet, forbearing face, with its pretty sprinkling of freckles, had taken on a sorrowful expression. 'I beg your forgiveness, Jenny. I would not distress you for the world but, in my foolishness, I have just done that very thing. You must think me very brash.'

It was not lost on Jenny that he had addressed her without any formality. Could this worldly man, so desirable to women despite his turn-of-the-blanket birth, really be interested in her? He had consulted her on every aspect of the work and completion of the new front door for Miss Tamblyn, bringing to her wood samples and paint charts, and hinges and escutcheons, for her approval. Miss Tamblyn was elated over her sturdy door with its brass plates and fox-head knocker. After the old lady's profuse and tearful thanks to Mr Jowan, Jenny had later told him, 'You've done a mighty deed for Miss Tamblyn. She couldn't be any more proud and uplifted. I swear she will live another ten years because of it.'

'It was my pleasure,' he had shrugged, while smiling at Jenny. 'I am pleased it has made you both happy.'

Maudie, the Wingfield House housekeeper, had voiced her views to Jenny about Jowan's unprecedented amount of visits to the house. 'Well, he isn't coming here to see me or Mrs

Brookson, is he? Mr Jowan would be a fine catch indeed for a girl of your humble beginnings.' She had hurried each time he called to titivate Jenny's hair. 'You are honoured, you know. Mr Jowan is not known as a man given to romance yet he is courteously attentive to you, Miss Jenny. You must be sure to give him a little encouragement.'

Mrs Brookson had intimated through direct looks at Jenny that she had noted these extra calls, but so far she had chosen not to mention them. It seemed to Jenny that Mrs Brookson was neither for nor against the notion. Overwhelmed by the idea, Jenny had pushed aside the smallest thought of any meaningful association with Jowan Kivell. After all, he might be just amusing himself and she did not want to make a fool of herself. Yet in her heart she was sure she could trust him.

Glancing shyly into the blueness of his eyes she found herself saying, 'I could never think ill of you at all, Mr Jowan.'

'You have made me feel very gratified, Jenny. Please call me Jowan. I feel we may make a closer acquaintance, if you get my meaning – if you do not object, of course.' He didn't linger over his smiles. He wouldn't be unkind to Jenny and make her feel self-conscious. She wasn't dynamic and fascinatingly unreadable like Clemency, but she was interesting in her own way and quite entrancing. She would hold enough innocence and constant appeal to never bore him. Jenny would never try to cut him down. As a wife she would give everything to her man and she would always be a treat to come home to.

Jenny's heart leapt in a way she had never imagined could happen. She had taken it for granted that romance and that sort of thing would not come her way. Men of high birth would not give her the slightest consideration, and Mr Logan and Mrs Brookson would never allow any interest from someone of meagre means. She had been content to stay as she was. 'I would have to speak to Mrs Brookson first.'

'Of course, but you do not wish me away from you?' he pressed gently, loving her natural shyness.

'I do not wish that at all, Jowan.' She met his warm smile with one of her own.

'Then I shall speak to Logan this evening to ask his blessing. I hope very much, Jenny, that when we next walk down the street I may take you on my arm.' He wanted to kiss her lips softly and briefly and to wrap her up and hold her close in his arms. He was looking forward to it as much as he would to any passionate encounter. He would love and cherish her, as he knew she would him. He would marry Jenny whatever Logan or Mrs Brookson might have to say about it. He had made up his mind.

There were various ways that the Juleff hut might be reached. This had helped Sammy to slip in quietly at home or make many a successful escape from his parents, Jenny mused

143

sadly. She and Jowan had gone by way of a narrow back alley, then along a series of rough tracks only one step wide. Mrs Brookson would be most displeased if she knew Jenny was grouping in her skirts and lifting them up calf high. There were shadowy places in the banks and hedges where two little boys might crawl under to huddle out of sight. 'Jacka? Joe? Hello? It's Miss Jenny. I've brought you food and milk. Don't be afraid,' Jenny called. She and Jowan then checked all the hidey-holes and were disappointed not to discover the two youngest Juleffs.

'The boys usually appear to snatch away what I bring them,' Jenny said sadly. 'By the look of it they haven't left the hut, poor things. I hope they haven't been beaten and are too hurt to move.'

'Don't worry, Jenny. Once we get to them I'll make sure those children will never suffer again.' During the search, Jowan had made up his mind to negotiate with Zack Juleff over some way to prevent further ill treatment of the children. He would do it for them, but most of all for Jenny.

'Thank you, Jowan. That will put my mind at rest.'

They arrived at the hut itself. It was the usual scene of dilapidation, the roof seeming about to cave in. As well as the gaping, splintered hole in the door, many of the weathered-grey wooden slats of the walls were broken or missing. The ground outside was covered in rubbish and filth.

Jowan caught his breath. 'Don't you go any closer, Jenny. I'll pick a way to the door and rouse the wretched man.'

'Wait, Jowan.'

He heard what she did. Horses were approaching from both directions on the road through the village.

'It's the squire and his manservant, and there's another gentleman with them,' Jenny was soon able to say.

'And it's Clemency with Harry Bonython,' Jowan said dryly. 'It seems there are more of us with the same thing in mind.'

He and Jenny walked on to the place where both parties had chosen to pull up and dismount, some yards from the hovel, where they would be out of sight. As Harry and Barker tethered the horses to a hazel branch, a man in dark clothing stole out from the trees and whispered something to Matthew. He then quickly went off through the trees on Matthew's instruction.

The gathering eyed one another. Out of respect for Matthew's position the others remained silent to allow him to speak first. Ignoring his despondency at Clemency being here with her new companion, Matthew spoke as the one in charge. 'I have come here to speak to Zack Juleff about the welfare of his children. I gather you're all present with the same intention.' Receiving affirmation from all, he went on. 'I am here to succeed in a plan that should be pleasing both to God and man. I have made arrangements that should suit all persons in that hellhole. This gentleman is a lawyer, here to act on my and the children's behalf.'

'I had thought to offer—' Clemency started up.

Matthew cut her off by raising his riding crop. 'All is settled. It only remains for me to confront Zack Juleff and obtain his consent. I ask you all to stand back. I am confident Juleff will cooperate with me but he might baulk at what appears to be a committee thrust upon him.'

'We'll wait quietly out of sight, Matthew,' Clemency said.

Throughout Matthew's speech, Clemency had not taken her eyes off him. She was impressed he had already put a plan into play and was carrying it out with authority. Matthew had not bothered to look at her or anyone else closely, but Clemency knew he was fully aware of who she was with. She did not wonder what his thoughts of her being with Harry were – after all he was part of her family – but she was concerned at Jowan's familiarity with Jenny Clymo, and how he was carrying her basket in a territorial manner.

News had come to Burnt Oak that Jowan was taking pains to flatter the pleasant, quiet girl. Jenny wasn't Jowan's type of woman at all. What point was he trying to make, and why was Logan allowing what seemed to be a dalliance on Jowan's part, to continue? Jenny Clymo was a vulnerable, naive young woman in the matter of love. She could end up hurt and heartbroken. Then Clemency saw Jenny was at ease with Jowan and that there seemed to be a genuine connection between them. Could it be that Jowan had moved on almost immediately after his proposal to Clemency? If so, he was serious about wanting a wife and family. By all account he had chosen someone who had ideal qualities in that respect. Jenny would never be troublesome. She would be eager to give her husband all due respect and loyalty. She was precisely what Clemency was not – ideal wife material. Abe was also now walking out with a miner's daughter. Clemency thought she would not care about it all but she did. She did not want to be incapable of doing or being anything. It was ridiculous to be running these matters through her mind while out on an act of mercy, but she couldn't help feeling left out and left behind.

All except Matthew, Barker and the lawyer moved forward to a vantage spot where they could view the proceedings out of sight.

'The squire seems a very able man,' Harry said, evidently enjoying this episode of local drama. 'Perhaps he intends to indenture the children to skills on his estate.'

'I had thought to do something similar for the eldest boy Eddie at Chy-Henver, and to ask among the family if they could take in any of the others,' Jowan said. 'There's plenty of room for them at Burnt Oak.'

'What they really need and deserve is to live somewhere in peace and security,' Jenny said with emotion.

'Do not fear.' Jowan lifted Jenny's arm and put it through his own. 'Before this day is over I swear to you those children will never suffer again.' He caught Clemency staring at him. It was likely she deliberated it as odd and unfitting that he should attend intimately to Jenny. Clemency was something of a cynic, and probably viewed his concern over the Juleff brats as a measure only to please Jenny. Except for making a new door for old Miss Tamblyn, he had done nothing for the villagers. But he had always been open-handed to charities, including some outside of the Kivell Relief Fund. That should count for something. He wasn't heartless.

'Why did you come here, Clemency?' Jowan's question was direct and he intended it as something of a challenge.

'To reason with Zack Juleff on behalf of the children and, if that didn't work, to take them away for good. In effect to buy them, because it's only hard cash that will speak to such a selfish brute. The squire is the one most likely to succeed with him. It doesn't matter who takes the children under their care as long as it leads to them living a better life.'

Matthew cautiously walked the path that Barker, with a staff in hand, had cleared for him. The stout-bodied lawyer followed on, clearly apprehensive and disgusted with the conditions he was called to tread on.

Barker rapped on the hut door with his staff. 'Zack Juleff! Open up. The squire, Mr Faraday, is here and wishes to speak to you forthwith. Open this door without delay!'

'Go to hell! I don't talk t'no one if I don't want to – squire, angel or God hisself – and I *don't* want to!' Zack hollered in anger from within. There were bangs and crashes as if things were being hurled about. Zack poked his brutish head out of the large, glassless window. 'Get away from here! This place don't belong to you, Squire, so you got no right to be here. Get away! Or else!'

Matthew made out the ugly, sneering face just inches from him. 'I don't wish to enter your filthy fleapit, Juleff. You will come out here to me.' The spectators watched astonished as Matthew reached in, grabbed the miner by the shirt and hauled him clean out through the window frame. Matthew dumped Zack on the ground, on to his knees, and placed a heavy boot on his shoulder. 'Hold still or I'll beat you senseless and deal with your wife instead.'

Barker pushed on the battered door and went inside.

'Huh?' Zack was confused for a moment, perhaps thinking he was in the middle of a beer house brawl. 'Here, you got no bleddy right to set yourself on me! Get off!'

'Silence, man, and listen to me and don't interrupt. I've come here for one thing and I will have my way. You have no intention of rearing your children as a father should so I am here to buy them from you, all four of them.' Matthew took his boot away and let Zack raise his head.

'Money, you say? How much?' A wide smile revealed every one of Zack's teeth stumps.

Clemency and the others had moved forward to see the confrontation better. After what had happened to Sammy and Nora, Clemency was sickened by Zack's eagerness to gain reward to be rid of the four little people he should love most in the world. Harry muttered something indecipherable under his breath. Jenny shuddered and a serious Jowan patted her hand. Clemency saw the lawyer, twitching his bumpy nose at the fetid smells, was unmoved by the drama as he pulled papers out of a leather folder.

'You disgust me to my soul, Juleff,' Matthew hissed. Then his voice grew hard and business-like. 'For the sum of ten pounds for each child I require that you and your wife sign them over to me for life. From this day forward they will be wards of the Faraday estate. You and your wife will have no legal binding over any of the four children. I want you and your wife out of the parish forthwith. Indeed, I will see you are escorted out well beyond its boundaries. I will give you a further sum of five pounds in re-compense of your and your two older children's month's wages; a generous amount. I also require that you sign over Sammy and Nora's bodies to me so they may be given a proper, dignified burial.'

Zack was still down on his knees, his hulk sagging in the middle as he laughed with glee. 'Where do I sign? Give me the papers quick.'

'Don't you want to know what I intend for the children's futures? Or to ask if your wife agrees to relinquish her children?' Matthew hurled down at him, toeing the ground as if wanting to give the miner a hearty kicking in the ribs.

'Not on your life!' Zack bellowed, staggering about as he got to his feet. ''S'right for the likes of you to preach and judge, but you don't know nothing of a poor man's life. I never knew my father. I was born a bastard and my mother was a whore. One of her lovers flayed the skin off my back 'fore I learnt to crawl and he preferred my body to hers. It was she what put me on the drink so I could bear the pain. I was on my own at eight years of age. I got a job on a mine surface, then I've worked down 'em ever since. I was never wed to the drunken bitch indoors. Don't know if any of them brats are mine anyway. That's why I don't care about 'em. Of course I'll take a good price to be rid of 'em. There's many who would do the same.'

'You have no excuse for your behaviour. You chose to follow a path of cruelty and all in and below heaven condemn you for it.' Deep repugnance exuded from Matthew's whole being. He was alert with tension, as if ready and hoping Zack would give him cause to beat him with his fists.

Clemency read Matthew's mind correctly that he despised the fact that the heartless greedy miner would benefit greatly from the deal. She felt for him and wanted to sympathize with him but now was not the time, and she wasn't sure of Matthew any more. He had showed her no favour so far today and he might not want her consolation.

'Excuse me, sir.' Barker emerged from the house. 'The woman is dead.'

'Dead?' Zack roared. 'She's raving drunk, been on the floor since I got in and can't be roused.'

'She's dead,' Barker repeated, discounting Zack as one would an insect. 'And has been for an hour at least. I've seen this sort of thing before. Blood poisoning. Her hands are blackened to the elbow and there are the other usual signs. I suggest the coroner is informed swiftly, sir.'

'I shall see to it, and that the woman is put in unsanctified ground before the end of the day.'

'I am sure there's no need to commiserate with you over your loss, Juleff.' Matthew's words were edged with ice. 'Sign these documents, pack your belongings and make your way to the crossroads. A cart will be there to take you far away from here. Meryen will be well rid of you.'

It took only five minutes for Zack to scribe a wavy X on the legal documents, witnessed by the lawyer and Barker, then to slip inside the house, and with a small bundle on his back, to be off down the road whistling a jolly tune.

* * *

'That man is despicable,' Clemency murmured, chilled that anyone could offload their responsibilities so gladly and be so callous. She and everyone else, now assembled by the horses, were relieved to be breathing fresh air again.

'He's evil to the core,' Harry said harshly. He went to Matthew, who was preparing to mount his horse. Clemency joined the men, feeling the uncomfortable emptiness of being forsaken, as Matthew had still not paid particular heed to her. 'This is a job well done, Mr Faraday. Sammy and Nora will soon be able to rest in peace, and the other children will know a good future. May I ask what arrangements you have made for them?'

Matthew focussed on him, then on Clemency, and Jenny and Jowan. 'You may indeed, Mr Bonython. The eldest boy and girl have already been collected from the Wheal Verity. A local preacher went with my man so the children would not be scared. They are being taken to a foster family at Redruth; good, Christian people, who will see they are educated and well cared for. The two infant boys are to be fostered by another family nearby so the children will be able to see each other regularly. The servant I had placed to keep watch here informed me that the boys left the hut some time ago. He has now gone to find them. It shouldn't be too difficult.'

'Forgive me for speaking up, Mr Faraday,' Jenny said. 'But it may not be easy to find Jacka and Joe. They are very small and in the past, in

153

a bid to escape a beating, they have successfully hidden away for hours. If they learn that their mother is dead, their father has abandoned them, and their brother and sister have been taken away, they won't understand it all and might stay hidden for days and starve to death.'

Matthew bit his lower lip. 'I thank you for the information, Miss Clymo. A wide and thorough search must be mounted for the boys without delay. God forbid there is another tragedy.'

'I suggest the villagers are best put to the task, squire,' Jowan said. 'They are familiar with all the likely hiding places and the boys will know them. Miss Clymo and I will be glad to organize the search straight away. First we'll go back the way we came, in case the boys are making their way back here by that route.'

Clemency watched as Jowan swept Jenny along to a narrow track leading to the side of the hut. They called out the boys' names, called that they had food and good news for them.

'What can Harry and I do, Matthew?' Clemency asked. How would he respond to her? In his former gentle and forthcoming, really-pleased-to-see-her way, she hoped.

Matthew met her eyes levelly. How easily it seemed she had forsaken him altogether. She probably hardly ever gave him a thought nowadays. 'Anything you care to.'

Clemency flinched inside. She had received a rebuke. Matthew had as good as accused her of doing exactly what she'd want to do anyway. She could not deny she was like that. She was selfish and high-minded. She must have hurt Matthew's feelings very deeply at the festival for him to be so offhand. He must have felt she had kicked him in the teeth. She hated that. Matthew had not deserved to be slighted. Her letter of apology could not have fully made up for her horridness after all the time they had been so close, totally trusting one another. Swallowing hard on the constriction in her throat, her voice came out small as she said, 'We will join in the search for the boys.'

'You have my gratitude.' Matthew bowed his head to her and mounted. Once his master was soundly astride, Barker followed suit. The lawyer was already prepared to leave.

'Matthew.' Clemency grabbed his horse's rein.

He lowered his head down to her and adjusted his sight until he got the best view of her face. Her cheeks had dark pink blotches and she was frowning heavily but she was as beautiful as ever. 'Yes, Clemency?'

Clemency's mind skimmed back to the time she and Matthew had kissed so passionately at Poltraze. It had been the best and most exhilaating experience of her life, but she, at sixteen years of age and with family troubles looming, had forgotten it so soon afterwards. Now she remembered all the times she and Matthew had shared together, all the fun and laughter. She enjoyed each and every thing they had shared even more now in retrospect. Every moment had been special; moments she should have cherished. Then in one foolish act she had denied herself the special relationship she'd had with Matthew. She missed him. She missed being in his house and all that was there. 'How is Hattie faring? Is she rested? I would so like to see her and renew our friendship. Would you kindly ask Hattie if I might call on her?'

'I'm afraid it won't be possible, Clemency. Hattie has made it clear that she doesn't want to see you at all. For some strange reason she becomes distressed at the mention of your name. I'm sorry but I have to ask you to refrain from calling at Poltraze until she has returned to her home. My parents would be pleased to receive a letter from you. I'm sure they would like me to pass on their regards to you here and now.'

Hattie's aversion of her was hurtful, but Matthew's unyielding formality ploughed an even deeper pit in Clemency's stomach. Matthew obviously did not want to see her either. Georgette was presently visiting at Poltraze. A stranger was welcome there but Clemency no longer was. Again she got the horrid, cold, dejected feeling of being left out. Cold waves of loneliness at the exclusion hit her like slaps to her face.

'Clemency?'

'What?'

'The squire has gone and we're alone,' Harry said. 'And you were away in your thoughts. Have you had an idea about where those two boys may be found?'

'No.' She brought herself back to the issue at hand. 'We could try along the stream. The banks are high and overgrown in places.'

'No, I should think we should go to the churchyard,' Harry said, passing her the reins of her pony.

'Why so? Have you had one of those strange feelings again?'

'Nothing like that, thank God. Those boys have been through even harder times of late. I was wondering where, what or whom they might turn to. Apparently poor Nora was willingly maternal towards them and Sammy was their big brother. I think they might have gone to them, as it were.'

Shortly afterwards, after shopping for a few things, Clemency and Harry entered the churchyard via Church Field. Neither wanted to pass through the gate in the wall where, just beyond, Sammy and Nora had died, but to make an approach by way of the lychgate might more readily alert the boys, who might then give them the slip. They trod stealthily in silence, looking all around until they reached the paupers' graves and the recently disturbed earth of Sammy and Nora's double grave. Two long rows of paupers' graves stretched back to a hedgerow heaped with budding gorse and flowerless wild herbage. The wind soughed through the trees and the ever-present crows cawed, up on the branches, and wheeled high up in the sky. Long grasses rustled and perhaps a small creature or two could be heard, but there was no evidence of two frightened little brothers having hidden themselves away.

Clemency glanced at Harry and he returned an encouraging expression. 'Hello,' she called softly. 'Jacka? Joe? Are you here? Please listen to me. My name is Clemency and this gentleman is Mr Bonython. We are your friends. We have come here to help you, if you'll allow us to. We were the ones who found poor Nora and Sammy the day they were hurt, the day that they died. We wanted to help them but it was too late. Now we both would like to help the pair of you. Nora and Sammy would want you to trust us.' As her words spilled out, she and Harry kept their heads in motion, hoping to spy the boys.

'Look, we have brought you some food and clean fresh water, and a warm blanket for each of you. We have come with news for you. Your mother has sadly died from an infection to the cuts to her hands and your father has left the village and he will never, ever be coming back. Do you remember Squire Faraday who held the festival? Well, he's arranged for you both to go to live with some kind people who will always care about you. You will never go hungry again. You'll never be beaten and you'll have a proper warm bed to sleep in. Eddie and Becky have already left the mine and gone to live with their kind new family. Please, won't you come out so Mr Bonython can take you to the nice people who will take you to your new home? Look, I'll put the food and blankets down beside Nora and Sammy's grave and then we'll stand back a long way so you know we aren't going to hurt you.'

Exchanging glances again with Harry, Clemency did as she had promised. They retreated several yards, and stood waiting, grim but smiling for the children's sake. Clemency put her hands together as if in prayer. 'Please let them be here. Please let them come out.'

'We'll leave the things anyway. Luck will have it hopefully that they will find them before someone else does.'

Minutes ticked by horribly slowly. Then Clemency thought she saw a movement at the foot of the hedgerow. She and Harry watched, astounded, as a clump of foliage was lifted and a tiny, dirt-smeared face rose up as if from the ground. Pinpricks of alarmed eyes darted from side to side.

'My God,' Clemency whispered, her throat raw with emotion. 'They're down in the ditch. They'll be damp and cold. How frightened they must have been to seek refuge there.'

A strange, distorted body emerged from the ditch and crept forward, crablike, on all fours. Clemency and Harry were puzzled until they realized that the youngest boy was clinging to his brother's middle. She and Harry stayed back, waiting patiently until Jacka had picked up a pasty, ripped off the wrapping and broken it in half, and he and Joe were stuffing the food into their mouths. The boys stared at Clemency and Harry in suspicion and fear, obviously knowing they couldn't make an escape, knowing that the man and woman could be on them in a moment. Hunger must have driven them out and Harry was as choked as Clemency was about it.

'Boys,' Harry said in a kindly tone. 'When you're ready, wrap yourselves up in the blankets and I'll carry you together to the others who will help you.'

'Is our father really gone?' Jacka called out.

'He's gone for good, I swear to you,' Clemency replied. She and Harry felt it was safe to slowly close in on the boys. 'I'm sorry about that. I know every child would rather live in their own home with their parents and all was well, warm, happy and safe. But sadly your father and mother were never kind to you. Squire Faraday has made sure that your father can never take you back, never, never. I promise you everything will be all right from now on.'

The brothers gobbled down the pasty, making sure they didn't miss a crumb.

'May I lift you up now?' Harry asked softly. 'Both of you together, of course.'

Jacka nodded.

Harry swept the double bundle of once discarded humanity up into his arms, holding them securely. Clemency wrapped the blankets about them, covering their heads so they would be spared the public gaze. Voices could be heard closing in as others thought to search the churchyard.

At Harry's side Clemency walked to the lychgate, sorrowful that it had taken Sammy and Nora's dreadful deaths for this to happen.

Twelve

'Julian! A visitor is being driven up to the house. Come and see.' Hattie clapped her hands ecstatically like a child receiving a surprise treat. Pale as mist, frail looking in a tragic heroine sort of way, she was reclining on a day bed in the master bedchamber, placed in the window nook where she could gain a clear view of the parkland. She was wrapped in wool and furs, for she had complained of being painfully cold.

Julian dashed straight to her side. He had discarded his coat and loosened his necktie and waistcoat in the stifling hot room, where the fire was well stoked. Hattie's girlish grin made him want to kiss her all over her face and hold her close against him. He settled for giving her a delighted smile, encouraged that she had at last found something of interest. She was placed here every day on doctor's orders but had ignored the birds and squirrels, and the flowers and trees he had pointed out to her. Her vacant eyes had sometimes swept the skies and she had murmured to herself in a strange language, seeing things, he knew not what. 'Oh yes, my darling. It's a young lady that your parents have invited here. A Miss Georgette Bonython.'

'She is very beautiful. Her bonnet is quite the thing. I wish to meet her, Julian. Send for my maid. I shall get dressed and go downstairs.' A little colour filtered into Hattie's wan cheeks and she began to push away her wrappings.

Julian was pleased but also worried and he gently restrained her. 'Darling, I'm delighted you feel that you are well enough to get up but I don't think it's wise for you to meet a stranger. I have to tell you that she is related to the Clemency Kivell you revile so much. Miss Bonython is actually currently residing at Burnt Oak.' The Kivells and their lot sounded a thoroughly rum lot to Julian, not at all suitable for genteel people and particularly not for his precious, ailing wife.

'But Miss Bonython *isn't her*. You saw her. She's a true lady. One can tell top breeding.'

'But she may say something that will upset you, darling.'

'I *want* to meet her Julian. Please do not forbid it.'

Some spark and stubbornness gleamed out through Hattie's blue gaze. Julian saw no sign of delusion or of her being overwrought. It was worth a chance, he hoped, while Hattie was calm and lucid to let her have her way. To keep Hattie cooped up against her wishes would probably drive her straight back into melancholy and worse. 'Very well, but I will not leave you for a single second. I'll ring for the maid.'

* * *

163

'What a fascinating house you have,' Georgette said and meant it. Seated upstairs in the drawing room with the elderly Faradays, she had been introduced to the spaniels, who had been ordered to sit or lie. She didn't care much for the dogs, and although the outside of the building was dull and strangely mismatched, with an uninspired extension here and there, tagged on down the previous centuries by the previous owners, she could tolerate the anomalousness. Not a roof or chimney or height of wall from wing to wing or addition tallied, and the windows were a hotchpotch of design.

Inside was rather better than she'd expected. The dark-panelled hall was a mix of the baronial, fine mouldings and the latest in chandeliers. The two corridors leading off from the hall were dark and shadowy but not in a gloomy way to Georgette. The bold side in her found them inviting and mysterious and she mused that one might discover all manner of distracting and delightful things pointing to the eccentricity of the Poltraze inhabitants. The housekeeping was highly commendable. The china, porcelain, plate and silver gleamed. Not a speck of dust existed on picture frame, sculpture or surface. Any musty smells from decades of wood-smoke fires and cold stone were offset by beeswax and burning lavender-scented candles, but she had detected a strong niff of dogs.

Here in the pleasantly fine drawing room, the walls were crowded with paintings of dogs and the Faraday family, present day and bygone, and at least a dozen by contemporary artists, all rural scenes and not to Georgette's liking. Mr and Mrs Faraday were portrayed as a young couple with spaniel puppies in their arms, a touching portrait of outmoded quaintness. Their four children were displayed in a row by age, when young, and all appeared pretty and pampered. The next complement showed the four upon reaching adulthood. The squire and his brother and sisters' likenesses showed quite different characters. The well-set man with the aura of confidence and success must be the banker Kingsley, who lived with his wife and family in Devon. The petite, harshly refined and dour-lipped young woman had to be Mrs Jane Hartley, the selfish, reclusive widow. The blonde girl in a white dress and wide, blue sash, trailing a wide, blue-ribboned hat in her delicate hand was like a fresh breath of air, and was obviously Lady Stapleton. The squire's portrait was hung above the fireplace and was the most striking of all. Commanding and powerful, he was in Lifeguards' uniform, his hand resting on the hilt of his sword. It was a picture of a hero, a man who would as readily die to protect the most insignificant human being as he would for Queen and country.

Georgette knew that Matthew Faraday was heroic and commanding still. He had taken complete charge over the recent tragedy, reassuring the shocked villagers as a true officer would survivors of his regiment after a bloody battle. Georgette found him an intriguing individual. Reluctantly friendly and cautious she had thought him, when they had been introduced, and definitely closed off to just about all. His eyes had been a shock to Georgette when he had lifted up his tinted eyeglasses out of politeness. She had expected ugly maiming but instead she saw eyes, although marred, of dove-grey gentleness, yet eagle-like and unbelievably gorgeous. She had, as she guessed others had before her, been mesmerized while he had drawn her face into his limited focus. There were such depths to his eyes. They were like corridors of sorrow and secrets. Matthew Faraday was entirely loyal and protective towards his family, unlike Harry was.

All the way on the drive to Poltraze, Georgette had become more frustrated with Harry – her feelings then turning to resentment and anger at his decision to choose Clemency's company over hers, a stranger to him until a few short weeks ago and a woman with some alarming unladylike ways. Clemency roamed about the world with little thought for decorum or the aspect that should be paramount to her: her reputation. Clemency was a bad influence on Harry, Georgette thought. She was stealing him away and Harry was a willing prisoner in her clutches. Clemency was a witch, and Harry was cruel to set aside his own sister so lightly for her. Once she got back to the farmhouse Georgette would make him see this, and he had better be repentant.

The Faradays were refreshingly unlike the Society climbers Georgette knew and this dippy old house was wholly appropriate for them. She would hate to live here, of course, yet it would suit her right now to stay here, to be in the more stately surroundings with a team of servants as she was used to. She would feel just as protected here as she would with Harry and the hardened, uncouth Kivells at the boring, countrified Burnt Oak.

'Our son keeps the house and grounds very well.' Phee beamed with pride. 'Matthew is a dear, you know. Have you met him?'

'I had the honour of speaking to the squire at the Squire's Day, but then unfortunately he was called away.' Georgette glanced down, as a lady should when mentioning a sad and traumatic occasion.

Just as a sensitive host should, Clarry changed the subject. 'Matthew is in Meryen on business at the moment, but he is hoping to return in time to join us for afternoon tea. Now, Miss Bonython, I do hope you are enjoying your stay at Burnt Oak. Never seen it ourselves, have we, my old bud?' Affectionately, he inclined his teetering, grey head to Phee. 'But we've heard many an intriguing tale about it from dear Miss Clemency. Now she's a captivating young lady, as you are yourself, if I may make so bold. We miss her; haven't had the pleasure of her calling here for quite a while, have we, my old treacle? I expect you and her are the very best of friends, eh?'

'Clemency and I are fond of each other. However, we do not have a lot in common.' Except wanting to be with Harry, Georgette thought sourly. The more she dwelt on it the more she resented Clemency from keeping Harry from being here with her today. Harry should be meeting the important local people, not indulging that wayward girl's whims.

'It's a pity your brother could not come with you today. Hopefully another time,' Phee said.

'I will insist upon it.' Georgette smiled meaningfully. 'Harry would like Poltraze. The gardens here seem delightful.'

'Thank you,' Clarry said. 'The gardeners and grounds-staff are highly skilled. There are many fine species of pine trees and subtropical plants. The hothouses contain the most beautiful delicate plants from across the world.'

'And,' Phee said as if awestruck, 'Matthew ensures we keep a very good household staff. Somehow he manages to avoid the plague of lazy, useless, disloyal misfits.'

'You are much blessed in that regard.' Georgette had heard too many boring laments at functions and in powder rooms from matrons on their troubles over inept servants. God forbid she must contend with those problems one day, although marriage and her own household was the last thing she could look forward to while Rupert Goring ... She tried to thrust him out of her head, but just like the persistent man he was, his image hounded her, his threats echoed in her ears. If only she could stay here.

It seemed a good place to hide. If she had to delay the return home – Harry had been to Portreath on the north coast but he planned to spend time yet at Falmouth – for at least a good many months, perhaps Rupert Goring would forget about her or reach a state where he could be reasoned with.

She was about to inquire on the health of Lady Stapleton but was saved the task when Hattie, followed by Julian, burst into the room.

'Ha, our dear girl, our dear Hattie.' Phee clapped her hands in glee. 'Come in, come in, how lovely to see you up and about, and Sir Julian too. What a lovely surprise. You look so well, Hattie, my rosebud. Come in and meet Miss Bonython.'

'So you think my little boy is adorable, Miss Bonython?'

'Well, I admit I know little of babies, Lady Stapleton, but your Freddie is quite the work of art.'

The two women had left the nursery and were strolling to a window seat, beyond the daybed's position, in Hattie's bedchamber. An hour and a half they had known each other but they were already like the best of friends. Hattie had dismissed Julian's misgivings about her desire to be with Georgette alone. She was feeling like her old normal self again, the self she had been – seemingly such a long time ago – before she had been heinously scarred. Her relief to at last be feeling that all things were natural and

169

unthreatening stole over her body in delicate little waves of hope and joy. Doors looked like doors and not gaping cave entrances to hell, or, when she was wrapped in ecstasy, like garlanded arches to mystical lands. Her footfalls sounded like their usual light taps rather than booming judgements or as if she was about to take flight and hurtle through the air.

Hattie remembered only a few of her episodes of madness. The one that stood out as the most terrifying was Julian stopping her from jumping off an attic roof and plunging to her death shortly after her lying-in. She had thought she could fly and had spread out her arms, seeing them as beautiful white-feathered wings. Coming to Poltraze to be with Matthew and her parents had helped to put her terrifying illness behind her. She was well again. Today she had made a new friend, a lady by birth. They had gelled from the first instance and had a lot in common. Hattie knew she would look forward to Georgette Bonython's future visits to Poltraze with joy.

'I hope you can come again soon, Miss— no, we are friends and should be on Christian name terms. Do come again soon, Georgette.' Hattie smiled through her paleness and clasped her new friend's hands. 'We could take a turn round the gardens. Or, as my legs are still a little weak, we could ride round in a carriage. Do say you'll come. You could stay all day. I promise I won't bore you. I hope you don't mind me saying so, but I think I need you a little. Say you'll come. It would mean so much to me.'

Before the pair had left the drawing room, after drinking a glass of the finest Cornish mead, Julian had whispered to Georgette, 'You must be aware that my wife is not quite herself, Miss Bonython. Things have been ... difficult for her. I pray you will be careful with her.'

'I think I understand your meaning, Sir Julian. You can trust me to call for assistance to Lady Stapleton if it becomes necessary,' Georgette had said.

Georgette now viewed Hattie with compassion. Last year she had heard about a washerwoman being carried off to the asylum after delivering a stillborn. The whole business of conception to confinement was a frightening risky affair for woman of all classes. It was no wonder women among the better off made out their last will and testament each time. If Georgette could cheer this sweet young mother, help soothe away the dark circles under her lacklustre eyes, bring gloss to her sorry, yellowy hair, and restore her vigour, it would be reward enough for setting out on what she had believed would be a tiresome, dreary day. And, to her quiet pleasure, today had proved she did not always need Harry's reassuring presence.

'I'd love to come to you often, Hattie. It will be good to be with someone of my own station.' Georgette leaned forward and kissed Hattie's cheek, finding it soft and cold.

Hattie leaned in to her. 'I've had a terrible

time, Georgette, but you have made me hopeful.'

'I will do all I can for you, I promise. I know what it feels like to be suddenly cruelly uprooted from all you once felt safe with.' She told Hattie about the tragedy of losing her real parents.

The two shared some moments of silence and stayed as they were. 'I cannot see how you can be particularly comfortable in a house where Clemency Kivell is,' Hattie said darkly and sympathetically. 'She's a hateful person, don't you know? Hateful.' Her head against Georgette's shoulder, her voice growing lower and huskier, Hattie's expression darkened and her eyes glittered like shards of smashed glass. 'I urge you to beware of her, Georgette. She's not what she seems. She's arrogant and sly. She can lie to one's face with an aura of absolute innocence. She pretended to be my friend but it was all deception. She used me to get at Matthew. She would desert me and go to his wing of the house. Then she'd seduce him, stay with him for hours, and finally return and tell me all about what they had done. I didn't want to listen but she would insist on going on. I knew, long before my marriage, facts that a young single lady shouldn't have known. She's a temptress, a witch. She kept Matthew under her spell for years, but as soon as your brother arrived in Meryen she cast him aside. I have seen my poor dear brother heavy and despondent with a broken heart.

172

'Please don't allow her to talk you into her joining you when you visit me, Georgette. I fear for my husband. Julian is polite and charming to a fault, as you have seen for yourself, and Clemency Kivell will want him as another conquest. She's mad, insatiable. She wants to keep proving to herself that she can have any man she wants. She told me over and over that she could easily take away any man who was interested in me. I am in great awe and fear of her.'

'I'm so sorry you should feel distressed in this manner. Don't worry, Hattie. I promise I'll always come alone.' Georgette knew Hattie was rambling. There was no possibility of Clemency being promiscuous – for one thing, the Kivells wouldn't allow it – but Georgette took pleasure in Clemency's name being sullied. 'I don't care for Clemency's company anyway. She quickly separated Harry from me and we used to do so much together. The journey down here was to learn about his Kivell forebears and the Kivell history, yet *she* has distracted him with her concerns about the poor in the village. It is none of her business. It is the responsibility of others to attend to that. It has certainly nothing to do with Harry. He is the patron of more than one charity at home in Yorkshire. Yes, I can understand it all now. Harry is utterly beguiled by her. They spend too much time alone. They might already have had ... knowledge of each other. She is despicable. I shall warn my brother about her tonight.'

'But you won't leave the area yet?' Hattie implored with planet-sized eyes.

'You have my word, Hattie, that I shall be spending a great deal of time at your side.'

Thirteen

In the late evening Georgette sent for Harry and he went dutifully straight to her room. Netty immediately made herself scarce, darting concerned eyes back at her mistress, and Harry knew his sister had something on her mind. Georgette was brooding in the way she did before making a demand, but it looked like this time she was not going to make it with pleading or cajoling. The atmosphere was cool and charged. Georgette was on her feet by the fireplace, her hands pressed together superiorly in front of her waist.

'I'm sure you haven't summoned me to tell me anything more about your time at Poltraze, Georgie, and I think I know what this is about,' Harry said calmly, while waiting for the dam of her ire to burst. Occasionally Georgette would throw a tremendous strop, and he would try everything to avoid that while staying here. It would be embarrassing for his kin to hear her childish and spiteful ranting. Strength of will and reasoning argument was the way here. Giving into hysterics was seen as a sign of weakness to those at Burnt Oak, and all would feel that, whatever Georgette wanted, she should not be pandered to.

'That's clever of you,' she replied crisply, moving her hands to her hips and leaning forward. 'Actually, I got very little opportunity to mention my time at Poltraze. Clemency and you monopolized the talk over the dining table with a prolonged account of your exploits with those children.'

'I'm sorry you feel that way about our, and the Juleff children's, harrowing experience, Georgie, and that is an unfair observation.' Harry remained composed but he intended the tilt of his head to show his displeasure. Georgette needed putting in her place. 'You kept pressing the point about how Lady Stapleton took to you in the first instance. How such good friends you both now are. How she couldn't wait to show you her son. Your remarks were aimed to hurt and belittle Clemency and I can't understand why. Clemency has not been unkind to you.'

Georgette had been smug about her jibes and she had enjoyed watching Clemency's expression cloud over with hurt. It was just punishment for her taking Harry over. Clemency had not seemed her usual proud self at all. The sadness of the village occurrence had dragged her down, apparently. It served her right for seeking to always play the heroine. She had been unfairly dealt with stunning feminine looks and she should be glorying in her blessing rather than interfering in a man's world. If ever she did marry she would make a very peculiar wife.

176

God help the man concerned. That man had better not be Harry, she thought.

'Why do you place her feelings over mine?' Georgette hissed; then raised her chin. 'And, pray, what is it you assume that I want?' Her eyes, Harry thought, were gleaming with superciliousness.

'First,' Harry replied, 'I shall say it is not worthy of you to have acquired a bad attitude towards Clemency, who has done nothing to deserve it. Obviously you are jealous of her and that is beneath you too. Now to the matter in hand. You wish to tell me you want to leave here, and in the circumstances I believe it is the only course to take. I cannot have us staying here now you have turned against a member of the household. This is not well done, Georgette, and I am exceedingly vexed and disappointed in you.

'I shall go downstairs and inform the family that we are to leave here tomorrow to spend a few days at Falmouth, there to look up a very aged acquaintance of our Grandfather Bonython, and to see the house where he was born. There are many good hotels there and it will be fascinating for us to see one of the largest natural ports in the world and to view the coastline. We shall return to Meryen and stay at the New Oak Hotel. I intend to spend more time with family members in and around Meryen, and to learn more about Kivell history.'

Georgette had stayed expressionless throughout his words. 'I don't wish to go to Falmouth,

Harry. I will be pleased to hear all about it when you return. Rather, I have been invited to stay at Poltraze. Lady Stapleton benefited greatly by my presence there today. Sir Julian and Mr and Mrs Faraday were so pleased and relieved to see her edging towards good spirits and normality again. It's an errand of mercy that I wish to undertake, to help return a young wife and mother to perfect health for the sake of her husband and child. You will understand my intention, what I hope to do, after the Godly thing you have accomplished today.' She exchanged her abrasiveness to a cajoling pout. 'I know I can be selfish, Harry, but I can't just turn away and do nothing for the poor lady.'

Harry was stunned and saddened by first her harsh attitude, and then her slyness. This was a side of Georgette he had not known before. Coming down to Cornwall had been for her sake as much as his own, to be part of the huge Kivell family that now stretched worldwide. To give Georgette a sense of belonging to more people than just himself, and a sense of reassurance that there were others who would willingly be available to her if anything untoward ever happened to him. Choosing to go to the aid of a sick woman was commendable, but he suspected what Georgette was really doing was shunning the Kivells for a more comfortable stay at Poltraze. He could understand her seeking the kind of surroundings she was used to, but otherwise he couldn't make her out. She was jealous of him spending time with Clemency, but before, apart from having reservations about some of the ladies he had shown an interest in, she had never seemed to loathe them, as she did Clemency. Clemency had strengths and depths to her that showed up other women as superficial moppets. Had she inadvertently made Georgette feel like that about herself? Yet Clemency was vulnerable too. Harry had witnessed how crushed she had been at Matthew Faraday's brusqueness with her today, her sorrow at the plight of the Juleff children, and her inner wounds at Georgette's malice about Harriet Stapleton.

Harry's mind returned to a point earlier that day. After little Jacka and Joe had been unwillingly prised apart, cleaned up in the vicarage kitchen and dressed in new clothes, they had been settled into a trap – clinging to each other once again – in the care of a village woman, and driven away to Redruth to start their new life. Pensive and rather sullen, saying little more than to wish the boys well, Matthew Faraday had returned to the vicarage drawing room. Harry and Clemency, and Jowan and Jenny, had waved the boys off, even though they had hidden their tiny heads under more clean blankets. The crowd of onlookers and well-wishers outside, waiting for this moment, had congratulated them for a 'good job well done'.

'I'll take Miss Jenny home. Clemency, Harry, will you come with us?' Jowan said kindly. 'It's been quite a day.'

Clemency had mentioned to Harry that she had gone to Wingfield House in the past to turn to Logan for comfort, but it was not her desire today. 'No, I'd like to return to Sammy and Nora's grave for a while,' she had replied, as if all the energy had been sieved out of her.

'I'll come with you, but I'll stay at a distance if you prefer,' Harry had offered at once.

'Come with me,' Clemency had said, as they neared the lonely, unmarked, little grave. With their arms linked, they had bowed their heads and kept silent vigil for some minutes. The sun gained strength in the sky. It shone in dappled shafts through the trees and danced a dance of light on the mound. 'Very soon Sammy and Nora will lie in a better grave after a proper service in the church. Their names will be inscribed on a gravestone and they will never be forgotten. I hope that somehow they know their sister and brothers will never know another cruel moment.'

'I'm sure they do, Clemmie. Sammy sacrificed his life trying to save Nora. That sort of brave, selfless action will surely be eternally rewarded.'

Clemency had leaned into him. She was misery itself. 'I wish I hadn't been so horrible to Sammy. The morning of the festival he approached me outside my shop. He was his usual cheeky self, trying as hard as he could to earn a few pennies. I was so scathing towards him. He was just a child, a child trying his best to make his own way in life. I shouldn't have been like that to him, so smug, so haughty, so uncaring. Sammy had had no chances in life and God only knows how poor Nora suffered. I wish I were more like Jenny. She has a heart as big as the ocean. She has always put others first.'

'Please don't be so hard on yourself, Clemmie.' Harry had hugged her. 'When you saw Sammy in his desperation you were moved by it and you did all you could to comfort him in his last moments. Then you decided to do something for the surviving children. Hundreds of people do nothing for anyone; they have no feelings at all.'

Like Georgette it seemed, Harry thought now. It was more for her benefit than for Harriet Stapleton's that she wanted to stay at Poltraze. 'You may have your way and I hope you enjoy your stay at Poltraze and will be of useful service to Lady Stapleton. But,' he went on firmly, 'an engagement is expected to be announced in the family between Jowan and Logan's ward, and there will be a celebration held in the biggest house here in the hamlet, Morn O' May. I'm looking forward to a typical Kivell party, and we shall not be leaving for Yorkshire or elsewhere before then.'

For one, long second, Georgette merely gazed at Harry without a flicker of eyelashes. Then she smiled elatedly as of old and rushed to be in his arms, to receive his adoring hug. 'Thank you so much, Harry, for seeing things my way. You are so good to me.'

'Yes, aren't I?' he replied, without enthusiasm.

Fourteen

Matthew woke from a deep, drugged-like sleep but did not open his eyes. His head was heavy and foggy from the lashings of champagne and cognac he had swallowed down the night before. His body felt light and numb yet also strangely weighty. His mouth was cloyingly dry. He was dehydrated but otherwise in no discomfort. He was in a floating stupor and didn't care if he stayed in it all day – whatever day it was.

Something touched his bare chest, a feathery touch that slowly, slowly traced a wonderfully tickly path down over his body. He felt himself smile then he tried to keep all his muscles still. He didn't want anything to break through this welcome dreamy state. He wanted to stay in this place where he could imagine anything he chose. To conjure up outlandish and mystical worlds, like he did in his poetry, and try to make them real for a while. He was without success, however. Reality had the maddening habit of breaking into his fantasies. Matthew became aware of rain spattering against the windowpanes – not the glass of his bedchamber at Poltraze or his parlour, where he often drifted to sleep, fitfully or really not slept at all. He was in a small country house, near to Hayle, that he was renting as a place to meet his lover, the youngish widow of a clothing merchant.

'Matthew, darling.' Gently, the naked Clara Pellingham nibbled at his throat. In smooth continuance she moved her practised lips and hands to inflame and pleasure him.

'Mmm?' He made to turn to Clara but she pushed him down to lie flat.

'I love it when you're drowsy,' she cooed. Her voice was naturally sultry, a compelling draw to any man from the first instance. 'Relax, darling, and let me tend to everything.'

When Clara started with him dawn had been near breaking, and when she finished with him the day was at full light and Matthew was near to exhaustion. Twice he had broken through her persistence to take dominance when her un-remitting expertise had got too much for him. As always, at the final end unselfish Clara had soothed him until he was totally at peace.

Now, as usual, they cuddled in contentment, with Matthew wrapping Clara against his chest. He kissed her hair and hot cheek and brow several times. 'You're wonderful, Clara. Wonderful. And beautiful.'

'You don't have to say that, Matthew.' She tenderly stroked his firm jawline. 'I'm more than happy with our arrangement, and the knowledge that it will end when it has run its natural course. After that we shall always be close friends.'

Hugging Clara gently, he allowed random thoughts to run through his mind – but they were hardly random, however, and he couldn't stop them if he'd wanted to. Clemency was here, clear in his mind. He wasn't ready yet to shut her out. Whatever he did for the rest of his life she would haunt his deepest self.

After a few lazy minutes, Clara said, 'You are always so quiet after we make love.'

'Does it annoy you, Clara? If so, I am sorry.' Matthew kissed her brow and ran his fingertip in light circles on her satiny shoulder.

'Nothing you do annoys me, Matthew.'

He had met Clara, known as the 'superlative Widow Pellingham', at the St Andrew's Hotel in Redruth, where, to get away from Poltraze, Meryen and the recent harrowing events, he had taken rooms for a week for himself and Barker. Graceful Clara had entered the dining room followed by a wake of besotted admirers. Matthew's curiosity had been heightened over the practically frenzied interest for this lady, an ethereal, shadowy, slim figure to him, who was wearing royal blue and sapphires and smelling divinely of an evocative perfume. After eating a meal of poached salmon and an iced cream sorbet at his lonely table he had made it his concern, with the aid of his guiding walking stick, to close in on her table of eight persons for the best view in the candlelight that he could gain of her.

'I don't think we know you, sir.' Clara had been too kind to allow him to be overlooked.

The genteel company of four men (two of them titled) were all members of the local chamber of commerce. The three other ladies – two of them wives, and one a sister, of the men – showed they thought themselves honoured to be in Clara's company. Matthew accepted that everyone was fascinated to meet him, the reclusive squire of the all-but-forgotten estate of Poltraze.

For the remainder of his stay, Matthew became a quiet part of the influential set and received many invitations to call at Society homes. He forged some business connections for his own local interests in engineering, foundries and quarrying. He met for the first time (apart from Logan Kivell) some of those who leased his land for the mineral rights to the Carn Croft and Wheal Verity mines. He found no particular satisfaction in the serious side of things, but he relished the company of the witty, stimulating Clara. He enjoyed listening to the echoing huskiness of her rich-toned voice. He enjoyed her witty and stimulating manner. It was heartening to find something satisfying and to his liking, to not be under hopes and pressure after so long. He learned Clara was well educated, well travelled and childless, and had taken her own money to her marriage to a much older American, who had already vested himself with a son and heir. Mr Pellingham, who had been tragically lost at sea on a voyage on the Atlantic Ocean to his homeland, had left a thoughtful amount of funds to Clara.

On the third night when Clara withdrew, late as usual, for her bed, she whispered an invite to Matthew to follow her to her room. He found Clara so easy to know that he had not been at all nervous. There had been no need for polite preliminaries or teasing delays. She understood his initial rush and ineptness after such a long length of abstinence. Afterwards, and on subsequent occasions, they had brought out the accumulated skills and sensitivities in each other.

They had since met at least three times a week. They had agreed their union would not be a permanent one, and when they talked it was only of life generally. When they were together the outside world, the past and the future did not matter – they had mutual trust and affection. It had, however, passed through Matthew's mind that Clara might make him a good wife. When Hattie was finally well and had returned home, and when Miss Georgette Bonython – who, although she was good for Hattie, he felt had something false about her – was out of his home, he could propose to Clara with confidence. She would be sympathetic towards his parents' eccentricities and have no trouble in dealing with the morose Jane, who had sent him letters of complaint about how she was shut out of the family. Matthew's frank reply had expressed the truth that her exile was self-imposed and she had only her own selfishness to blame. He did not take it for granted though that Clara would accept a proposal of marriage. She probably would refuse, with a gentle laugh. His family aside, he could not see Clara desiring to make the lacklustre Poltraze her home. In any event, he did not want the peace of his home disturbed. He did not want parties and dinners and social events. He would have to find someone who preferred a quiet life to become the mistress of Poltraze, if he decided to get married at all.

'I don't pretend anything with you, Clara,' he said. 'I meant every word.'

'I think well of you too, Matthew.' After a dreamy time of idleness, Clara raised her body and waited patiently for him to find her face. 'May I ask you something personal, Matthew?'

Trusting her not to probe too deeply, he answered, 'Of course you may.'

'You don't have to answer this, and please don't be offended. Matthew, are you in love and have you had your heart broken? I sensed from the moment we met that there was a great sadness in you. That something vital was missing from your life. When we are intimate, you make light of kissing my lips. In my experience, a denial of this very personal kind usually means a person is in love and not ready to move on. Am I right, Matthew? Or nowhere near the mark?'

Matthew closed his eyes as he contemplated her question. He could laugh it off or simply reject Clara's suspicion, but she was too special to him to lie to. On further reflection Clara was the ideal person to talk to about Clemency. He needed to speak to someone. He needed help in easing the turmoil in his heart. He opened his eyes. 'You are right. I am very much in love.'

'Do you want to tell me about her, Matthew? It may be good for you to unload your burden. You suffer a crushing heaviness, don't you? I hate to think of you being so terribly unhappy. I swear on my life not a single word will go further than this room.' Clara moved away from him, demonstrating her sensitivity. Pulling the bedcovers up over her chest she sat up against the pillows. Matthew did the same.

He cleared his throat. Then glanced at Clara. He took a sip of water. Cleared his throat once more. He gazed up at the ceiling. 'This isn't easy for me. I've never been given to sharing my private thoughts, my inmost feelings.'

'I understand.' Clara looked upwards too. 'Start by telling me her name.'

Matthew exhaled a tremendous sigh. 'Clemency. Her name is Clemency.' Then the words began to spill out of him. He shared everything about Clemency from their first, contentious meeting and all that he later knew about her, gleaned over three, long years. 'We didn't like each other at first. I thought her a most unsuitable friend for my bright and breezy, naive young sister. Coming from such an unconventional background Clemency considered me weak for living as a secret recluse, and she told me so, ruthlessly bluntly. That's often Clemency's way. She took me to task over many things and each time I bit back at her. And then there happened one of those unexpected moments when a man and woman at war slip suddenly into an unstoppable attraction for each other and find themselves in a passionate embrace. For me the kiss was the most sublime moment of my life, the time when I found out who I really was. But we were almost immediately interrupted by troubles in Clemency's family and that took precedence for her. To Clemency our encounter had put us on a closer footing, but she wanted no more than friendship. Well, she was very young, only sixteen years at the time.

'Finally, my devotion got too much for her and in great irritation she shrugged me off. She's apologized since, by letter. We haven't had the chance to speak privately. She wrote that she still desires a friendship with me, although on a different level. But now the situation is hampered by another unfortunate occurrence. The serious condition of my ailing sister Hattie forbids Clemency to call at Poltraze. It's personal. I had to tell Clemency this to her face. Clemency was upset and horrified. I wasn't particularly sociable about it. I was jealous because Clemency was with this distant relative of hers, a successful, eligible man, who's been her constant companion of late. I can't expect Clemency to want to be my friend at all after that.'

Clara listened intently. 'I feel for you, Matthew. Every word you've said abounds with your love for Clemency.'

'I'll never love anyone else like I love Clemency,' he said, his voice choked with tears that did not reach his eyes. 'I'm like a lost soul. Once I chose to stay alone, but until this I'd never understood what real loneliness is. It's cruel. It's debilitating. It's eating away at me.'

'That's easy to tell and I'm sorry for you, Matthew. I have to say, however, that I don't understand why after all this time of hoping to get really close again to Clemency, of doing things her way, that why, after her moment of pique, you have totally given up on her.'

'I've had no other choice. Clemency is worth fighting for and so much more, but to continue to pursue her would only push the wedge between us even deeper. I couldn't bear that. Clemency's only really content when she is with her own people. Harry Bonython is much more to her liking.'

'Yet, according to you, she's already turned down a marriage proposal from a kinsman, a man who had also made his intentions plain, and it ended their closeness on a sour note.' Clara mused on in silence.

Matthew turned to her. 'What are you thinking, Clara?'

'That, as well as being a young woman with a strong mind, and one who is quick to action, Clemency is also confused and lonely.'

'No, I don't see Clemency like that, not the Clemency I know. She's surrounded by a large, extended family everywhere she goes. She has never known the frustrations of being held back

190

from her dreams and ambitions.'

'But Matthew, it was Clemency herself who told you that you didn't truly know her, and I don't think she truly knows herself. She's lived all her life in the same small area. I grant you that she has conquered trials and dangers that would have been the undoing of many, but no one is so strong that they don't succumb to human emotions. Clemency is used to going her own way. To have been faced with making a lifelong commitment as part of a couple may have been a little frightening for her.'

Clemency with frailties was a compelling picture to Matthew and he loved her all the more for it. 'So you don't think I should give up hope?'

'It's up to you what you decide, but my advice to you is to ask yourself if it's really what you want to do.'

There was no hesitation in Matthew. 'I love Clemency. I really love her. I'll have to think very hard how to do it, but I'm going to fight for her.'

Fifteen

C. A. Kivell's Music Emporium. Outside on the narrow pavement, Clemency could not re-capture the joy and excitement of the shop's opening day. It seemed rather like a joke to her now: a sad, mocking joke. Her own tiny empire, her mark of independence – she might have been one of the very few women to set up a business of her own but it was not as great an achievement for her as it would be for others. The odds had never been against her. It had not been an unreachable dream. No one in her family had tried to stop her. Having rescued more than one victim of villainy she was con-sidered a local heroine. It was the conclusion in all ranks that her strong will and driving energy would lead her to accomplish something out of the ordinary. The shop wasn't a hard-won accomplishment, something she had set up from nothing. She'd had the money to build it, own it, equip it and pay a staff. There were dips and rises in sales but it was never a binding worry. She still had a tidy sum in the bank to fall back on. The business now seemed no more than the sort of enchantment in a hazy dream that passed away on waking to reality.

How selfish and ungrateful she was to be thinking like this when people who passed her by in the street were striving to make ends meet, and in often impossible conditions. The air was chilly and biting. It was one of those unpleasant spring days when a late frost threatened to destroy delicate shoots and buds; when the weather was no friend at all. If Clemency was cold at home she could light a fire, or if she got cold when here in the village she had the shop and several family hearths she could go to for warmth and a hot drink. But the miners, labourers, farm workers and smallholders had to eke out their meagre supplies or go without. Innocent little children, like the Juleff brood had been, took lack and discomfort for granted. And here she was whingeing to herself and steeped in self-pity. She was disagreeable and not worth knowing. It was no wonder Matthew had hardly bothered with her outside the Juleff hut that day. Her arrogance had brought her down and it served her right.

Mr Keast came outside to her, his lavish eyebrows raised in what looked like consideration, rather than officiousness or snobby disapproval or fawning. 'I bid you good morning, Miss Kivell. May I ask if all is well? You have been standing there for quite some time. It's rather fresh today. It's beginning to drizzle and you have no umbrella. If I may be so bold, I suggest you come inside. Mrs Keast would gladly make you a warming cup of tea.'

The unexpected kindness from the usually

pompous shop manager nearly brought Clemency to tears. It shook her; why was she so emotional nowadays, so weak? 'You are very thoughtful, Mr Keast, thank you. Actually, I am on my way next door to the hotel. I'm sure you have all in order in the shop. I bid you a good day.'

After Clemency had departed, Mr Keast hurried inside and went straight upstairs to his apartment to inform Mrs Keast that Miss Kivell was subdued and listless, pale and wistful. 'I've never seen her like that before. Well, she was in a state over the murders. Who wouldn't be? And getting those other children away from their wicked father must have been something of an ordeal. But this was so different for her. She usually copes with everything admirably. Now she seemed ... well, the only way I can describe it is defeated.'

'Huh. She's either ailing for something or it's an affair of the heart,' Mrs Keast pontificated. 'It's time something brought that young madam down off her high horse, in my opinion.'

'But I hope it's not something that will lead her to selling the shop or shutting it down, dear.' Mr Keast fingered the knots gathering above the bridge of his large nose. 'Life is good for us here.'

Clemency went up to the reception desk of the hotel.

'I'm afraid Mr Kivell is not on the premises, Miss Kivell,' Oswald Clench, with an important sweep of his head, said in reply to her inquiry about Logan's whereabouts.

'Do you know if he is due to arrive later?' Clemency was desperate for kindly company, and Logan never failed to cheer her up.

'He has a meeting in Truro today, Miss Kivell. I'm not expecting to see him until tomorrow. May I get you anything?'

'Um, no, no thank you, Mr Clench. I have other calls to make.' She did not. She had nothing planned.

Outside, the drizzle was getting heavier and the darkening skies foretold an imminent downpour. Clemency dragged her feet across the forecourt and carried on down the High Street. There were fewer people about. The old men and women generally to be found sitting outside their doors, gossiping together or reminiscing, had given in to the weather. Mothers of the cheeky, mostly poorly clad, infants usually seen out playing had shooed them inside. Those who were hurrying about seemed intent on their affairs and bid Clemency only a quick greeting. She so wanted someone, anyone, to stay and chat to her, to say something that would make her forget her misery for a while. She had plenty of relatives she could call on but the talk in all their dwellings and places of businesses would include the engagement of Jowan to Jenny Clymo, and Clemency did not want to hear about others starting out on happy, new ventures. It would make her feel more of a failure.

It was as well Logan was not in reach today, she reflected dolefully. He was thrilled about Jenny securing herself a good marriage and he would have spoken of little else. He had immediately held a quiet champagne celebration at the hotel. Mrs Brookson, apparently, was pleased for Jenny not to be facing a lonely spinsterhood, but had murmured some uncertainty about Jowan's ability to make her a good husband. Mrs Brookson had also said she would miss Jenny's company every day, but she had the constancy of Serenity and the children.

'You can see how much Jenny loves him and how much Jowan dotes on her. Your turn to find someone next, eh, Clemmie?' Logan had slapped a drink in her hand. 'Those two getting together was the last thing I'd have imagined. Could've knocked me over with thistledown when Jowan asked to talk to me alone. He was so nervous. It was what made me feel he was right for Jenny. They are very different in character but in this instance it will work wonderfully well, don't you think?'

Seeing Jenny held tenderly and proudly on Jowan's arm, Clemency agreed with Logan. Jenny had the look of a woman who had found everything she'd ever wanted. She was in love. Her man, and hopefully a family, was all she would ever want. Clemency was glad for Jowan. They had reconciled and had hugged, and she had wished him lifelong happiness. Many times she had joined in the celebration of a family engagement and had laughed and danced all the way through it, but the happiness of Jenny – a girl born into poverty, and who had expected so little out of life – filled Clemency with an envy and an emptiness that scoured the roots of her soul. She had felt a moment of fear: that cruel enemy that delighted in leaping on any victim it could grasp. Emptiness was a scourge that could grow unchecked. It had no substance and yet, bit by bit, it devoured its victims. The same revolting feeling had caught Clemency unawares many times since then.

Inevitably, plans were being made for a traditional, noisy Kivell feast, with drink flowing like a river, at Burnt Oak. Harry would be back from Falmouth in time for it. Clemency knew part of her melancholy lay in the fact she was missing Harry. She had gone through so much with him on the very same day she had soured things with Matthew. She and Harry were on the same level. Without his sustaining presence she was at a loss. She had been stunned by the news that Harry and Georgette were to suddenly move out of the farmhouse. She had to admit to herself she was jealous and annoyed that Georgette was leaving to stay at Poltraze.

An intense dislike for Georgette had grown in all the Kivells at the farmhouse as she said her farewells. Georgette had been wearing a bonnet and outfit more suitable for a garden party and she had peered down over her nose. 'I can't thank you enough, all of you, for having me and for putting yourselves to a lot of inconvenience. I'm afraid I can't say when I'll be able to return for a visit. It all depends on dear Lady Stapleton's condition.' Then she had looked from under her eyelashes directly at Clemency. 'She needs me so much. She has such terrible fears and I am the only one she feels safe with outside of Sir Julian and the Faradays.'

'I shall pray for Hattie's quick recovery,' Clemency had said, keeping her voice and expression bland. She had shrugged her shoulders as if she had no real interest in any of the Faradays, but the lie had hurt, nearly as much as the dreadful knowledge that Hattie hated and feared her. She had an enduring affection, a love, for all the Faradays. She missed them all very much and she missed being at Poltraze. Life could change quickly and she had lost a lot this spring. Mostly, somehow, she had lost herself and it frightened her like nothing else had before. The tragedies, even the threat of violence that had beset her over the years, she had met head on. Now she felt less than alive; like a waft of vapour, small and barely there.

'Well, I think we've seen that young lady in her true colours,' Verena had whispered to those seeing the Bonythons off.

As his sister and Netty were driven away, Harry had said, 'I shall definitely be back in a week or two.' Evidently none too pleased with Georgette, he'd added dourly. 'I hope the Faradays will not be overwhelmed.'

Verena had then ushered all the others inside to allow Clemency and Harry to say a private goodbye. 'Come with me, Clemmie,' Harry had implored her. 'You've been so low lately it would do you well to see new sights, to breathe the sea air.'

Clemency was aware of Verena peeping out of the sitting room window. Her mother had earlier questioned Clemency's closeness to Harry. 'Don't worry, Mama,' Clemency had replied lightly. 'I'm not planning to elope to Yorkshire with him.'

'I know it's selfish of me but I couldn't bear to have my only daughter living far away from me. Of course, if Harry felt inclined to settle in Meryen ... I'd be more than pleased.'

'Harry and I don't feel that way about each other. Why must everyone assume that if a man and a woman get along well they will have a romance?'

'Don't be so touchy, Clemmie. It's the usual thing that happens. And it's every mother's hope that her daughter will find a husband who will love and cherish her. Jowan was never right for you. But Harry is quite different. It's my wish that you clear your mind from all the clutter you seem to have whirling round in it and seriously think about him.'

'I'm very sorry, Mama. I like being with Harry. He likes being with me. We've become uncommonly close through our experiences with the Juleff children. However, we have an empathetic friendship that won't progress to anything more.'

'Even so...'

Her mother still wished her to marry Harry.

She had watched their farewell, no doubt, in the hope that Clemency and Harry would share a particularly warm embrace. It was what Clemency had wanted more than anything at that moment: to be enclosed in the warmth and strength of Harry's arms. She had hugged him tight but, with her mother's hopeful eyes on them, she had kissed Harry's cheek only lightly.

'I have things to do at the shop, Harry,' she had fibbed. 'I shall be eagerly waiting for you to come back and tell me about all your discoveries. Enjoy all you do.'

'I shall find it fascinating, I'm certain of that. It's really strange for Georgie to be so far from home and for us to be going our separate ways. She will be all right there, won't she?'

'She'll be well taken care of at Poltraze,' had been Clemency's last wry words as Harry had trotted off.

Horrid, trivial-minded Georgette at Poltraze, pretending to care for Hattie but actually being there for her own ends – whatever that reason was – while Clemency herself had been placed under banishment, ate at her like barbs scoring her heart.

She wondered why she was being so introspective. If she tried to clear her mind, the things that disturbed her so much just relentlessly rushed straight back in. Her feet carried her aimlessly and she found herself trudging along Miners Way – a short straight street, fairly new to Meryen – and cutting through former common land, where the proudly built

Miners Institute was and a half-dozen terraced, whitewashed cottages faced each other. The people who lived here, the men who gathered in the Institute for a drink, a game of cards and for camaraderie, did not have time to waste on melancholy and failures. They just got on with life and its struggles. They had no other choice.

Clemency felt dizzy, could feel her heart thumping inside her chest. She recognized the signs of becoming panicky. Stop it, she told herself. Things had happened to shake her out of her complacency. That was all. She only had to take measure of herself. Regroup her opinions and values and hopes and dreams.

She became still, frozen, not moving a muscle. Did she have a dream? Something she wanted to do, or achieve, or see happen? Something that seemed virtually unattainable but not impossible? Most people did. But she had always taken it for granted that life would either fall into a pattern to suit her, or that after a struggle – some challenge she would enjoy – she would come out on top. Life had dealt her a lot of sorrow, and some almost deadly blows, but she had got through them all, emerging even more confident. But strong emotions had not got in her way and floored her before as they did now.

'Clemmie! What are you doing standing here like this in the pouring rain? You're drenched.'

'Oh, it's you, Abe.' Never had she been more pleased to see him.

He took her arm and propelled her towards

the Institute. 'Quick, let's run. I'm doing some work inside. You can dry off while the rain eases.'

'Should I be allowed in here, in this men's holiest of holies?' Clemency asked in the lobby.

'Don't be daft. I don't expect you to pass by and get more saturated and I don't care about others' opinions.' Abe took her into the bar room, where eight tables – for four, six or eight persons – with chairs and forms were spaced closely together. Charcoal, chalk and water-colour pictures hung on the cream-painted walls, as well as a portrait of Queen Victoria as she was now, in her mid-thirties, and the local mines' banners. There was the smell of stale tobacco and ale, and the turpentine Abe was using.

Looking down at her dripping hemline, Clemency glanced behind and saw her telltale wet footprints on the planked-wood floor. She was an intruder here. Once she would have been amused and defiant about it, but now she was nervous that some stalwart miner, not on his core, would come in and bawl at her and order her out. How could she have been reduced to such weakness? She shivered with shame and anxiety as much as she did because of being so horribly cold.

Abe had rushed straight outside to her in his work apron. Now he fetched his coat to wrap around her, then, holding her at arm's length, he studied her fallen face. 'What on earth is it, Clemmie? What's upset you so much?'

'What makes you think something's wrong?' she snapped, cross with herself for displaying her raw emotions so plainly.

'Same old Clemmie, always ready to bite someone's head off,' Abe grinned. 'I've got some crib with me. Want to share a slice of pork pie and a mug of tea with me?'

'I'm sorry. Thanks, Abe. I am a bit hungry.' There was no need to explain anything to Abe if she didn't want to. He was the best sort of friend. He never got cross with her if she was moody.

'Here.' He pulled out a chair from a table in a corner, away from the windows, so they would not be seen.

Clemency pulled off her bonnet, which was now a bedraggled mess of felt and ribbons. While Abe sat on the next chair and divided the pork pie and poured out tea from his flask for her, she used her fingers to detangle the soaked, curly ends of her hair.

'You look lovely,' Abe said.

'Thanks.' Clemency knew that she looked dishevelled, hunched up under Abe's rough coat, but she took the compliment for how it was meant: a true compliment from a friend. She took a bite from the pie. 'This is tasty. From the baker's?'

'No. Your brother Logan's cook, actually. Jenny left it when she called on my parents yesterday.'

'That's typical of her. I don't suppose she'll stop all her kindnesses when she marries my cousin.'

'You think they'll make each other happy?'

'Yes, absolutely. Their differences will work for them. Whether Jowan will keep his roving eye in check remains to be seen, but I can't see him ever getting fed up with Jenny or hurting her deliberately. Are you still seeing the balmaiden? Sorry, I don't know her name.'

'You mean Loveday Endean, a great granddaughter of the old midwife, Frettie. She seems set to continue the tradition. No, it fizzled out between us. My parents are so frail now. Don't think she fancied taking care of them as well as me and the house. Don't blame her for that.'

'I'm sorry. I keep forgetting your burden of responsibility.'

'Don't be,' Abe shrugged, apparently totally unbothered. 'I'm happy to do the best for them. The neighbours are good enough to keep an eye on them when I'm working. Can't see either of 'em lasting out the year. That'll be the right time to only please myself. It wasn't like me and Loveday were in love.'

'Love,' Clemency mused, over the tin mug she held up to her chin, 'it's what makes all the difference, isn't it? Do you particularly want love and marriage, Abe? You've got so much to offer a woman. Loveday Endean was very near-sighted not to have taken things further with you. You're a wonderful man. You have a nice home and your job isn't dangerous, like when you mined underground.'

'Yeh, I'll be all right as long as I don't fall off

204

my ladder.' He winked, laughing. 'That's better, I've got you smiling at last. I'll take what fate hands me. If it's a wife and family, fine. How about you? I suppose you'll want romance and the rest eventually.'

'So you think I'm still determined to hang on to my freedom. Love. I'm not sure I'd recognize it if it did happen to me.'

'Of course you would. You're no fool, Clemmie.'

'Aren't I?' She looked away from him, feeling a sob rising in her chest.

Abe left his seat and dropped down on his haunches at her side. He gently tugged on one of her straggly ringlets. 'Want to tell me what's troubling you?'

'Nothing.' She gazed into his eyes – eyes that were open and honest and offered simple caring. 'Everything.'

She reached out to him and he rose and cradled her against him. Clemency couldn't keep back the wall of tears that was crumbling inside her. She cried and sobbed and clung to Abe. Finally, her face against his strong chest, she wrapped her arms around his waist, and she told him about the rift between her and Hattie and Matthew, and about her loneliness now Harry had gone away. 'I know I'm being silly about Harry. He'll be back very soon. I just feel that I've lost so much and thrown so much away.' She looked up at him. 'I know I've got all my family but otherwise ... thank God I've still got you, Abe.'

He ran his hands over her hair, pushing it back from her brow. 'I hope whatever you do, whoever you might marry, you'll remember I'm always here for you, Clemmie.'

She recalled the things she and Abe had in common. They had met while he was poaching pheasants on Poltraze land. He wasn't a hardened criminal but he took joy at cocking a snoot at the law. He was free-willed and easy going, just as she had been. 'I'd hate it more than anything if I lost you, Abe.'

'Well,' he said, his dark eyes twinkling as he gazed deeper into her own, 'you never will.'

Clemency realized she enjoyed being this close to Abe. His body was lean and well muscled. He wasn't handsome in the hero-god-like sense but his features were nicely honed and he had lots of attraction. His mouth was wide and lush. She looked at his lips the same moment he looked at hers.

They closed their eyes and closed the space between their lips. The instant the first contact was made their kiss was intense, and a shimmer of shock travelled up and down Clemency's body.

'My God,' Abe murmured against her lips, adjusting his body to draw her in more and more to him. 'Is this all right with you, Clemmie?'

She wound her arms round his neck, pushing into him, grasping him. 'Don't stop Abe. I don't want you to.'

Sixteen

My Dear Clemency,

It is my great wish that this letter will find you, and all of your family, enjoying good health and in good spirits.

First, please allow me to pass on the news from the report I've just received of the four Juleff children's progress, as I am sure you will be eager to learn how they are faring in their new homes.

There have been difficulties with all four children – as one would expect – with matters of behaviour and hygiene, but the foster parents are confident these will ease under a caring but firm hand, and with patience and understanding. Eddie and Becky have started to attend a dame school. This small, non-regimented setting is hoped to be beneficial to them learning the basics of education. Neither child is showing any particular aptitude yet, but it is too early to expect significant advances.

Jacka and Joe are facing more complex problems on their road to rehabilitation. Their lack of intelligence makes it difficult for them to understand the need to drop

207

certain behaviours and adopt new ones. These little boys still cling to each other. Indeed, it is thought that Joe thinks he is one half of a whole person. Security and a non-aggressive environment is what they have now and that is paramount to them.

Clemency, is it my intention to call on the children in their new homes in a few weeks, when they have had time enough to settle in and get used to their new way of life. If you would like to see the children's progress for yourself, you would be most welcome to accompany me.

Now, there is another matter about which I feel most strongly in which I must appeal to you, Clemency. I owe you my heartfelt apology over my curtness towards you on the day the Juleff children were rescued. I would like to explain more to you about my attitude and I beg the favour of being given the opportunity of doing so in person.

Also, I can understand how distressing it must have been for you to be told about Hattie's anxiety over the thought of seeing you again. I...

Once again Matthew could not carry on with the letter and, for the umpteenth time, he tore up the sheets of paper and scrunched them into a ball. Again he threw his work across the room in utter frustration.

Damn it! Everything he wrote to Clemency sounded clumsy and pathetic and ingratiating, and she would despise him for it. Of course she would be interested in information about the Juleff children. She would see a letter from him as a front to toadying his way back into her favour. No, she wouldn't, he damned himself. Why did he think of Clemency, the beautiful woman he loved and desired, as shallow? She wasn't. Confused, maybe, as Clara had said. Haughty, certainly, but she was artless and open and honest, unlike the cunning madam staying under his roof and professing to be Hattie's mentor. But he didn't need to compare Clemency with any other woman. He knew her every way and he loved them all. He loved her but, like a first-class fool, he had let her slip away from him. He loved her with his whole being, yet simply because she had rebuffed him, and because he had seen her in the company of another man, he had been deliberately unkind to her. He knew she would have been crushed over Hattie's strange notions about her, yet he had made her wound deeper. He didn't deserve her. He should keep out of the picture and allow her to follow her life's course her way.

But he could not. He should at least tell her how sorry he was and hope to ease her hurts. There was only one thing for it. He called for Barker.

Very soon, with long, eager strides, Matthew, dressed for riding, was leaving the east wing. Sandy plodded along with his head down, knowing it was the company of the spaniels again for him. Matthew pulled at his cuffs. He shuffled his shoulders to ensure his coat sat square on him, even though there was no need. Barker always turned him out with regimental smartness.

Barker, a former corporal and Matthew's servant in the Lifeguards, kept pace in his own sharp, thickset march. He also kept glancing at his master's face.

'What is it? Have I a mark on my chin? Why are you so amused?' Matthew demanded from the man he trusted with his life, and (nearly) all his secrets.

'Just thinking that it's good to see you more your old self again, sir,' Barker replied, in his broad, man-of-Kent burr.

'I certainly know that *you're* pleased with yourself,' Matthew countered.

Squire and valet descended the stairs to the first floor. 'What makes you say that, sir?'

Matthew knew the middle-aged Barker, whose dark-brown whiskers were preened to pointed precision, was grinning from ear to ear. 'I know you don't want to play games with me, you old goat,' he said with barrack room bawdiness. 'You're assuming we're on the way to a certain address again. *You* know that *I* know that you were humping Mrs Pellingham's maid.'

'And 'twas very satisfying too, sir. So I've got the destination wrong today?'

'You have. We won't be going there again. Of course, you are at liberty to continue to seek encounters with your amour if you so wish.'

'Oh, there's no need for that, sir. I've got one or two arrangements locally.'

'I know that too, Barker.' Matthew squared off for the main hall. 'Take Sandy to my parents, and inform them that I'm going to Meryen.'

'Yes, sir.'

Once on his own Matthew paced about, rehearsing his opening words to Clemency. He was actually intending to go straight to Burnt Oak and find Clemency there, otherwise he might have to chase all over the village to locate her. He decided it was useless to plan a speech. It was best to try to read Clemency's mood and take it from there.

Matthew's blindness meant he had keen hearing and he swung round towards the Long Corridor. Someone was about to come along it and he recognized the light, tripping steps of Georgette Bonython. He had no wish to speak to her. He did not really know why he could not accept her, but he found her uninteresting, anyway, and hoped she would leave the instant her brother returned to Burnt Oak from Falmouth. The report he had asked for on Hattie this morning was promising. She had been a little confused on waking but had soon grown restful and had eaten a good breakfast. While Matthew was grateful that Georgette might have speeded up Hattie's recovery, he was concerned that she might, inadvertently, make Hattie feel inadequate. Hattie might compare her flawed looks to Georgette's unblemished

211

complexion, and she would never feel comfortable in the rounds of social life that Georgette would return to. With the help of his walking stick, Matthew slipped away outside.

Georgette walked the length of the Long Corridor. With rooms either side of it there was little natural light and it was cast with gloom. Netty had been told by the Poltraze housekeeper that the ghost of a long-dead architect haunted the corridor, and Georgette always felt a sense of chill and foreboding until she reached the end of it. The entire house was rumoured to be haunted, but what great house wasn't supposedly afflicted? There was a definite aura of something woebegone in the Long Corridor, but Georgette had detected nothing similar elsewhere.

Emerging into the better light she glimpsed movement outside: the top of a man's fair head, clearly the squire's. She hastened to a window to see if he was about to leave the property. Resting her hands on the cold stone of the deep-set window ledge, she raised her brows. He was standing down in the gravelled courtyard, idly moving the granite chippings with his stick. For the squire to be waiting like this, before his mount or a carriage had been brought round to him, meant he had hurried outside. He had to have known she was approaching him and he had deliberately avoided her.

Georgette's hands curled into fists. How dare he snub her? Why did he disapprove of her? He was always polite to her but otherwise he showed her a cool reserve. She deserved better. She had presented herself in exemplary fashion during every minute of her stay here. She had given Matthew Faraday no cause for complaint. He had nothing against the Kivells, so it couldn't be her family ties he objected to. Hattie had told Georgette that the squire had set his heart on marrying Clemency. He must be jealous about Harry taking his place in Clemency's life. Georgette was pleased he did not dine often with his family so she did not have to look at him across the dining table.

If Matthew Faraday was avoiding her because he feared she thought of him as a likely husband, he was a conceited buffoon. He had nothing to offer her. He would do only for someone as dull and unsociable as himself; some impoverished gentlewoman, a governess or a widow perhaps, or the daughter of upper-middle-class 'new money'. It didn't occur to Georgette that she herself was not of higher birth. It was understandable that Clemency preferred Harry's company to Matthew's. Georgette doubted that Clemency would come here often now, even if she were not under an enforced restriction. Physically, she supposed Faraday was masculine and handsome in a fascinating sort of way. He was a clever man, not calculating but astute. With no one about to notice she scowled at his confident figure. He had offended her. There was no need for him to eschew her. She would not tolerate it.

Flinging up her head, she passed through the hall, then the vestibule and out of the huge double doors, and descended the steps. Even though she knew Faraday couldn't see her well she kept up her look of harsh disdain.

Matthew turned round to her, sighing inwardly. What was she about? He wasn't aware of Georgette Bonython usually taking a step outside until after luncheon, when she took the air with Hattie.

'Good morning, Mr Faraday,' Georgette said, brightly and strongly, before he could speak to her. She kept shifting her feet and angling her head to prevent him gaining any measure of sight of her. 'It's a very fine day, is it not?'

Matthew waited until she had left the bottom step and was facing him on the crunchy ground. He bowed to her, 'Good morning to you, Miss Faraday. Indeed, we are graced with the best of spring today.' Her perfume was soft and fresh, perfectly complementing the season, but nothing could endear her to him. 'I am waiting for my horse and my valet.'

I won't let you send me away, Georgette thought. 'It's a good day to be venturing out. If I may I would like a word with you, Mr Faraday.'

'All is well with you, I hope, Miss Bonython. Have you worries about Hattie?'

Georgette ignored his inquiries. 'What I want to say is to congratulate you on your wondrous gardens.' She sincerely did find the Poltraze gardens splendid and delightful with their

214

several species of azalea, camellia and flowering bulbs, and the amazing collection of explorers' trees and shrubs, but she did not elaborate. It wasn't a pleasant conversation she wanted with this man but to show she did not care what he thought of her, and that she thought herself his superior.

You bitch, Matthew thought. It was spiteful of her to keep in motion, denying him some sight of her. She was out of luck, however, if she thought she could put him down. Her arch smugness highlighted exactly how honest Clemency was, with her candid intentions and responses. His mouth curled up in a satisfied smile. 'I'm very proud of the whole estate.'

Georgette knew if she didn't withdraw now in stalemate it would, for her, end in defeat. She had forgotten that Matthew Faraday was shrewd. He did not need two good eyes to realize when another was baiting or deriding him. 'That's all I wanted to say. If you'll excuse me...'

With pleasure, Matthew thought. 'Of course. Enjoy your day, Miss Bonython.' The young lady had proved his instinct was right. There was something untrustworthy about her. He would have a word about her with Julian when he returned, to see if he shared the same concern.

Somehow Georgette managed to ascend the steps without stamping up each one, which would make the rotter below smug with satisfaction.

She swept into the house and past the footman, who had stationed himself there to close the doors after her. She went fleetly across the hall and up the staircase and turned off, halfway along the picture gallery, to enter the corridor where her guest room was. Once in the room she beat her hands against some cushions and raged under her breath.

She hated being in Cornwall. Even though she'd had to get away from the loathsome Rupert Goring, she had thought the trip down here would be diverting. Pleasing, even. Always fascinated by the tales of Harry's roguish forebears, she had quite liked his provincial relatives. The country festival had been quite enchanting, until it had been ruined when some sordid trollop had been responsible for her children's savage deaths. Just punishment it was, the woman dying alone in her filthy hovel.

If only Harry had not had some stupid premonition and got involved with the scandal. It had changed him, making it easier for Clemency to claim him for herself, the little shrew. Before, Harry had granted Georgette her every whim and had never got impatient with her wants. But now, he had positively resented her wanting to stay here at Poltraze. She regretted, however, not going with him to Falmouth, where she could have mingled with naval officers and sea captains. Instead, in a moment lacking in foresight, she had tied herself to a boring, unstable woman, and she had to pretend to lavish adoration on her baby. Babies and small children were sweet when asleep or polite and prettily dressed, but otherwise they held no interest for Georgette. She hated the bad smells, the burps and the dribbles that also went with their charming aspects.

Thankfully, Hattie was quite sane much of the time, but she didn't have an ounce of social talk in her. She had no wit and offered nothing to have some fun about. Sometimes, usually when she was sleepy, she would ramble about such silly, impossible things. She would see fairies dancing in a ring in front of the hearth. One night, she had seen two moons in a sky of thousands of shooting stars. Another time she had been convinced Sir Julian was an angel, a real one, with wings hc could fold away out of sight. Georgette would have loathed it if Hattie had succumbed to her former hysterics and terrors (those episodes she had heard about from Netty, courtesy of Poltraze servant gossip), but she still had a tendency to whip into little panics at sudden noises or simple movements like fluttering drapes. And she would go on and on about how she hated and feared Clemency, for her own sake and Master Freddie's.

As much as Georgette resented Clemency, she did not believe a word of Hattie's prattling about her. Netty had gleaned information about Clemency's conduct while she had been here. The housekeeper and cook thought her unsuitable for genteel folk and rather vulgar, but they had not mentioned anything about her being loose in morals. Georgette's opinion was that Clemency would only give herself to the love of her life. Georgette had decided to marry to further her own interests. She suspected that Clemency would marry only when she chose to. In moments of humiliation, like now, Georgette envied Clemency over her less restricted life.

Calming down, checking that her appearance was immaculate, Georgette left her room to go to Hattie.

'A very good morning to you, Miss Bonython,' came a sudden, light voice, out in the corridor.

'Oh!' Her hand flew to her breast.

'Oh, my dear Miss Bonython, I beg your forgiveness for startling you. You will think me a heartless brute.' Julian Stapleton said, his voice awash with regret. He bowed his head low to her. 'Shall I send for a glass of water for you?'

Whenever Georgette found herself in this baronet's company she was always impressed by his supreme manners, humbleness and kindness. What a perfect husband he was. Titled, wealthy and sensitive. He put women on a pedestal and saw them as goddesses to be cherished and adored. He was, without a doubt, undemanding in all respects and, she was sure, was easy for his wife to keep in line. He was wasted on the overwrought Hattie Faraday.

Spreading her skirts she performed a modest curtsey and then, fluttering her eyelashes as if in shock, rather than the ire she had felt at the sudden interruption, she smiled faintly. 'I confess I was a little surprised by your unexpected greeting, Sir Julian, but please worry not, I am already quite recovered.'

'I'm so relieved to hear it,' Julian said. 'Miss Bonython, my wife has asked me to express our mutual gratitude to you over your kindness in attending her and spending so much time faithfully at her side. Lady Stapleton would also like to extend to you an open invitation to stay at our estate whenever you would care to, to repay something of all she believes she owes you.'

Georgette's mind worked rapidly. This unanticipated invitation might be the very thing to end all her worries. 'It will be my pleasure, Sir Julian. In fact, when Lady Stapleton is well enough to face the journey home, I would be very pleased to travel with her and see her safely settled in at her home again.'

'Would you really?' he replied lightly.

Basking in his gallantry, Georgette missed that the same light did not register in his mood.

Seventeen

'What does Harry say in his letter, darling?'
Verena asked Clemency. Breakfast had been an
hour ago, and this was the second day that
Clemency had made no plans to go out, after
returning home from the village soaked to the
skin and bedraggled. Verena was glad to see
that although Clemency was unusually subdued
she was not miserable, grumpy, or sickening for
a fever. She put her daughter's quietude down
to her missing Harry. He had been a constant
and a support to her after their tragic discovery.

'It's full of excited detail.' Clemency smiled,
picturing Harry's delight in all his new experiences. 'He's enjoying everything about Falmouth – its ancient streets, and the sea in
particular. He's been sailing in the harbour and
out to sea, and has taken a pleasure steamer to
Truro. He's met up with lots of people who
either met or knew of Reuben Bonython, his
great-grandfather. He's traced the house where
Reuben was born, the church where he was
baptized, where he was schooled and where he
spent his life before he married our Keyna
Kivell and took her up country. He's also
visited the graves of his Bonython forebears.

Reading between the lines, I suspect some of the fascinating creatures he's mentioned include some women of dubious repute. Anyway, he passes on his regards to everyone here and is looking forward to returning to us.'

'You'll be glad when he's back, I suppose?' Verena said.

'I've got used to having Harry around,' Clemency replied. 'I shall miss him terribly when he finally returns to Yorkshire. I hope to go up to see him at his home one day. Would you fancy making the long journey up north with me, Mama? You've never travelled very far.'

'It's good that Harry's pilgrimage to Falmouth has been such a success,' Verena said. 'And yes, I think I'd like to make the journey up to Yorkshire. I've received a few lines from Georgette. Written just to be polite, I'm sure,' Verena ended, tongue in cheek.

'Mmm. She's not the sort to put herself out willingly.' Neither Clemency nor Verena would forget how Georgette had snubbed them by leaving the farmhouse so eagerly. If they weren't good enough for the puffed-up madam, as far as they were concerned she could stay at Poltraze, or the hotel, until she left Cornwall.

'Do you think she's setting her sights on the squire?' Verena wondered aloud.

'Doubt it,' Clemency retorted, admitting inside herself that she was jealous that Georgette had easy access to Matthew while she did not. 'I'm sure she considers Matthew and

Poltraze beneath her league.' Clemency didn't want to hear how well Georgette was getting on with Hattie, but she couldn't stop herself from muttering, 'What does she have to say for herself?'

'Oh, the usual things about enjoying her stay and so on. She stresses that Miss Hattie couldn't possibly do without her, and that she's happy to do whatever she can for the dear suffering lady. She mentions that the squire keeps himself aloof, and is out quite often, including many an overnight stay. That there's whispers among the staff that he's taken a mistress.'

Mistress? Clemency felt as if she had been punched in the guts. It took an effort of will not to recoil and cry out. She felt as if her life force was seeping out of her. That Matthew would go to some other woman had never occurred to her. She didn't want to think about it. How could he have turned elsewhere so soon after she had made it clear marriage was not for her yet? She felt betrayed. Jowan had done the very same thing. But why should Jowan not seek a wife after she had turned down his offer, and Matthew the comfort of another woman's arms?

She could not bear to think about it, not about Matthew. Abe. She had to go to Abe. His gentle kisses and caresses had been special to her. He'd held her quietly for some time until she had felt a sense of relief, some peace. They had agreed to meet alone on the downs on Sunday afternoon, just to be together. She needed to be with Abe now. Immediately.

As airily as she could, she declared, 'Do you know, it's too good a day to stay in? I think I'll go for a ride.'

'Very well, my dear. I'm going into Meryen today to have lunch with Logan and Serenity at Wingfield. Will you be joining us?'

'I shouldn't think so, although I don't know exactly what I'll be doing yet. Bye, Mama.'

On reaching the lane Clemency encouraged her pony to grow wings on its hooves. She was halfway to the village when Matthew, escorted by Barker, turned into the Burnt Oak hamlet looking for her.

Two young gentlemen were shown into a swish single room at the New Oak Hotel. The man who had booked the room, as well as one for himself, flipped a florin to the bellboy who had carried up the trunks.

'Thank you, sir!' The bellboy's eyes lit up at the generosity. 'If there's anything I can do at all for either of you two gentlemen, the name's Pascoe.'

'I may well have a need for someone to run errands for me, with the utmost discretion, of course,' the man said with a benign smile that Pascoe, although a sharp looking youth, failed to see was quickly erased. 'Mr Wallace and I will be fine until luncheon. Our valets will unpack for us.'

'We're hardly fine, Goring.' Mr Wallace's voice sounded as if he had a mouthful of marbles. He had a habitually twitchy expression. He flopped his heavy, well-fed bulk down on the bed. 'Can't see the point in us coming all the way down to this godforsaken place. I've always thought of Cornwall as a stub of land inhabited by savages and goblins, and, apart from a few pretty bones in the wenches here and there, I can't see that I was far wrong. All those dusty, gut-wrenching miles of railway, ferry and coach because old Good Queen Bess had once said the gentry were a handsome lot. S'pose there might be one or two like that somewhere. Mind you, I don't mind feasting my eyes on the luscious Matty Faraday again. He was simply *divine* in uniform. Some time after that silly little fire, when he hid himself away from the world, I did manage a crafty glimpse of him and he was strangely even more beautiful; a hero, so sad and ruined. I just wanted to cherish him. He could have fulfilled my fantasies for over a year, I can tell you. Now, your spy informed you that Georgette has connived her way into Matty's house. She might be taken with him. Have you thought of that?'

'What rubbish you do talk. Faraday hasn't got a fraction of the necessary to suit Georgie's extravagant needs. I have, but she'll only get what I choose to allot to her ... but that's a different story. Now, Peregrine, please do not forget again that I am Jonathon Howard for the purpose of this journey and, until we leave with what I've come here for, you must forget you're not really Bertie Wallace. I won't risk Georgette slipping away from me again.'

Rupert Goring had excellent posture and a good hold on his composure. His closest friend from boarding school days, Peregrine Deedes, was the pampered heir to a baronet. While Goring was effortlessly unperturbed by almost everything, Deedes tended to be anxious and apologetic. While Rupert was careful and meticulous in covering up anything he did that was unscrupulous, the only drama Peregrine cared for was the kind gained from drunken orgies and gaming palaces. The two men were not unalike in features and could even be mistaken as brothers. Both had lots of style, and volumes of brown hair with full, precision-barbered sides.

'Yes, Bertie Wallace it is,' Deedes agreed, falling down flat on his back, settling to doze. 'Can I have that boy back in here to help undress and bathe me?'

'No scandals, for heaven's sake, man! No boys and no serving maids. In fact, be very sure to keep yourself circumspect every minute that we're in this quaint village. We must never forget that Georgie is a part of this roughneck Kivell clan who protect their own to the utmost, and, indeed, we are staying in Kivell-owned premises. I'll send your valet in. You take your nap and wake up with a clear and sharp mind.'

Deedes shot back up to a sitting position. 'Yes, of course, Ru— Jonathan. I'm sorry, very sorry.'

* * *

'Your sister is watching us again, Hattie. She's over there, snooping out from behind the box hedge.' Georgette and Hattie were strolling through the gardens, slightly behind the nursemaid who was pushing baby Freddie in a perambulator, purchased by Sir Julian for their stay at Poltraze.

Without lowering her parasol to look, Hattie tilted her chin in disdain. 'That wretched woman is no sister of mine. She has not come once to my side while I've been here. She's obviously jealous of me because I have an adoring husband, whom I've given a healthy heir. No doubt she also resents that I have a wonderful friend in you, my dear Georgie, while she has only another shrew like herself at her side. I don't know why Matthew doesn't seek to put her off the property and put her in some cottage somewhere without servants. She doesn't deserve any consideration at all. She gives nothing to life and is a drain on the estate's resources.'

'Don't you find this spying of hers unsettling; even somehow sinister? It's not a healthy thing to do, in my view.' Georgette had been amused at first when she had glimpsed Jane Hartley on a previous outing – clad in dark mauve and brown, like some mouldy rook – but now the servants were murmuring about the woman popping up in strange places and just staring, seeming troubled. There was something viperish in her demeanour. Jane Hartley was stalking her family. It was a mad thing to do when she only had to enter the house and speak to one of them. She might be filled with loathing for everyone living in the big house. There was the unsettling possibility she could turn from absurdly preposterous to a danger to anyone at any moment. 'Hattie, dear, I don't want to alarm you but I think you should get your brother to confront her and demand to know exactly what she's up to.'

Hattie was hit by a wave of panic. 'You're right. I should have given more thought about it. Jane could be planning to harm my darling Freddie, to abduct him.'

'Oh, please don't let what I said distress you about the baby. It's Clemency you fear where Master Freddie is concerned,' Georgette said, pleased to further Hattie's campaign against Clemency.

Hattie seemed aghast at this notion and shrilled on a high note, 'Clemency? Clemency Kivell, my old friend? She would never do such a thing. How could you say such a thing, Georgette? Her beast of a father hurt me very cruelly but it was Clemency who saved me. I owe her everything. If I had died that day I would never have gone on to meet Julian and give birth to my precious Freddie. No, you've got it all wrong. It's that witch over there who is full of ill intent towards me and my son. Nursemaid, take Master Freddie inside and inform Sir Julian that I need urgent assistance from him.'

Full of outrage, and as fierce as a tigress protecting her young, Hattie marched off across the lawn, waving her parasol in threat. 'Jane! Jane! Hold there, I wish to speak to you.'

Under the brim of her feathered bonnet, Georgette raised her eyes. Hattie's post-natal delusion had switched from Clemency and now she was annoyed at her, Georgette, over her remark. It wasn't madness, however, to worry about the peculiarity of the Arctic-faced widow for spying. This was all so tedious. Georgette craved the gloss and brightness of Society. Bored, yet disquieted, she followed after Hattie. 'Hattie, do be careful.'

'What do you want, Harriet?' Jane had come out of her hiding place and stood her new ground with iced condescension. 'Why are you coming at me like a harpy? I do have the right to wander these grounds. Are you forgetting the respect you owe me? I am your older sister!'

'If you thought yourself my sister you would have done more for me than send a badly-stitched garment for my child.' Hattie was on fire with contempt. 'You may do as you please, anywhere you please, but I will not tolerate you spying on me. Why do you conceal yourself? What are you up to? What mischief do you have on your mind? Come on, speak up! I've sent for my husband but I warn you I am not afraid of you.'

'Mischief? How dare you! I am merely taking the air. You have no right to attack me verbally. You really are mad, aren't you, Harriet? What next can I expect from you: a physical attack on my person? You ought not to be outside without a guard of some sort. Certainly someone more appropriate than this whey-faced lady should take charge of you.'

'Oh!' Hattie shrieked, stamping her foot in indignation. 'There is no need to insult my friend, who has been more of a helpmate and sister to me than you have ever been. You are despicable. You are a witch. I shall speak to Matthew about you the instant he arrives home. I will waste no more breath on you. Come along, Miss Bonython, we're leaving.'

Hattie turned round smartly and, linking arms with Georgette, she marched them both off.

Jane stayed cemented to the grass with disbelief, and a tempest of hate flowed more thickly through her veins than her blood did. What had she done to deserve such spite, she asked herself. And now, like a mob, Sir Julian Stapleton, Rumford and Mrs Secombe had reached Hattie and her pinch-faced friend. Hattie took her husband's arm, pointing at Jane as if she was some murderous felon. Stern as a hangman, Sir Julian disengaged himself from Hattie and came forward in haste.

'Mrs Hartley, madam, I would like to have a word with you.'

'I have nothing to say to you, sir,' Jane rejoined, frost edging her words. She sidestepped behind the box hedge and ran. She heard shouts – she didn't know from whom. She ran on over the vast length of the lawn and out on to the avenue of rhododendrons on the approach road.

She cut across the carriageway and into the facing rhododendrons, running faster than she had in all her life, surprising two gardeners throwing trimmings up on a compost stand as she took the shortest route home.

A maid saw her red-faced, panting mistress heading for a rear door of the house and scurried to open it for her. 'Madam –' she curtsied – 'what's wrong? Are the dogs chasing you?'

'Insolent wretch!' Jane smashed the flat of a hand across the girl's face, spraying her with spittle. 'Don't dare to question me again. Get out of my house. You're dismissed!'

The maid ran off crying to the kitchen. She was in pain and she was scared, but she was not fearful about her position. Only Mrs Secombe had the power to sack the servants here, on the squire's orders. Minutes later, every one of the Wellspring House staff was on their way to the big house to inform Mrs Secombe that Mrs Hartley had arrived home in a violent mood and was smashing up her bedroom, and that they could not tolerate another minute in her service.

Jane had stormed up to her room, thrusting the door open so fiercely it crashed against the wall, the vibration and draught sending delicate ornaments, and a vase of narcissi, plunging on to the carpet square and polished floor. Her blood thundering in her ears, her eyes glazed and snake-like, she went on a rampage. With deliberate crazed glee she grabbed every small, every large and every moveable object in the room and threw them against the walls. Wall

230

mirrors and a hand mirror ended up splintered and buckled. Paintings followed them. Powder and cream pots spread their mess and perfume bottles disintegrated and turned the air into a choking mixture of odours. Little round tables, cabinets, the bureau, chairs and stools were turned over. She ripped the bedcovers off the bed and trampled over them while throwing off the pillows and bolster. Clawing at the bed drapes she yanked and screamed while tearing them off the bedposts. She tore down the damask curtains at the windows and went at the lace with her fingernails. Blood gathered on her fingertips as her nails were ripped off. Finally, she snatched up a brass figure of a ballet dancer and hurled it at the window. The smashed glass plummeted down to the terrace below and noisily fragmented, satisfying her need for destruction.

Her body half bent over, her chest heaving with her laboured breaths, blood trickling down her cheek from a cut from sharp shrapnel of porcelain, her hair hanging in straggles, Jane let out a high pitch howl. She sounded like an animal caught in a trap. 'There! There, all of you, every one of you in my rotten family!' She stamped her feet in raging anguish. 'Are you happy now? You hate me. Now you've destroy-ed me. I hate you all. Die, every one of you. Die soon. I curse you. I curse your offspring. I curse Poltraze and everyone who ever sets foot in it. Die or I'll kill you myself!'

It was over. Her last drop of energy whooshed

out of her. She was completely empty. Her heart was numb as stone. Her head felt it was about to implode. She did not notice Adela Miniver cowering just outside the door.

Limp and heavy, operating on instinct alone, Jane shuffled into her adjoining boudoir, the one place she adamantly kept private. Once inside she leaned her weight against the door, the only way she could close it. Knowing she would soon faint she put out her hands, stumbled to the chaise lounge and collapsed down on it. Somehow she got her legs up, and with her back and neck blessedly against the cushions she let her brainless mind drift.

It could have been a second or hours later but suddenly her mind was jerked back into function by a sound. Her eyes sprang open. She listened. Hoping it was just a raindrop against a windowpane or some other natural occurrence. Please God, she prayed, no disturbance now. I'll get up from here eventually and put everything right in the next room.

The sound came again. It was a tap-tap on the boudoir door. 'Jane, it's me, Adela, can I come in?'

Jane sighed in irritation. Go away, silly woman.

Tap-tap. Tap-tap. 'Jane? Jane, please. I only want to know if you're all right.' Tap-tap again. 'Please, Jane, I'm very worried about you. All the servants are gone. I don't know what to do,' Adela wailed, her voice full of sobs. 'Can I come in? I think I ought to. I'm coming in.'

The unstoppable rage was in Jane again. She flew to her feet. She reached the door as Adela cautiously turned the brass knob, and wrenched the door back.

Adela shrieked in alarm. 'I–I'm sorry...' She winced in panic at the sight of Jane's darkened contorted features. She was snarling, her gums pale and bloodless, saliva frothing at the corners of her twisted lips. She was like a savage, a maniac. In that terrifying moment, Adela feared for her life.

Jane clutched Adela by her thin, trembling shoulders. 'You dare to come in here! How many times have I told you never to step across this threshold? You ungrateful bitch! Have I not given you enough? You use my house, you avail yourself of my servants and you eat my food. You're a parasite, Adela Miniver. You've leeched off me for years and given me nothing in return, but not any more, do you hear me?'

Adela opened her mouth to say that yes, she had heard Jane, and to plead to be let go. She was ready to beg to be allowed to stay on because, as afraid of Jane as she was, at that moment Adela had nowhere to go. Her words were not aired. Jane thrust her head forward and butted her viciously on the brow.

Jane tossed her companion away from her and saw with satisfaction how the smaller woman fell over the debris down on the bedroom floor. The mess and destruction was a lovely sight. It was pretty and sparkly. The glass pieces were like diamonds; the china and porcelain like a

233

scattering of snow with sprinkles of the colours of summer and Christmas. The picture frames made silvery and golden stars, and silk ran here and there like streams. Jane took it all in, so pleased with herself. She had never considered herself as an artist before.

Then her eyes travelled down the splendour to very near her feet. What? There was a lump of ugliness here. It was scrunched up but it moved in repulsive shudders and whimpered like a cranky child. It wasn't a child. It didn't look human. It was a goblin and it was ruining her masterpiece. It had no right to be here invading her creativity, the finest thing she had done in her life. It had to go. She had to put an end to it, destroy it at once. Stepping past the writhing creature she crouched down amid her show-piece and selected a beautiful, cool, smooth, heavy, jade obelisk to finish off her work.

Eighteen

Clemency was on Poltraze land, wandering a few yards distance from a bridleway that led through to parkland. It was where she had first seen Abe and encountered Hattie the second time. Hattie, a wilful, impressionable eighteen-year-old, had taken a tumble from her pony and was lying stunned and winded on the ground. Clemency had mistaken Abe (who had poached a brace of pheasants) as Hattie's attacker.

Recalling how she had raced up to them on her pony and hurled herself directly at Abe, Clemency smiled emotionally. She had landed a punch on Abe's face and got an arm lock around his neck. Abe had shoved her off him as if she was no more than a troublesome insect, explaining crossly he had come to the fallen young lady's aid. Clemency had found Abe couldn't be bossed. He had refused to let her take charge. As she and Abe had escorted Hattie home, Clemency, and a grateful Hattie, had warmed to the young miner, with his kindly, devil-may-care approach to life.

Clemency walked on through the bridleway, trailing her pony's reins, finding the old oak and beech trees a towering, leafy fortress of comfort. Being here was the next best thing to being

235

with Abe.

A short while ago in Meryen she had gone straight to Abe's back garden at Edge End, a row of terraced houses, to see if he was in his workshop. No luck. Knocking on the back kitchen door, hearing no answer from his disabled parents, she had crept inside. As long as they weren't startled and made anxious, Mr and Mrs Deveril liked to have visitors. Both long past climbing the stairs, Abe had brought their little double bed down to the front room. They had all the things that were precious to them there and they had not left the room in ages.

In the narrow passage, not wanting to give the old couple a fright, Clemency listened carefully at the door, which was always kept slightly ajar. All was softly still and quiet. 'Hello,' she called in delicate tones. 'Mrs Deveril. It's a visitor for you. May I come in please?' There was no use in calling to Mr Deveril, he was stone deaf, and it was no use in Clemency announcing her name. Mrs Deveril had very little memory.

'Hello?' came a croaky reply.

Clemency went slowly into the room. Partly darkened by half-drawn curtains but partly brightened by a serene, flickering log fire in the hearth, it was dominated by the small brass bedstead, a large, circular rag rug, and a strong smell of camphor. There was a dresser, lined with medicinal stuff, clean towels and linen, and a sturdy commode that had been fashioned by Abe and topped by a plain wood seat and then a flat knitted cushion. As on every occasion she stepped into this scene Clemency discounted the walls and fancied she was actually inside an old oak tree. It was like something out of Matthew's mystical-themed poetry. Propped against pillows, a faded, multicoloured patchwork quilt drawn up to his white-beaded chin, in an overlarge, bobbled nightcap, his toothless mouth agape as he slumbered, was tiny, bespectacled Mr Abraham Deveril. Side by side to the bed, in the one upholstered armchair, was the equally tiny Mrs Seraphine Deveril, her feet up on a stool. She too was swathed up to the chest by a patchwork knitted blanket, and a well-used, gone-off-white shawl was crossed over the top of her. Her white hair was under an ancient, white cotton cap with long, wide side flaps trimmed with age-spotted lace. Her hair at the back couldn't be seen, but Clemency knew it went down and down, plaited to a long, tapering point. The couple were like centuries-old, elfin great-grandparents. They were more whimsical than Clarry and Phee Faraday. It seemed impossible for them to have parented the overtly manly Abe.

Never had people commanded more respect than these two, was Clemency's opinion, and she curtseyed to them both, even though Mr Deveril couldn't see her. 'Good morning, Mrs Deveril. My name is Clemency. I'm a friend of Abe's. Do you happen to know where he is working today?'

'Hello, *cheeil*, my you're a some pretty maid.' Mrs Deveril had sadly mothered endless babies

237

until finally her last, Abe, had survived infancy. She had child-sized hands. They were a marvel to Clemency, for they were pure white and without the slightest gnarling. She raised her left hand, encased in a knitted fingerless mitten, to her ear. 'What did 'ee say?'

'I have come to see Abe,' Clemency said, mouthing her words slowly. 'Do you know where he is?'

'Eh? Oh, Abe, the boy, you mean? He's not here, is he? Might be out the back. The dear of 'un might be digging the garden.'

'I've already looked, Mrs Deveril. Abe is not there. Do you know where he could have gone?'

'Gone? Abe, the boy? He's gone out, I b'lieve.' The last word was barely out of Mrs Deveril's tiny puckered mouth when her head sunk down to her chest and she was soundly asleep.

Clemency stayed put for some moments, looking from one shrivelled old Deveril to the other. Neither snored nor puttered, they were totally at peace; so sweet and other-worldly. It was no wonder to anyone that Abe loved his parents dearly and was wholly devoted to them. *If I grow old and my mind goes, I hope I go to a place like they're in,* Clemency thought. Stooping, she placed a soft kiss on the cheeks of the dear old pair. 'Fare thee well, fare thee well,' she whispered to them at the door, the parting blessing they'd always given to others.

A neighbour, a young housewife, arriving to

make the Deverils' mid-morning cup of tea, and known to Clemency as Betsy, and a friend of Serenity and Jenny, told her that Abe had a job over at the hamlet of Meadowsweet. Disappointed beyond words, Clemency thanked Betsy and, feeling she couldn't interrupt Abe while he was working outside the village, she rode away, heading for the downs. She went straight to the place that was a favourite of hers and Harry's. A tableau of granite boulders resting with one large one as a flat surface, and the others offering shelter from eyes and the wind but not high enough to block out the sweeping views of the heather and gorse-strewn landscape. 'It's as if God sprinkled these rocks from his fingertips in a loving gesture to give a perfect place for peace and to soothe the soul,' Harry had once said about it.

'That was poetic,' Clemency had replied, and her thoughts had gone to Matthew. At any given moment of the day, Matthew slipped into her mind.

Where once she had laid down beside Harry, her head resting on his arm, gazing up at the sky, watching billowing clouds drifting along, insects flitting about, larks soaring, and buzzards hunting on the wing, she sat with her knees drawn up, arms hugging her knees, and felt the loneliest moment of her existence. It was all to do with the men in her life. She had sent Jowan away and that had been the right decision. She had spent a lot of time alone with Harry. Once they had stared at each other

239

summing up each other's physical attributes, silently acknowledging that usually this sort of perusal led to a measure of intimacy, but the spark of that sort of attraction had been missing. They had hugged, simply hugged, saying not a word but glad that their relationship would always be as loving distant cousins.

In her case there was another underlying factor. She had not admitted it to herself then but she did now. Matthew. He had always been there in the back of her mind, wedged in her soul, sheltered deep in her heart. She had thrown Matthew's love and devotion back in his face; she had betrayed him and all they had meant to each other.

Crouched up here on this hard rock she felt as if her life was over and she may as well not continue to breathe. 'Fool!' she screamed aloud. She had denied herself the love of her life.

She could have had Matthew. She could have had everything she'd ever wanted. Love. She could have shared in that simple yet mysterious emotion of endless meanings, that thing of beauty, bliss and divinity, the only thing really worth having. She knew now that she loved Matthew, was absolutely and irrefutably in love with him, and it was too late. He was the love of her life and she had tossed his love away as if it was the most irritating thing on earth to her and had even lost his friendship.

She had never thought too much of that age-old thing called love. She had never chased a dream of meeting her soulmate. She had either accepted what life had thrown her way or had gone for what she wanted and got it. Life had been almost too easy for her. Yet love had been available to her for over three years in the shape of an extraordinary, fascinating, gentle-eyed man who had stayed faithful to his love for her for all that time. Matthew had cherished her as his dream, believing her worth the long wait. The kiss she had so willingly shared with Matthew back then had thrust her into all the realms of heaven and worldliness. She had immediately chosen to ward it off and forget Matthew's exceptional sensuous attraction. Forgotten it to her cost. She had abused Matthew and struck him down. She deserved her terrible loneliness. She deserved to stay in wretched misery all her life.

Now she was here trespassing on Matthew's land, walking one of his bridleways, but not in her old manner of going exactly where and when she wanted to and to hell with the consequences. She was crying, the tears hot and searing and streaming down her face, in shame and despair because she had hurt Matthew and couldn't bear the thought of him suffering.

The trees were alive with grey squirrels, rooks, blue tits and, here and there, plump-breasted robins, and the air was alive with the song of several more species of birds. The sun wove merry shafts of bright light through the burgeoning leafy branches. Carpets of bluebells reached through the parkland and the woodland

241

floor, out of sight. In the ditches either side of where Matthew was walking with Sandy, celandines blazed yellow like guiding lights on the path ahead. Long, widely spaced, fairly straight wire fencing on the sides of the hard, stony path kept out straying sheep and cattle from the fields and meadows. Normally, Matthew used his imagination to make up for what he couldn't see and he enjoyed all these delights to the full. Today he trudged along with his hands clasped behind his back and his head down, and moved on instinct alone. At times Sandy had to nudge his legs to lead him back safely in the right direction.

At Burnt Oak Farm, Verena Kivell had informed him that he had not long missed Clemency, who was on her way to Meryen. 'I've come with news of the Juleff children,' he had explained, unintentionally gruff to disguise his frustration. 'I thought Clemency would be interested to hear how they are faring. They are well. I will write to Clemency instead. I'm sorry to have troubled you, Mrs Kivell.'

'Please be assured that you have not troubled me at all, Mr Faraday,' Verena Kivell had replied, and he had sensed in her sympathy and understanding for him. It had soothed him a little, yet it was also humiliating that his intention to try to get on good terms with Clemency again was so transparent. 'Clemency will be delighted to hear the good news about the children.'

His hope to come across Clemency in the

242

village had also failed. All he had learned was that she had called on the elderly Deverils and had then ridden off somewhere. 'Don't think she had gone to none of her family here, sir,' he had been told.

He had decided to return home and make another attempt to write a letter to Clemency, having no idea how on earth to begin, word and finish it. When he and Barker reached the thatched gatehouse, they were met by the gate-keeper with the urgent tale of his widowed sister's drama.

'Well, Rumford, Mrs Secombe, what has gone on?' He addressed his head servants in the morning room, he alone, as he must be when bearing the brunt of his family's various theatricals. He was so frustrated he wanted to scream and to leave the house and all its problems forever.

'I'm very sorry to have to tell you, sir,' Mrs Secombe began, to Rumford's obvious chagrin, but it was to her the Wellspring House staff had rushed to. 'That following an altercation with Lady Stapleton in the grounds, in which Sir Julian had to be called to go to her Ladyship's assistance, Mrs Hartley returned to Wellspring House and it appears she went berserk. She slapped the housemaid so hard across her cheek that a red hand mark can still be clearly seen. Then she dismissed the girl, but of course she does not actually have the right to do that.'

'Mrs Hartley then went upstairs, sir, and was heard to be breaking things, many things.

Apparently she was hysterical,' Rumford said, taking up the report, his nose twitching in superiority. 'The servants were all somewhat frightened and they ran all the way up to the kitchens here.'

'I see. The servants did the right thing. They must move in here. The injured maid should rest for the day. I'm sure you and Mrs Secombe can find tasks for the others to do. Mrs Hartley can be allowed to recollect herself. If she does not put in an appearance here, she should be sent for. She can attend me in the estate office at six o'clock this evening.'

Matthew went up to Hattie, concerned to find her alone but also relieved she was calmly sewing. The baby had been brought into the room in his cradle on her orders and every other second she was glancing down at his little sleeping body and smiling. 'He can be taken back to the nursery this evening but I want him with me for now.'

'I'm so glad you are taking it all so well, Hattie.' Matthew then frowned. 'Where is Miss Bonython?'

'Oh, she went down to the library to fetch a book for herself. Julian is there attending to some business. I charged her to report to him that all is well with Freddie and me.'

'I'm pleased you don't mind staying on your own for a while,' Matthew said. Before this, Hattie had panicked to be left alone.

'Oh, I'm becoming more and more my old self. I'm sorry I've been such a bother to you,

244

Matthew. You look tired and drained. It's been overwhelming for you to have my shocking illness thrust upon you on the very day your Squire's Day was so dreadfully ruined. And now there's this trouble with Jane. What will you do about her?'

'I haven't decided yet.' Apart from the relief of Hattie coping with a crisis without losing her mind, this whole new episode made him incapable of making any important decisions. He was dangerously near breaking point.

'Matthew, Georgette said a very strange thing to me in the garden. She said that I actually believed that Clemency would harm Freddie. I have no recollection of saying such a thing. It is true?'

'Yes, I'm afraid it is. It's why she hasn't been here since your arrival.' He could have groaned at how this made him miss Clemency more and more.

'Dear Lord, that's awful.' Hattie put a hand to her mouth. 'I haven't thought of Clemency as my dearest friend since the abduction, but after all I've been through, now I realize I'm so fortunate and blessed to have my precious son and Julian, I'm more than grateful that she saved my life. I found it hard to forgive her for that, you know, when I was left scarred and scared that there'd be an attacker behind every bush. Clemency is the best of people. Mama and Papa must be missing her; she was so loyal to them. And you must miss her too. I would really like to see her. I shall put this sewing aside and write to her immediately.'

His spirit lighter than it had been for weeks, Matthew went back downstairs and ordered Barker to fetch Sandy. 'I'm going for a long walk, a very long walk. I'm not to be sought out under any circumstances.'

'I understand, sir. You're looking a lot brighter if I may say so.'

'I feel it, Barker. Now I wish only to be alone.'

Hattie would have her letter taken to Burnt Oak Farm straightaway. If Clemency accepted Hattie's explanation and apology hopefully, *please, please God,* she would turn up here tomorrow.

Clemency had reached the other end of the bridleway, her tears now all dried up. She left her pony there and walked on and out on to the parkland, reaching the path Matthew was using. A jolt ran through her to see him coming this way in the distance. He looked so lost and lonely and she felt an overwhelming leap of love for him. She wanted to gather him in against her heart and cry that she was so sorry for making him miserable. She wanted them to go back to the time when they had kissed, to the moment when their lips had met, and for them to renew their passionate feelings, and quite simply to be in love.

Sandy saw her and barked. Clemency caught her breath. She must slip away before Matthew knew she was here. How different she was, she mused, from when they had first met, when she had stamped about his house in her confident and to-hell-with-it-all manner. Now she did not want to disturb Matthew, to put him through any more sorrow. Yet she did not want to leave here, to leave *him*.

She'd left it too late. Sandy, recognizing a friendly presence, while loyally standing by his master, barked an enthusiastic welcome to her. Startled out of his pensiveness by Sandy's exuberance Matthew fell over his own feet.

'No!' Clemency cried in horror at what she had inadvertently done. 'Matthew, stay put. I'm coming to you.' She pelted along the several hundred yards distance to him and was soon on her knees where he lay sprawled on the rough, stony ground.

Matthew lay where he had fallen, stunned and uncomprehending. Why and how had he ended up down here? Why had Sandy got so out of hand?

'Matthew, it's Clemency.' Her hands were gently pushing his hair away from his eyes. 'Are you hurt? Have you any pain?'

'Clemency, is it really you?' She was a shadowy form to him, and her voice was different, it was the warmest he had heard, anxious and hesitant.

'Yes, Matthew, it's me. It's my fault you tripped over. I'm so sorry. It seems I'm always doing something to upend you. Have you broken anything?'

She was stroking his face, running a gentle hand over his legs and shoulders. To Matthew, after the sudden jolt and horrible sensation of being pitched down in the fall, it was heavenly. 'I don't think so, just a few bruises and a little sprain to my dignity. Clemency, you really are here, aren't you? This isn't a dream?'

'It's not a dream, Matthew, I promise you. Let me help you up. You must be so uncomfortable. Hold on to me and move slowly and carefully.'

He could easily get up on his own but he was happy to obey, to be in such close proximity to Clemency, to slide one arm round her waist and rest his cheek against her neck, breathing in the very feminine essence of her. With a little effort on both their parts he was up, and he kept a firm hold of her, afraid she might vanish in a puff of smoke and leave him desolate.

Clemency examined him for blood and scratches, and gently brushed off the debris on his coat. Then she gazed into his eyes. 'Are you quite steady?'

'I'm fine.' Sunlight beamed down on her and he saw her with keen clarity. She was utterly beautiful, a living vision of supreme femininity. She seemed to be looking at him with utter tenderness. 'Is all well with you, Clemmie?'

'No, it isn't, not at all.' Her tone wavered with emotion. 'I've made a terrible mistake, Matthew. I came here wanting to feel close to you. I didn't realize how much you meant to me, you see, until it was too late. It's not too late for us, is it? Please say it's not. I'm begging you to forgive my immaturity and self-centredness. I know that you might have someone else now and, as much as I don't want to come between a genuine affection, I have to know if there's any hope for us to be together. Properly. I'll take any form of relationship you desire to have with me and think myself blessed for it.'

He was hardly daring to breathe. 'There's no one else, Clemmie. I had a brief affair but it's over and all because I couldn't get you out of my head and heart. I went to the farm today hoping to see you. I tried to write to you but I wanted to see you in person. I brought good news to you but I was also praying that you'd be pleased to see me.' He could not take it in, Clemency suddenly being here with him, touching him, pleading that she wanted him. Again, he had to know he wasn't in some wonderful dream. He lifted his hand. Would he actually feel her hair under his fingertips; her hair, which always seemed freshly blown by the wind? Would he feel the softness of her cheek? And the warmth that radiated off her fabulous body? Would he feel his hand on the silky slenderness of her neck? Or would she suddenly not be there and he would realize he was just daydreaming about his most precious fantasy: that Clemency had come to him and said she wanted to be his?

As he touched her hair she turned her head and kissed the palm of his hand. 'I love you, Matthew. I really do love you.'

His doubt broke into fragments and melted

away. And, for Clemency, his immediate, joyful response chased away all her doubts and filled up all her emptiness. There was no need for explanations, speeches and soul searching. They were in each other's arms and their lips were meeting. The time lost since their first and only kiss was of no significance. All that had happened between then and now had been necessary to bring them to this point of wondrous reality. And the love they would always share was stronger for it.

'I love you so much, Clemmie. I've dreamt of having you like this for so long.' He rained kisses over her face, down her neck and in her hair.

'When I came to my senses about you I was so scared I'd lost you. I'm so sorry, Matthew. Thank you for staying patient with me.'

'I'll always be true to you, my darling Clemmie.'

'You're all I'll ever want, Matthew, darling.'

'Then I'll ask you what I've longed to do for so long. Will you marry me?'

'If you'll marry me,' she said, bright-eyed, holding his face in her hands.

Matthew kissed her, hugged her and laughed. 'I can't believe I'm so happy.'

They walked on into the woods, to a place where a gap in the trees enabled the grass to grow soft and lush. Once there, Matthew sent Sandy away to explore. Then, starting by clasping their hands, they cherished each other, relishing the sweetness of each other's mouths and learning the contours of their bodies, each shivering with the pleasures they evoked.

Their loving went on and further still. From standing to kneeling to lying down they showered and took passion and held nothing back.

'Clemmie, my precious darling,' he breathed into her glorious hair, the amber-fair tresses tumbling free from his caresses and, supporting her with an arm underneath her, he went into her at just the right moment.

She gave a woman's cry of triumph, taking the moment of pain as her right and fully giving herself to him.

When they eventually left the woods, hand in hand, Clemency leading her pony and Sandy bounding on and sniffing about, Matthew told her all the good news. 'There is one important thing, Clemmie. Will you be happy living in the house? Poltraze has suited me, and Mama and Papa, but most people disparage it as gloomy and ugly. We'll live in the main part of the house, of course, and you can make any changes you want to. With you at my side, Clemmie, I'm ready to change. All your family would be welcome at any time. Poltraze could really start to live at last. We could hold parties; do anything that the Kivells do.'

'And we'll have a large brood of children tearing about the house and garden. It's not bricks and stone that make a home, Matthew, but the people in it. Clarry and Phee know that. They'll be so pleased to see you living your life again. Now Hattie wants to see me again every-thing is set to be perfect. I'm really looking for-ward to seeing her and Clarry and Phee again.'

'It won't be long now.' Matthew laughed aloud for he was so happy. He shouted at the top of his voice, 'I love Clemency Kivell and she's agreed to marry me.'

A mass of crows were frightened out of the trees, cawing in protest, and the couple laughed together.

'When we leave the house for the farm so I can speak to your mama and brother Tobias, perhaps you'd care to take Georgette Bonython as well,' he said drolly.

'Oh? I can tell you don't like her. Is Georgette not good for Hattie after all?'

'I suppose she is. I'm sorry to think ill of your distant cousin, darling, but although I can't figure what is wrong my senses tell me she is false.'

'False.' Clemency pondered on the descrip-tion.

'How did *you* find her?'

'I haven't given her very much thought with so much going on lately. My impression is that she seems a typically well-brought-up young lady. She's gifted and seems quite sweet-natur-ed, although rather self-seeking. I thought she took it well, moving out of the hotel to stay in the lesser grandeur at the farmhouse. She was very clingy to Harry at first. I thought it was because of the tragedy. But Harry explained she had always been like that because of the way she was ripped away from her parents' home after their tragic deaths. I did think it strange she should be so enthusiastic about helping a woman she barely knew, and to suddenly hardly need Harry at all. I thought perhaps she had set her mind on you, darling.'

He made a wry face. 'She's been polite and quite entertaining generally. You are right about her good nature. She has made no demands on the staff here and fits in readily with the routine. I was sure she would be bored but there have been no reports of that. She seems genuinely fond of Hattie and the baby.'

'There is one thing that stands out about Georgette. Just after she arrived in Meryen she begged Harry to take her travelling overseas as soon as they had met the family. Then she urged Harry to take as much time as he needs at Falmouth, and when he returns to look up the family history. She is in no hurry to leave here. I'd have thought she would be eager to return to the high social scene. The more I think about it, the more it makes me wonder if she's hiding from something.'

'I agree. So that begs the question, if she *is* hiding from something then what could it be? It makes me worry for Hattie.'

'But we also could be being unfair to Georgette. She may simply be a sweet creature who wants to help a sick young mother.'

'I suppose I should be glad that Hattie is getting well again and that she enjoys her life with Sir Julian and her son.'

The west wing of the house came into sight. It was too long since their last kiss and they stopped for another passionate embrace. At the same moment there was a high-pitched wailing coming from the garden up ahead. Sandy barked in Matthew's defence and Matthew called him to order. 'My God, that sounded like Hattie.'

Clemency left Matthew and climbed up the wire fencing, keeping herself steady by grabbing the wooden post. 'I can see someone tearing across the lawn. I'm afraid it is Hattie and there's a man running after her who I assume is her husband. She's in great distress. Oh, Matthew, this is dreadful.'

She jumped down off the wire and found Matthew shaking his head in disbelief. 'But she was so well when I left the house.'

Clemency was disconsolate for Matthew. 'We'll take my pony and ride there as fast as we can. I'll keep out of the way in case Hattie's fear about me has returned. Don't worry, Matthew, you have me now to help you get through everything.'

Nineteen

'Will you all please sit down now?' From the winged armchair she had chosen to sit down on, Hattie used lowering movements with her hands as she addressed the gaggle of anxious faces all about her. She took her feet off the padded stool that Julian had ordered to be placed for her. 'Please do as I say. I am not ill. I was in fear for my son. The nursemaid had had the necessity to leave the room for a short while and, almost at once, I was in fear for my son. I thought I had to save him. Now I know he is safe and well I have calmed myself. Please, I don't need all this fuss.'

'How can you say you're calm, darling?' asked Julian, his high brow rutted with worry. He had caught up with Hattie when she had suddenly stopped in her flight across the lawn. Acting against her insistence that she could walk, he had carried her inside. Georgette Bonython had been ascending the stairs. 'Miss Bonython, have you just come from Lady Stapleton's room?' he had asked her.

'Why yes I have, Sir Julian. What is all the to-do? I had slipped to my room to change my slippers and was surprised to find only Master

255

Freddie and the nursemaid there. The nurse-maid was perturbed to find Master Freddie all alone. She said Lady Stapleton had given her permission to take a short leave of necessity. Then I saw from thc window Lady Stapleton in dire distress outside. I've come down at once to see if there is anything I can do.'

Hattie had struggled so strongly that Julian had been left with no choice but to set her down on her feet. She had rushed to the bottom stair. 'Are you absolutely certain Freddie is there in my room?'

'Yes, Hattie, I mentioned to the nursemaid how peacefully asleep he was.'

'Thank God, thank God.' Hattie had almost collapsed in relief.

While sharing her relief, Julian had once again wished he had not let Hattie talk him into travelling here. She had made some way to recovery but if she were still at home she could have been completely well by now. His brother-in-law, the squire, flushed from a swift ride, had arrived, reigning in his pony on the lawn. Matthew had then suggested everyone go to the morning room. The butler had hurried to open the doors ahead of the party, which included Mr and Mrs Faraday (for once without any dogs), the housekeeper, and Hattie's personal maid.

'You were distraught, Hattie,' Julian remind-ed her, clasping her hand.

Georgette stooped a little towards Hattie, her hands folded together. 'Dear Hattie, you seem-ed quite out of your mind. You need to be more careful in future,' she said.

'That was an insensitive thing to say, Miss Bonython,' Matthew admonished.

'Oh, I didn't mean...' Georgette fought back a small sob, letting her chin sink down. Her remark had not been aimed to hurt Hattie. There was a hidden meaning in it. Georgette could explain it to no one but Netty. She despised Matthew Faraday for admonishing her. She was obviously no longer welcome here as far he was concerned. She would not stay where she was not wholly wanted. That meant failure, something she hated but which seemed to have plagued her this year.

'You said you were haring across the lawn, Hattie, dearest, because you saw, a minute after the nursemaid had stepped out of the room, that he had vanished from his cradle and a note had been left where he'd been lying saying he had been taken,' Julian said. Georgette thought he looked strained with the effort of understanding his wife. Hattie had told him such an implausible story!

'You said you spotted a man from the window carrying something,' Julian continued, 'and you were convinced he had Freddie. When you saw it was in fact a gardener simply carrying an armful of plants you knew you had made a mistake. But you see, my love, Freddie was there all the time and there was no note. You imagined it. But you can take comfort from the knowledge that this delusion did not last long and you have recovered quite quickly. Now, I really

257

think you should go up and rest. As soon as you've seen Freddie for yourself I think he should go back to the nursery. I'll sit with him myself if it will soothe you.'

'That will be for the best,' Hattie said, evidently happy with the conclusion. She pecked Julian on the cheek. 'This time I remember things clearly, while before I had to be told what had occurred. I really am getting better.'

The more Hattie spoke, the more every muscle in Georgette's face tightened. Pathetic woman. So undeserving of a perfect Society husband who adored the very marrow of her bones. It was Hattie who must have taken her baby out of the cradle and hidden him behind long curtains in the corridor. Georgette had heard the baby fretting and made the astonishing discovery of his whereabouts. She had put the baby back, covering him carefully. Hattie had been mad enough this time to write and leave a note. Georgette hadn't bothered to read it and had thrown it on the fire. She had gone to look for Hattie and had heard her screaming outside. Georgette had tried to protect Hattie from possibly being denied access to Freddie if her husband thought her a danger to him, but Georgette also wished to soon extricate herself from boring, old Poltraze, and not just for the night of Jowan Kivell's engagement celebration. She didn't want Hattie clinging to her again. Georgette had done a good thing, even if it were partly for her own ends. She tightened her lips. She didn't care what the people here thought of her. She would leave Poltraze today.

Hattie rose, holding on to Julian's arm. 'Matthew, I noticed you arrived on Clemency's pony. Were you with her? She is your close friend, after all. Does that mean she's close by? I would like to see her very soon. Perhaps she would like to call on me tomorrow.'

'Clemency would be delighted to be welcome back in the house again,' Matthew said, happiness evident in his face. 'Now I know your distress is over I shall be riding to Burnt Oak with Clemency to ask for her hand in marriage. Poltraze will very soon have a new mistress.'

Shortly afterwards in the servants hall, Mrs Secombe sounded off. 'Could be worse, I suppose. We won't get no airs and graces from Miss Clemency, and it was so good to see the squire happy at long last. He'd been too many years in the doldrums. Mr and Mrs Faraday were elated, weren't they, Mr Rumford?'

'Indeed they were. Lady Stapleton too was pleased for the squire. Sir Julian has intimated that, as soon as he's confident her Ladyship can withstand the journey, they will be returning to Devon.'

'It will be for the best for our dear young lady to be home and to get Master Freddie settled into his own nursery,' said Mrs Cooper. The cook was in charge of the huge, brown teapot, under a green, knitted cosy. She frowned at the scullery maid's silent and humble request for a top-up of tea, and ceremoniously filled the girl's cup by half an inch.

'Thank you, Mrs Cooper.' The pale, skinny girl bowed her head, acting as if she had been given a vat of heavenly nectar; to everyone else's satisfaction.

'I'll be glad when that Miss Bonython has gone,' put in the parlour maid. 'Miss Netty is an angel and very nice to us here, but her mistress ... Mind you, I liked the young lady at first, though she thinks she is a saint for how she's dedicated herself to her Ladyship. Well, Miss Bonython is not all she wants people to seem, if you ask me.'

'It is not our place to speak so of our betters, Lizzie,' Rumford chided, polishing the monocle he wore on odd occasions, something he did when signposting his superiority. 'As it happens Miss Bonython has made arrangements to leave today, to return to Burnt Oak for a family engagement.'

'I can't say I'm sad to hear that, but Lizzie is not wide of the mark, Mr Rumford.' Mrs Secombe leaned towards him and lowered her tone. 'Did you notice her expression when the squire quite rightly took issue with her? And again, when her Ladyship mentioned Miss Clemency in her old kindly manner? And when the squire said he and Miss Clemency were to be married, well, you know the saying, if looks could kill. Miss Bonython was jealous; green with envy that others are happy. If I was one to interfere I'd warn the Kivells to watch that one.'

Twenty

Julian Stapleton was treading out a circuit of Poltraze House, anxiously scanning the gardens and crooking his head to peer round bushes and trees, and peering beyond garden walls, concerned that Jane Hartley might be lurking about, intent on some new wickedness. He was decidedly unhappy that it would be some hours before Mrs Hartley was taken to task over her unseemly and violent behaviour.

'It is not something that I consider should be allowed to rest, Matthew,' Julian had said, arguing the point in the morning room. The women had all gone upstairs. A while earlier Matthew had sent Barker outside to Clemency, where she was lingering discreetly in the summerhouse, to invite her inside the house. Hattie and Clemency had had a polite and warm reunion, and Hattie had been eager to show off the baby to Clemency. Mrs Faraday, all proud and happy smiles, had taken Clemency's arm. Not intending to trail on last, Georgette Bonython had hurried to walk out at Hattie's side. Mr Faraday had not joined in the men's conversation. Instead, he had petted the dogs in his effusive way. 'Mrs Hartley has overstepped the mark,'

Julian had continued. 'And ita very serious state of affairs when her servants are sent running away from her in fear of her anger.'

'I don't intend to pander to my sister's tantrums,' Matthew had said, making himsclf comfortable in an armchair with the brown and white, curly-eared spaniel that had leapt on to his lap. 'Given plenty of time to reflect, hopefully she will rectify the damage she was heard doing. I don't see why the servants should clear away her mess. Jane can ponder about what her life would be like if she was permanently denied servants. I haven't had the chance to think through what I shall say to her, but one thing I will make absolutely clear is that she will only remain in Poltraze property under the most strict of conditions. Indeed, I might come to the decision that it would be better done if she and her companion were moved to some distant location.'

'But what if Mrs Hartley sees fit to come up to the house and tries to cause further trouble?' Julian had protested. 'Hattie has come through Mrs Hartley's ill-will most admirably, but she might become troubled if there was any more offence today.'

'Jane will not be allowed admittance. I have ordered Rumford to station a footman at each door. My sister will sulk and seethe for a long while yet. There would be no reasoning with her. It's better this way, Julian. Why not sit and take some mead with Papa and me?'

Displeased at the outcome of the debate, but

not showing it – Julian was well trained not to show emotion in public – he had withdrawn politely. 'If I may decline your kind offer, I would like to retire to somewhere quietly for a while. Before I go, Matthew, please accept my congratulations on your forthcoming engagement. I hope you and Miss Kivell will know every happiness together.'

'That –' Matthew had stretched his legs out blissfully – 'is a foregone conclusion.'

Julian had gone straightaway to the conservatory and paced among the fern trees and tender plants and Wardian cases. In his opinion his brother-in-law's judgement was blinded by his new found happiness, although he couldn't really be blamed for that. Clemency Kivell was a beautiful and vivacious creature, open and forthright, her character the direct opposite of the disingenuous Georgette Bonython. It was no loss that the young lady was to leave for her family home. However, whatever the reason, Matthew had made his decision about Jane Hartley. Now, Julian made his.

Cautiously certain Jane Hartley was not nearby, lying in wait to perpetrate some mischief, he put his hands nonchalantly behind his back and sauntered away from the house as if taking a relaxing stroll. He made for the nearest stand of trees and threaded his way through them until well out of sight of the house. Then he went down to Wellspring House to remonstrate heavily with the widow Hartley. Hattie was his wife! He had sworn to protect her and to always endeavour to ensure she lived a harmonious life. He was unlikely to obtain the promise of an apology to Hattie from the Hartley woman, and indeed he did not want the embittered harridan to go near Hattie again, but he resolved that the resentful and twisted witch was not going to be allowed to get away with her insults.

Julian approached the house from the back quarters. The stark heavy door was flung open, no doubt left so after the flight of the servants. He mounted the outside high stone steps and paused to listen for sounds. There was no ranting, no shrieking, no hysterical destruction. He heard nothing at all, not as much as a ticking of a clock. Somehow, he knew his quest to take the widow to task was not to be. The stillness of a graveyard – not the peaceful kind – and a darkly simmering atmosphere hung thickly in the stale air. He stepped inside, putting his foot down carefully. Hunched over a little he crept along the dim, narrow passage and went up the servants' stairs, wary of not letting the wooden structure creak under his weight. The arched door to the landing was half open. He took an extra moment on the last steps before he reached it, listening. The brooding quality in the mawkish air, the disquietude – birthed by a lone woman's bitter, wild wrath – seemed to be growing into something real and threatening. Julian had no idea what to expect but he was sure he was to be horrified to some extent.

Of the seven rooms leading off from the landing one door was open, open wide, and Julian could see shards of broken china and glass, pieces of ripped fabric and a cushion with the stuffing pulled out, all put together in a heap about a yard inside the room. It was like a peculiar morbid memorial – God knew what to – and its existence brought on clammy chills, which rode up Julian's spine. Strong light spilled from the room, pointing to curtains having been pulled down. Splinters broken off the trophy display gleamed in the paisley-patterned wool. Julian felt the horrid sensation of his scalp prickling, his flesh creeping and his stomach heaving. He half-expected some dangerous creature or monster to suddenly leap out from any direction and attack him. Jane Hartley could be inside any of the rooms. She could be stealing up the stairs or creeping up behind him. He might be knocked to the floor, or blinded or deafened, or half his legs cut out from under him. It was like being in a childhood nightmare.

Without noise or warning a woman, a dark outline of a woman, was there in the doorway.

Julian gasped, one hand instinctively going to his throat and the other to his stomach as if he needed to protect these vulnerable places. Jane Hartley's twisted gargoyle expression seemed to hold all the hate in the world; icing him, slicing him. Her thin-cut eyes had the unblinking expression of a reptile. She appeared beyond reason, bereft of humanity. Her hair was tangled and her lace cap, although still tied under her jutting chin, was down on her shoulders. One of her fists was clenched and there

265

was blood on it and blood was splashed on her dress. Clasped in her other hand and pointed to the floor was a brass poker from the fireplace. Julian was relieved to see there was no blood on the instrument, which she had probably used to cause a lot of the damage he could see. Piercing warning sensations got at his insides. The blood on her was, apparently, not hers. He detected no cuts or injuries on her.

'What are you doing in my house?' Jane intoned, as if addressing something that had stolen in from the gutters.

Her deadly eyes bore into him and Julian wasn't sure if she recognized who he was. He was ashamed to feel a moment of sheer terror. It was as if he could smell the lunacy on her; all the bitterness and corruption in her. She was as dangerous as a savage and he needed to keep his wits sharp. It was paramount he did nothing to bring her to a rage. 'I thought it remiss of Matthew not to send someone to see if all is well with you, Mrs Hartley. You were very upset in the gardens a little earlier.'

'Liar,' Jane uttered in a noxious tone, pointing at him. She threw back her bloodless lips and smirked. 'You've come to see what I have done, haven't you? Do you want to know?'

Julian's heart was beating hard, thumping against his ribs. He did not doubt the crazed woman had enacted out some monstrous crime. Nevertheless, he kept his voice calm and caring. 'What have you done, Mrs Hartley? Where is Miss Miniver?'

266

beast. How much of her word could be trusted? 'If you really *have* murdered Miss Miniver.'

'Come and see for yourself.' Jane laughed hysterically, flailing her arms. With some unnatural energy surging throughout her skinny body she shot off into her bedroom. Julian went after her, wary, incensed at what she'd raved about Hattie and his son, but now unafraid and ready to take her out of the house by whatever force proved necessary.

'Here she is,' Jane trilled manically. 'Dead as a tombstone with pretty red ribbons and shades of blue and purple.'

Julian glanced down to the crumpled form Jane was lurking over. A glance was enough. The remains of the head of the dead companion was the most obscene thing he had ever seen; something that was going to be difficult to push out of his mind for the rest of his life. The red ribbons the mad woman had spoken of were rivers of blood. Keeping his eyes rooted on the Hartley witch he whipped off his coat and threw it over the top of the corpse.

'Oh, a fine figure of a man, aren't you?' Jane jeered. 'Was it enough for my rotten little sister to welcome you into her bed? Or did you take her by force as my dead husband did to me? He hurt me in the most humiliating way possible and then he mocked me and told me I wasn't good enough to satisfy even the oldest man.'

Julian ignored her ranting, which went on and on and turned into the sickest obscenities. He rounded the body and advanced on Jane. She trod back, matching him step for step. He stopped before she reversed their positions and she was nearest to the door. 'You might as well hold still. You won't evade me forever.'

'You think not?' Jane hissed through clenched teeth and balled her fists. 'I won't let you take me to my brother. I won't let you see me in prison and sent to the gallows. I shall escape you and do it my way!' She lurched for the window.

Alert to any sudden ploy, Julian lunged at her and caught her arm before she reached the window. She shrieked in words that were unintelligible and kicked and clawed at him. 'I won't let you throw yourself to your death,' he cried, using all his strength to clamp both her arms to her shaking body and imprison her in an unbreakable grasp. 'It's justice for you, woman, and not by the rope. You'll be locked up, but it's an asylum for you where your mind and body can further degenerate until the moment you die, and I hope that's not for many years to come.'

He was not sorry he was forced to manhandle her; that he had no choice but to restrain her by tying her arms tightly to her sides with shreds of curtain. All the while her mouth fouled the air and he would have gagged her if not for the objection he thought he would get from Matthew at going too far. Still she struggled and he had to drag, and then haul, her up off her feet to get her to the door. As he carried her outside he caught a glimpse of himself in the hall mirror. The harridan had scratched and bruised his face and neck unmercifully, his collar was yanked loose and some of his hair had been pulled out.

He was the angriest he had ever been. His beloved wife and child could have met with a terrible disaster because of lazy negligence on Matthew Faraday's part. 'Right you bitch,' he said, the words torn through gritted teeth. 'To the big house. I've got plenty to say to your wretched brother.'

Twenty-One

Peregrine Deedes, the man using the alias Bertie Wallace, took his place in the dining room of the New Oak Hotel. Putting on his gold-rimmed spectacles he perused the luncheon menu with avid anticipation. There were lots of fish and seafood dishes to choose from, all caught locally and offered in either traditional or regional recipes and sauces. He patted his spreading stomach happily. He was a great lover of all such food. The hotel had a fine chef, and Deedes had worried unnecessarily that his palate would be starved of delicacies while staying here. On the whole, the New Oak Hotel supplied good service, and the time spent in this village, he supposed, was tolerable.

Deedes felt he could bear it here a little longer. Indeed he had to – he was too totally in awe of Rupert Goring-cum-Jonathan Howard to complain. Goring was superior to all, and a complete bully. He was clever, and a ruthless winner in all things, and Deedes lacked the courage to end their association. Deedes fretted about what he was missing at home and, worse still, that he might even become forgotten. The 'fun' promised from this little adventure had not started yet. Goring was waiting for the right time to pounce on the delectable Georgette by first approaching Harry (gorgeous Harry, the fact that Harry seemed to loathe Deedes made him all the more appealing), but Harry had suddenly taken himself off to Falmouth. It was vital that Harry and Georgette were in the same location for the confrontation by Goring. Georgette was as devious as the Garden of Eden serpent and she mustn't be allowed time to wriggle out of the threat of Harry receiving the blaring truth about her character. Goring's trump card was Georgette's pressing need – her only passion – for Harry to always see her as an innocent, perfect young lady. Harry would be mortified if he learned of his sister's cunning and heartlessness: that a servant lay dead and disgraced in a pauper's grave because of Georgette's greed and barefaced lies.

To pass the time away, Goring had dragged them out on excursions to Redruth, Camborne and the next parish of Gwennap every day, finding places in which to eat, to drink, to be idle and to have sex. Both men had diverse tastes for both sexes and they had been fairly successful in locating suitable partners and the occasional group.

Today they would be stuck in the hotel for it was teeming down with rain. Deedes didn't mind that at all. He was quite happy to recline in the hotel lounge and soak up the Society gossip columns, even though the news-sheets and magazines were a few days old after the journey down from the capital. He enjoyed having a drink with the proprietor, Logan Kivell, who was a handsome stag of a man, of overt and thrusting masculinity. The loss of an arm did not hamper Kivell from indulging in some heavy drinking and cards, winning almost every time. Goring hated to be beaten, but Deedes found the wilder man's victories added to his terrific sensuousness. Such a pity Kivell was for women only, and he was a bit of a bore, going on and on about his adored wife and family, quite proud of the fact that his wife, and some shy little ward of his, were former mine workers. Deedes was a little nervous about whether Kivell believed Goring's explanation that their presence in the wilds of Cornwall was for 'a change of air, and a rest from a hectic life'. Kivell often gazed at them curiously but, like a good host, he never asked questions.

Altogether, Deedes found Meryen rather fascinating. Although slothful and a nightjar, he often woke early. The first morning here he heard what sounded like a low, rumbling thunderstorm, but at ground level. The sound grew and grew. He'd pulled on his corded dressing gown and slipped out into the corridor to a gable-end window. Added to the noise now was a hubbub of low voices, and the occasional clip-clop of hooves and the rumbling of wagon wheels. He realized he was witnessing the daily migration of copper mine surface workers: men (mainly older men) and women, even old women, girls of all ages and boys (some

274

rather sweet little urchins) not old or strong enough to work deep down in the hellish glory holes, all on their way to the two mines. Hobnail boots and stout shoes beat out a proud march across the cobbles and rough ground. Canvas bags swung on backs, likely holding some sort of food supply. Tools were carried, and the women and girls in their needfully short calf-length skirts and petticoats, their modesty preserved by strips of cloth bound round their lower legs, in white aprons and colourful bonnets, had – he learned later – their rough work aprons and long-flapped protective bonnets folded over their arms.

In the cool dawn light, Deedes saw that the workforce, in the main, had bright eyes and straight postures. A proud lot setting about one of their regional industries, their spirits raised by Methodism and Bible Christianity, yet also tempered as much by superstition as accident, illness or poverty. Not one person looked up and spotted him. These people took their lives as fate or as God-given, and they disregarded the place where gentry were sleeping in a comfort they didn't even dare to imagine. They thought only of the day ahead. Deedes learnt that there were artists and diary writers staying at the hotel, eager to illustrate all aspects of the local way of life, and he had taken the time to get to know some of them and to discuss and view their works. Rupert Goring was not in the least bit interested in the same, and the men went their separate ways on these occasions.

Deedes knew Goring's mind would be filled only with plotting and planning the exact time to take his grip on Georgette Bonython. Goring knew her every word and movement, via Pascoe the bellboy, Mary Nettle, who was currently at Poltraze attending her mistress, and Rumford, the butler, who was known to Goring from a previous post at a big house, and was an easily bribed individual.

The waiter, smart in pinstripe trousers and pristine white shirt and apron and a towel on his arm, who had seated Deedes and laid his napkin over his lap, asked in a tone that would very well suit a parson, 'May I inquire what wine you would like, Mr Wallace?'

'I had a fine French white at dinner last night. I think that will do the trick nicely. Mr Howard will have the same, I should think. He should be joining me shortly.'

'Very well, sir.'

Five minutes later Rupert Goring joined Deedes. 'Ah. There you are,' Deedes said, pleased that his appetite would soon be appeased.

Nothing more was said until they had tasted and approved the wine, reordered by Goring to a fruity Portuguese white. The waiter left them to decide on the menu. Deedes eyed Goring. 'You've had news, really *good* news this time, haven't you? I can tell by the glint in your eye. So, the Nettle woman has come through for you again?'

'Indeed she has. There was a very unpleasant

scene concerning the Faradays at Poltraze yesterday and consequently Georgette has returned to the farmhouse at Burnt Oak. She has summoned Bonython back to her side. He may be disappointed to cut short his visit to Falmouth but I couldn't be more pleased. Bonython is a blinkered fool where Georgette is concerned.' Goring peered up superciliously under his lashes. 'But he will soon learn the extent of his foolishness if Georgette doesn't comply with my wishes.'

'So, you'll soon be forging ahead to get what you've always wanted, a wife who is highly esteemed and will be an asset to you, and the lady will get what she deserves. I almost feel sorry for Georgie.' Deedes smirked, but these weren't his true feelings. He was something of a gallant of old where women were concerned. He could never hurt even the seediest whore as Goring so sadistically did. The notion of a beautiful young lady having to endure agony and humiliation in the marriage bed, and being cruelly controlled to breaking point, repulsed him.

'Do you?' Goring challenged, clenched-eyed.

'Well, no.' Deedes squirmed, hating to have to say it for his sake. 'She's a manipulative, lying little bitch.'

'Quite. I could have ruined her with a scandal. She would never have made a good social outcast. She knew the price she had to pay for my silence. She imprudently deceived herself to think she could throw me over. She reneged on our agreement because she knew her wings would be clipped. But she will repay me and on my terms – for the rest of her life.'

'So, I take it we'll soon be making a foray to this Burnt Oak place. Should be interesting, I'd say, even though it sounds rather like something out of the dark ages. From the looks of mine host here, and the other Kivells I've seen hereabouts, they seem a handsome breed.'

'There's to be an engagement party there in two days' time, for a Kivell and Logan Kivell's ward. The Kivells hold very wild celebrations at their original community, apparently. It suits me very well, for I have determined it will be the ideal time for us to arrive there. On explanation for our subterfuge – my broken, longing heart, and Harry having thought before that I'd make his sister the perfect husband – I'm confident we'll be welcomed and included.' Goring smiled a smile that was drenched in wickedness and the anticipation of wreaking revenge on Georgette. He pictured her panic and revulsion at having to accept his formal proposal in front of the entire Kivell family. He would do the full down-on-one-knee act, a glittering engagement ring in his hand. She'd know she had no choice but to willingly accept or suffer the consequences. Georgette was a designing bitch but entirely innocent of what a man could do to her. She'd have the rest of her life to find out and secretly lament. She was as easily deceived as her brother; unaware that her lifelong, faithful servant also retained a most selfish streak.

'We shall have to ensure we keep out of Bonython's way if he happens to come into the village before then. I can see it all now at Burnt Oak. Georgette preened and stunning in her best gown, seeking praise and honour, the things she most craves. I can't wait to come face to face with her. Then to be alone with her and to tell her exactly how her life will be.'

Deedes had trouble preventing himself from visibly shuddering. His 'friend' was evil to the core.

'Netty also informs me in her note that a Kivell girl, the sister of Logan Kivell, is soon to become formally engaged to Matthew Faraday.'

'Eh? Matty's getting married?' Deedes pushed away the glass that had rarely left his plump lips; he was drinking for disguise and courage. 'Well, she must be a very special sort. Will Matty be at this party?'

'I presume so. Anyway, I shall insist Georgette and I marry here in the village church so her whole family can attend. What a joy it will be for me to spend my wedding night in this very hotel and then return to Yorkshire with my beautiful bride.'

Deedes put on a giggle like a maiden. 'It will be riveting to watch you keeping her in line over the years.'

'Indeed, but you won't enjoy it as half as much as I will,' Goring said darkly, perusing the menu. 'And once she has given me an heir and a spare, Georgette can go to hell for all I care. You have a care for local facts. Did you know that, apart from the odd drunken fight amongst the miners, a lot of skulduggery goes on hereabouts?'

'Skulduggery?' Deedes guffawed, mightily relieved for the subject to be changed. 'You make it sound like old legends. Do you think witchery and smuggling goes on here? The sea is never too far away in Cornwall, I understand. What about ghostly haunting? No one's been horribly done to death in this very hotel, have they?'

'I'll order the mussel soup and then the mackerel.' Goring snapped the menu shut. 'There was a to-do at Poltraze yesterday involving Faraday's widowed sister, Jane. Do you remember that frigid frump the hopeless late Hugh Hartley tied himself to? Well, she'd been behaving oddly for a while, which led to a confrontation with the Stapletons. It was immediately followed by a violent episode in her house. The servants deserted the place. When Faraday was informed he decided to let things rest for a few hours. Stapleton wasn't happy about that and he discovered that the widow Hartley had gone as mad as a red full moon and had brutally murdered her companion. On the grounds of insanity she's going to be shunted off to some private asylum. A fine scandal for Faraday to contend with,' Goring said, grinning maliciously. 'The village will soon be awash with the news.'

280

'Oh,' said Deedes, somewhat deflated. 'That means Matty might not attend the party after all.'

'It will make an interesting tale when we return home.' Goring shrugged his straight shoulders with cruel satisfaction. 'I can't imagine Georgette has enjoyed her stay down here in the slightest. She might even be glad to see me.'

Deedes felt obliged to laugh at Goring's private joke.

Twenty-Two

Clemency climbed up and over a lonely outcrop of rocks far out on the downs. She was alone and would be for some time, having come early to keep her meeting with Abe. She needed to be alone, to settle her mind after all the wonderful and terrible things that had happened in the last two days.

Matthew, and the wonderful love they now shared, never left her for a waking or sleeping moment. To be his, to have made love with him and lain in his warm, powerful arms afterwards, was like a dream: a dream that would forever hold the most meaning to her. A dream that was real and mystical and timeless. It had been right and beautiful for them to make love, the essence of them being alive. They were totally bonded in soul and spirit and whatever happened to them from now on it would be a journey of magical steps.

Her love for Matthew had grown to poignant heights over his distress at witnessing his sister being hauled into the house and branded an insane murderess.

It had been with a little unease that Clemency had climbed the stairs to view baby Freddie on the morning of the terrible incident. Up until a short time before, Hattie had loathed Clemency and feared that she would hurt her child. Hattie had apologized again and again for her belief. 'I just don't know how I could ever have got such an idea into my mind, but I haven't been well, you understand, Clemency, not myself at all. And I should never have blamed you so for my scarring. It wasn't your fault. I'd quite forgotten that you had suffered great trauma too at the time. You've always been the best and most loyal friend anyone could have. If not for you, dear Clemency, I would have perished along-side Logan, and that would have been a terrible loss for you. I should never have been so wrapped up in my own little world. If not for my misfortune I might not have met Julian! My blemishes meant nothing to him. It proved how much he loved me. And if not for Julian I would not have had my precious Freddie. Oh, Clemency, I can't wait to show you my darling angel. And now at last you and Matthew have discovered your true feelings for each other. You're so right for each other. This is proving to be such an exciting day. I held up strongly against Jane and her spite, and then we all learn there will be a wedding.'

As Hattie had gushed on elatedly, Clemency saw just how much the renewal of hers and Hattie's friendship was not to Georgette's liking. She was obviously feeling usurped, an understandable emotion as no one liked to be suddenly forgotten.

Once at the cradle, Clemency was enchanted when she peered down at Freddie, who was lying on his back, chuckling and cooing and raising his arms and feet. 'Oh, he's simply amazing, Hattie.' Clemency was used to babies and children and totally comfortable with them. 'May I touch his hand?'

'You may do more than that. You must hold him.' Hattie lifted Freddie out and passed him over. 'Feel how heavy he is. He's thriving. And don't you agree he's the very image of Julian?'

Several minutes were spent cooing over the baby and there was a long discussion over his development and routine. Clemency noticed Georgette did not join in and was barely listening. Her boredom and displeasure were evident. It was no surprise she had announced she intended to leave here today. Hattie was oblivious to Georgette's distraction, and Phee was beyond picking up moods unless they were thrust upon her.

When Freddie was settled down with the Nurse, Hattie invited the women to sit in the armchairs near the window. 'Tell me how things are at Burnt Oak, Clemency.'

'Yes, Clemency, I would like to hear about the family,' Georgette cut in. 'I feel quite guilty to have deserted them when I left to be at Hattie's side. Particularly, how is dear Aunt Verena? How will she and your brothers react to the news that you are to become mistress of Poltraze?'

While Phee hummed, off in her own rambling

thoughts, Clemency and Hattie saw Georgette's remarks for the curt accusations they were. Hattie glanced down, chastened for ignoring Georgette, whom she had thanked every other day for being an invaluable help to her.

Clemency, however, would not be put down. 'The family are all very well. An announcement of an intended engagement between Matthew and I will not raise surprise or an objection,' she said loftily.

'How very reassuring. I'm sure Harry will find it all quite riveting.' Georgette was smiling but her eyes were slightly narrowed and the jut of her jaw angled too sharply to exude sincerity. 'Now, ladies, I wonder if I could crave your understanding in allowing me to retire to my room to see how my maid is getting on with my packing?'

'Of course, dear Georgette,' Hattie replied, putting on her warmest smile. 'Would you like me to call you when luncheon is ready? We must have one last intimate meal together.'

'I should like that,' Georgette replied more lightly, raising and smoothing flowing hands over her dress.

'It has been a pleasure to see you again, cousin,' she said to Clemency, then to Phee, 'Do please excuse me, Mrs Faraday.'

'Um, um,' Phee murmured, not taking in that there was to be a withdrawal.

'Oh dear,' Hattie said wryly. 'I fear Miss Bonython's nose has been quite put out of joint.'

A short time of agreeable chat passed in the room. Then came the interruption, brought in with much drama by Georgette, who returned with her hands held up in horror.

'Oh, dear Hattie! I hate to be the bearer of bad news but it seems something particularly untoward has occurred. I happened to be looking out of my window and was astonished and perturbed at the sudden appearance of Sir Julian coming fast up to the house with your sister, Mrs Hartley. She's screaming like a fishwife and he is bundling her along in a most ungentlemanly like manner. What could it possibly mean?'

Currently perched amid the silent rocks and sweeps of gorse and heather, the breeze sifting through her hair, Clemency recalled Julian Stapleton's outrage. She had rushed downstairs to alert Matthew before Georgette could perform her spiteful dramatics on him. Together, with a summoned Barker, Rumford and Mrs Secombe, they had met Julian as he hauled Jane along in the worst of undignified manners to the bottom of the stone steps. Jane went limp and fixed her mouth shut but, from Julian's dishevelment, she had clearly struggled against him most of the way. It was clear that, before he had apprehended her, she had attacked him. Now she was passive; strangely catatonic.

'Whatever my sister may have done, Stapleton, surely there is no need for such force to be used on a lady,' Matthew rebuked him angrily. 'Barker, take Mrs Hartley away from Sir Julian and untie her.'

'A lady!' Julian bawled, and the range of his fury for a usually quiet man was shocking. He released Jane into Barker's care as if ridding himself of something foul and unholy. 'That woman is nothing less than a demon. She's murdered her companion, bludgeoned her to death beyond recognition, and thanks to your crass misjudgement, Faraday, she was about to come here and slay my son out of pure jealousy of Hattie. She planned to burn this house down. And she can do just that for all I care, but not until I've safely removed my wife and son. We shall be leaving immediately. I won't have my family staying here among all this madness a moment longer. I brought my wife here as a very ill woman in the hope her family would soothe her to recovery. I had no idea there was true insanity, borne out of abject evilness, here. Your sister said this place is cursed, Faraday. Indeed it is. I thank you for your hospitality. My family and I shall never darken your door again. And take my advice and rid yourself of the presence of the Bonython woman. She's more poison.'

Julian would not be reasoned with. Throwing up his hands against all explanation he strode inside the house. Mrs Secombe scurried in after him to obey his orders that immediate arrangements be made for his party to pack and leave.

Clemency clasped Matthew's hand. He had gone cold and clammy with guilt and shame, and she hoped to transfer her love and support to strengthen him. He motioned to Barker to bring Jane close up, and he rooted his sight on her. Barker had not yet untied her, and Clemency was glad. Jane's white face had splodges of livid colour and her eyes were glazed over, except for tiny rabid fathomless pits in the centre. Clemency shuddered. Those pits seemed to reach all the way down to hell.

'There's no use in talking to you, Jane. I believe Sir Julian's every word,' Matthew said in chilled tones. 'Barker, take Mrs Hartley to the parlour in the east wing. Restrain her gently in a chair. I shall send for the doctor. I'm sure he will have her certified insane. Then I'll have her removed forthwith from the county.'

Later in the day Jane Hartley was taken away, in the care of a formidable-looking nurse. Seemingly oblivious to all and everything around her, not eating, drinking or moving a muscle, she was, in the doctor's opinion, mercifully fading fast and would not linger much longer in the world. Clemency sent word home that she would be delayed at Poltraze and why, and to expect Georgette's imminent return. Georgette went the moment her things were packed, merely bidding all a polite goodbye. Clemency then diverted Clarry and Phee for the rest of the day so they would be unaware of the terrible events and not fret too much over the upheaval. The reason for Hattie and Julian's sudden departure was put down to news of a business crisis that Julian alone could deal with. Hattie was sad about the sudden leave taking, but angry with Matthew over Julian's ordeal and, for the sake of her baby, she was glad to go.

In the evening, soon after Adela Miniver's body had been removed from Wellspring House for a post-mortem examination, Clemency had gone to the house with Matthew.

A police constable from Redruth was station-ed inside the porch to guard the murder scene. 'My condolences to you, Mr Faraday. It's a very strange and distressing affair for you, sir.' Constable Percival Noon, a man with a lightly-whiskered face, twitched his long, tapering nose, his tone regretful. He drew in his mouth as if this was the most mystifying case known in the universe.

Matthew was in no mood for patience or officious sympathy. He was angry with himself; mortified with guilt. The instant there had been a quiet moment he'd told Clemency, 'I should have gone down there immediately and sorted out the situation while it had been no more than gross unpleasantness. I might have saved Adela Miniver's life.'

'You must not blame yourself, darling,' she had implored him. 'There can be no doubt that Jane killed Miss Miniver soon after the servants walked out, and it probably would have still been the case even if they hadn't left. No one could have got down there in time to save her.'

Matthew would not be pacified then or now. Nodding curtly to the constable, he drew Clem-ency into the hall. Silently, they went up the stairs. 'Stay here, Clemmie,' he said numbly, once on the landing. 'There's no need for you to view my sister's destruction and the evidence of her deliberate bloodshed.'

'I will go with you, Matthew. I will be at your side forever. We do everything together from now on,' she said firmly, hugging his waist.

He leaned and murmured into her hair, 'Thank you, darling.'

They had both seen similar distressing scenes before. With the daylight fading it took Matthew a long while to take everything in: the destroyed room, the upheaval of the struggle, the volume and the spattered distance of the bloodstains. 'Let's get out of here, right out of this house,' Matthew said as soon as he had absorbed the full gruesome setting.

Matthew gulped in several deep breaths as they slowly began the walk back to the big house. Clemency felt his hand trembling where he held her round the shoulders. She had been horrified at what she'd seen – where a human life had been brutally ended and another had passed the brink of sanity – but she didn't have the same emotional link and sense of responsibility as Matthew did.

'I shall have that house pulled down,' Matthew said, sighing, his tall frame sagging a little in his helplessness. 'The former squire's first wife died, tragically young, in it. It was built in the first place for an elderly, mentally incapacitated Nankervis widow. I shall have trees planted over the site. Nothing must remain of it. Julian could be right. The whole of Poltraze seems to be cursed. So many terrible things have happened in the buildings and the grounds. Clemmie—' He stopped suddenly and gripped her upper arms.

'Yes, Matthew?' She gazed up at him, hoping that even if he couldn't see her eyes he would know her look was sending out all her love and devotion.

'I can't ask you to live at Poltraze. It wouldn't be fair. You mustn't go against me on this. I beg you not to try to talk me round.' He was trembling in his intensity.

Her heart plummeted to her feet. 'You mean you don't want to marry me?'

He put his hands gently either side of her face. 'No, no! I couldn't live without you for a moment. What I meant was that I don't want us to live in Poltraze. It's too morbid. It's known too much sorrow. For something so bad to happen so soon after we had become so happy bodes ill for us, Clemmie. I want us to raise our children in new and bright surroundings where echoes of violent past times won't taint their lives.'

She placed her hands over his, smiling with happy tears on her lashes. 'I'd be happy to live as your wife in a tiny cottage or anywhere you choose. So you want to sell Poltraze? Leave Meryen for good?'

'No, not that at all. I like Meryen. I have an affinity with it now I've been involved with some of its people. I'll move my parents and

291

myself out quite soon. What I need, what we all need, is a fresh start. I'll have a new house built on some other part of my land.'

'And that fresh start Squire Faraday includes taking our sister as your wife, eh? We'll have to think about that.' The couple had been so absorbed in themselves that they had not heard Tobias, who had spoken, and Adam, approaching them on foot. 'Georgette has not long returned to the farmhouse and filled us in on all the details. We're sorry about what's happened here. Mother is worried about you, Clemmie. We've come to see if you're all right, and if there is anything we can do, as a family, to help.'

'Everything is under control.' Matthew thanked the brothers. 'I hope both of you feel this is not an inappropriate time to ask for Clemency's hand in marriage. I love her more than my life and I swear I'll always do the utmost, whatever the cost, to make her happy. For one thing, we don't plan to live here, in this miserable place, after we're married.'

'Is this what you want, Clemmie?' Tobias asked sternly.

'More than anything in the world,' she responded, joining herself to Matthew protectively, her expression fierce and unchangeable.

'As if anyone could stop you,' Tobias added dryly. He grinned, with a note of caution in it. 'All we and Mama ask is that you're happy, Clemmie.' He went forward and kissed Clemency and shook Matthew's hand, as did Adam.

'It's a wise decision, Squire, to leave this place. Our father wanted it, craved it, and it destroyed him and brought tragedy to others. Too many bad ghosts and memories haunt the place.'

Even though so much had gone on today, both terrible and wonderful, Clemency was struck yet again by the complete difference in her brothers. Tobias was muscled and toned, tanned and toughened by years of farming, a typical confident and proud Kivell. Adam was pale, thin and dull-eyed, and almost lifeless. 'Are you all right, Adam?' she whispered to him. Mention of their father always shot a barb of grief and despair through Adam's heart. He blamed Seth Kivell for the sudden death of his wife and loss of his child and would never come to terms with it.

'I for one would be glad to see Poltraze as no more,' he whispered back. He spoke normally, 'We've come to take you home, Clemmie. Georgette is distraught. She's sent for Harry. Mama doesn't quite know what to do with her. Perhaps you'll be the best one to console her.'

Clemency sighed with displeasure. She didn't want to leave Matthew yet. Damn Georgette. She was a nuisance and, even more, she was a troublemaker. It had been with malicious glee that she had rushed into Hattie's bedroom and dramatized the first instance of Jane's wicked deed. She did not deserve to be pandered to. And what had Sir Julian meant by Georgette being poison? What had happened to make him say such a thing?

'I've got something to tell you, Abe.'

'I know what it is.'

'You do?'

'That our kiss was a mistake, that we'd never be suited and that things would be better if we remain as friends. I agree with you, Clemmie.'

'It isn't exactly that – well, it is – but there is something else.'

'I know that too. You're going to marry the squire. Congratulations. Mr Faraday seems a good man. I hope you'll have a very long and happy life together.'

'What? How did you know?'

'The whole village knows, Clemmie. Knows everything. You didn't really think something so horrendous wouldn't soon leak out and spread, did you? People are hoping the squire won't let it drive him into seclusion again. But you wouldn't allow that anyway, would you?'

'Matthew doesn't want to hide away,' Clemency said happily. 'Quite the opposite, in fact. After a quiet time to allow things to calm down he's going to make a lot of changes. It's just a pity that we won't be able to announce our engagement for a while.'

'Why not? Who cares about all that decorum stuff? What Meryen needs right now is some great occasion to look forward to. Get married soon, Clemmie, and have a huge wedding with a week-long celebration. Everybody will approve and love you and the squire for it.'

She laughed aloud. 'I'll tell Matthew that

when I next see him. I'm sure he'll want you to be a guest of honour, Abe. After all the chaos of late it's good to hear a voice of reason. May peace come to Meryen and reign for a very long time.'

Twenty-Three

'We should be staying here. It's so much nicer than that smelly, old farmhouse,' Georgette grumbled to Harry. They were in the music room – the former banqueting room of Morn O' May – which was the largest room of the largest house in Burnt Oak, where the extended family, descended from the original clan leader of the Kivells, lived. 'It's the size of a small house just in this room and the other rooms aren't so basic and austere.'

'The farmhouse isn't at all austere, Georgette,' Harry hissed, battling to hold up a heavy load of brightly-coloured streamers. 'Do stop whingeing and help me put these up. It's unbecoming and ungrateful of you. The farmhouse is very comfortable and well you know it. You haven't stopped finding fault with everything since I've returned from Falmouth and you haven't been a bit interested in anything that I've wanted to tell you.'

Georgette conceded this. 'What is it you wanted to say?'

'This isn't the right time and place for a discussion. We're supposed to be helping with the preparations for Jowan's engagement party. If you'd only allow yourself to relax and think of others for once you might find yourself actually having some fun.'

Georgette's piqued expression fell as if a barrage of dung had been slung at her. 'It wasn't my idea to come here and help. If that's your attitude you'll do better without me.' Sobs formed in her throat as she hastened out of the music room, feeling hurt and humiliated. She passed through the various wide passages of the house, often having to turn sideways in her wide skirts to allow room for a Kivell man, woman or child carrying tables, chairs, tableware and linen, crockery and vases of flowers for the celebration, to pass by her. Some spoke to her and she grimaced a reply; all gazed curiously at her, making her feel all the more out of place. She was glad to finally stumble out through the front porch. What had got into Harry? How could he be such a brute to her?

Walking blindly, she scraped along over the cobbled court and moved away from the buildings that circled it, a formation that gave a medieval look to the earliest dwellings, along with the craft shops and the smithy. Three of the many lurcher dogs that were bred freely in the hamlet tagged along with her but, instead of shooing them away as she usually did, she ignored them and let them go with her. She trudged to the meadow: land she had disdained traversing over before because there were sheep browsing on it and their droppings. Grabbing up an armful of her skirts to keep them off the ground she moved fast, her soft-leather ankle boots tramping down the green, lush grass. She was careful to keep away from the watchful ewes and skipping lambs, not wanting to be accused of frightening the creatures, even though she had been told they were harmless and shy. The more she trudged on the more her misery escalated. She let her skirts fall. Here and there were clumps of thistles and, although she edged round them, she didn't care if her hems got snagged. Two of the lurchers deserted her. The remaining one kept up with her as, in her misery, she increased her steps to strides. Faster and faster she went, and then for the first time since she was a little girl she was running. Running away from everything. Running towards nothing. Her breath came hard and sounded as loud as drumbeats. She was aware of the persistent canine company and she welcomed it, in her desperation, not wanting to be alone.

Woman and dog sped down and down until they reached the long, meandering hedgerow at the foot of the meadow. Georgette stopped, panting heavily, and her companion stopped, panting lightly and waiting companionably. In amongst a scattering of bramble and blackthorn was a stile of wooden steps. Georgette glanced at the dog. 'What shall we do? Stay here or climb over?'

My God, what's happening to me, she thought. Scaling a stile and clambering over a hedge would have been anathema to her before now.

The lurcher, a young female, put its head to the side. It was a friendly gesture and Georgette liked its gentle, brown eyes. 'If you knew me you'd be amazed at my behaviour right now.' A moment of rapid reflection assailed her. 'But perhaps you would not. I have a tendency towards displays of selfish theatrics. Tearing through the meadow like some lost, lamented soul would have been seen as such by everyone else.' She studied the stile. The wooden steps were solid, not too far apart and curved at the edges, so there was nothing hazardous about them. 'They say nothing ventured, nothing gained. Let's go over, shall we?' Afraid her new friend might take off and leave her alone, she called, 'Come on girl, come on.'

Bundling her skirts, she used her free hand to haul herself one careful step at a time up to the top step. It meant an undignified hoist of her leg over the final post and lowering it down on the other side to the corresponding step, but she did it, dragging the weight of her clothes, and wondering why she bothered to dress up so fussily and meticulously until the evening. She understood Clemency's desire for simple attire to allow freer movement. As Georgette mounted and descended each step the dog followed just behind her. At last safely grounded on the other side of the stile she found herself in a large pasture hedged in on four irregular sides, the facing hedge having a five bar gate incorporated in it. It sloped away to another field with cattle in it. Georgette had an idea the cattle would be put here to graze in a matter of time, she knew not how long, when they'd munched down to the roots where they now were. She was heartily glad of that; she was definitely afraid of cattle. Here and there stood a solitary elm tree – for animal shelter, she assumed. 'Shall we go over to the top tree?' she asked the lurcher. Asking a dog a question, its permission indeed, was totally out of character. It scared her. This was how much her heart was troubled.

The dog seemed eager to stay with her, thank God. All Kivell dogs had silver nameplates on their leather collars. She wanted to know the name of her faithful friend. 'Thea. That's a nice name,' she said, touching Thea for the first time. Her coat was wiry and warm and she licked Georgette's hand. Georgette would have squealed in horror before and rushed to soap and hot water. Now she didn't mind at all. It was liberating and refreshing. She was learning a lot of new things about herself today. 'Off we go then, Thea.'

On the way to the elm tree Georgette lifted the hems of her skirt and starched petticoats off the ground. It wasn't fair on Netty to inflict more damage to her clothes. She would get a chiding from Netty anyway, although since they had returned to Burnt Oak Netty had taken to nagging her and seemed to get easily cross with her. This, combined with Harry's unusual impatience with her, her crushing boredom, and her longing to go travelling and discover new distractions, had brought her down to her present low mood. Her great fear of a threat from Rupert Goring grew with every passing day. His vindictive and dogged nature might make him decide to follow her down here and demand she follow his cruel desires. She had a need to talk to someone, to offload her muddled thoughts.

'I suppose I have been difficult since I arrived back here, Thea. I've been showing a side to Harry and Netty that they don't like. Well, I can't be all sweetness and light all the time, can I? It's really not my fault. They've always treated me as a delicate creature to be cosseted. Well, I'm not a doll! No, not at all,' she repeated more softly. 'But I've cultivated the illusion that I'm precious and deserve to be showered with every indulgence. If I hadn't been brought up to be totally genteel, perhaps I might have been more like Clemency. I'm sure that Harry wishes I were more like her. I've been rotten to Harry. I was furious about his wish to return to Falmouth as soon as possible for a few more days. I shouted at him and accused him of being heartless. I believed he truly was, Thea. But I was the one who was heartless, wasn't I? I'm spoilt and selfish, and if I don't change my ways I shall become impossible to live with and I'll lose Harry's love and respect. That would be the worse thing in the world to me,' she ended wistfully and pained.

She glanced at Thea often and Thea looked up at her, as if in understanding, while wagging her long, tapering tail. They reached the tree. The ground was a little mossy and worn down and she fancied people had stopped and sat here – Kivells and their farmhands, and perhaps lovers too. Sitting on the bare ground was unthinkable ... but was it? What did it really matter? And she had already damaged her dress. Wearily, she lowered herself down and even put her back against the hard trunk of the tree. Thea sat at her side and edged her body in close to Georgette. Moved by this trusting companionship, Georgette put her arm round Thea's strong shoulders.

'If you knew what I'm really like you'd run away from me and bark at me if you saw me again. I'm quite horrid, Thea, but thanks for staying.' Georgette collapsed in hot, bitter tears, acknowledging that most of her weeping was out of self-pity. She cried and cried into her handkerchief and finally, with a groan of despair, wrapped her arms round Thea and cried against her strong warmness.

'Miss Bonython.'

Georgette felt Thea look up and get excited. Georgette had heard a voice but, with her senses dulled through her distress, she thought she must have imagined it. There was a touch on her shoulder. 'Oh!' Her heart leapt against her ribs and she threw up her head.

'It's all right, Miss Bonython. What troubles you? Are you lost?'

It was Adam Kivell. He was eyeing her warily, as he always did, and with what she hoped was a little concern.

'I just...' she dabbed at her eyes, fraught at being discovered like this but not mortifyingly embarrassed, as she once would have been. She must appear quite a sight, she thought: red-eyed, puffy-cheeked, a blotchy complexion, hair somewhat bedraggled. It would have caused a lot of sniping gossip in her usual circles. 'I needed a little time alone. Thea kindly kept me company.' She was pleased Thea did not seek to leave her side.

Adam put his hands in his pockets and tilted his head back slightly, regarding her as though she was some curiosity. 'You have not welcomed any of the dogs near you before.'

Georgette hoped he was not being disdainful. 'No, it was wrong of me. I didn't realize before what faithful creatures they can be. Thea seems to really like me.'

'You said that as if in surprise.'

She nodded. 'It's not as if I've gone out of my way to be admired by animals, or even people. You don't like me, do you?' She could hardly believe she was talking in this open way to this man of all people. It was hard to get much more than monosyllabic sentences and blank stares out of Adam Kivell, but he seemed prepared to carry out a conversation rather than quickly excusing himself from her presence.

Adam shrugged. He hated anything that upset his normal routine of quiet reflection – he knew the family worried about him, believing his continuing grief was morbid and bad for him, and they were probably right – but he didn't

303

think about people long enough to ever consider if he liked them or not.

'I wasn't lost,' Georgette said. 'I can find my way back when I'm ready to leave.'

'Good. I've—'

'I suddenly saw myself as others do, you see.' It was silly but she longed for this unresponsive man, already wanting to desert her, to ask her what was wrong. She was confused and wanted someone to help her get her thoughts on an even level before she had to face Harry and Netty again. First she would apologize to them, and she wanted to be composed so they were left in no doubt she was sincere.

'That's never a comfortable thing,' Adam returned. He was not about to allow this young woman, even a family member, to unload her cares on to him. There was her brother and her maid for that, or she could turn to his mother or Clemency. 'I've been asked, if I happen to see you, to give you this.' He drew something out of his pocket. 'Everyone else is busy getting things ready at Morn O' May,' he ended accusingly. He had put in his day's work with the stock and the paperwork on the farm, and now all he wanted was to be alone with his memories of Feena. He would show his face at the party for Jowan's sake and so his mother wouldn't worry about him, and then he would drink himself senseless.

'What is it?' She was puzzled and a little anxious.

'It's a letter.' He went close enough to hand it

304

over. 'It was hand delivered by a member of the staff at the New Oak.'

'The hotel? Thank you for bringing it to me.' She frowned as she took the letter from him. 'I can't think who would send me word from there.' Then she was terribly afraid. Could this be from...?

Adam made to politely withdraw but he saw the high colour flooding up her from her neck and the trembling of her hands as she tore the letter free from the sealing wax. He paused. As much as he wanted to leave it wasn't the way of a Kivell to abandon a woman troubled.

'Oh my God!' Georgette quelled, and then panic sent her shooting to her feet. 'Please, *please*, Adam, will you help me? I'm in grave danger.'

He took the letter from her. 'What is it? How are you in danger?'

'R–read it.'

In a low voice that remained bland throughout, Adam read the letter aloud:

'Dear Miss Bonython. You may remember me as one Peregrine Deedes, a close associate of Rupert Goring, and I wish to issue you with a warning. We are staying at the village hotel under the pseudonyms of Bertie Wallace and Jonathan Howard, respectively. Goring is planning to turn up at your family celebration tonight and, on the pain of revealing the secret he holds over you to your brother and the elite up in Yorkshire, he is determined that you will agree to marry him and your engagement shall

305

be announced forthwith. He is so confident that your brother will be delighted with the arrangement that he also plans for you to be wed almost immediately in the local church.

'You must be wondering why I am informing you of this. It's simple, really. I like to think I am a true gentleman and that I retain some honour. I want to give you the chance of escaping him, although it will not mean escaping the scandal that will inevitably follow. Goring bullied me into accompanying him down here. I had no choice. I am afraid to make an enemy of him, but my conscience will not let me allow a young lady, through one regrettable mistake she had made, be forced into marrying Goring and suffering a lifelong hell. You do not deserve such a fate, Miss Bonython. My advice to you is to flee or confide in your brother, who will surely protect you. My best wishes go with you. Do, I beg you, destroy this letter and spare me the dire consequences. B.W.'

'You had better tell me what this all means,' Adam said.

Georgette did not know what to make of the grim set of his motionless face. All she knew was the utter relief of him being willing to listen to her, yet she said, 'You don't have to try to help me, Mr Kivell. I don't wish to cause you any concern. I'll go to my brother.'

'You are part of the family. Whatever kind of person you are, Georgette, whatever you have done, that puts you under my care and protection. Do you want to follow this man's advice and run away? You've been running away all along, haven't you?'

'Yes, I...' Normally she drowned her fears in tears designed to gain sympathy but this time, although she wanted to cry her heart out, she was completely dry inside. She had been found out, not least by her own self, and there was nothing for it but to confess and bring up the whole truth. Her only comfort was that Adam Kivell wouldn't be shocked or dislike her all the more. This man who had been robbed of his life love was a good judge of character; he had seen through to her soul from the first. It shamed her to know that he couldn't be the only one to sense how she really was. It was plain to her that she had not fooled Matthew Faraday and Sir Julian Stapleton, or Clemency and her mother. Harry, after spending time away from her in an area dear to him from his past, had seen her in a different light. 'It's not a tale to be proud of, Adam.'

'I take it this Goring fellow has some sort of fascination with you and also has something on you with which he's prepared to use to force you into marrying him. What happened, Georgette? What did you do?'

Swallowing hard, her legs weak and rubbery, Georgette sank back down to the ground. Thea resumed her place beside her and Georgette took Thea's head on her lap and stroked her. 'My biggest sin at the time was that, despite the fact Harry and his parents had always given me everything I ever wanted, I coveted others' possessions. On my eighteenth birthday Harry threw a huge sparkling party for me. His gift to me was a diamond and pearl necklace with matching earrings. A recently married young lady had newly returned from her honeymoon, having taken in the whole Grand Tour. Throughout the evening she boasted of the splendid and expensive gifts her husband had bestowed on her in every city they had visited. The highest fashions from Italy and artwork from Florence and so on. Her most prized trophy was a pair of diamond bracelets she had chosen herself in a leading Parisian jeweller. At one glance it was obvious the value of her bracelets outstripped the value of my birthday jewellery. I was seething with envy over the bracelets and the admiration they received.

'I made a point of befriending the bride and, at the earliest opportunity, I stole one of the bracelets. I did not want to wear it. I just wanted to destroy the bride's delight. I knew she would never wear the other singly. People would ask questions and she would feel a fool. I meant for it to look as if she had been careless and lost it, you see. I threw the bracelet in the lake. Then ... th–then...' She chewed on her lips.

'Then?' Adam prompted, as still as a statue.

'I never meant for anyone to be blamed for what I'd done. I had no idea there was suspicion in the house of one of the maids being light-fingered. The girl was accused of theft. I was away at a weekend house party and didn't hear the girl had been thrown in gaol. As soon as I heard I intended to make a call at the house in the hope of spotting the bracelet in the lake and somehow retrieving it. I knew it was a long shot and I was frantic. Then the terrible news was brought that the girl had torn her skirt into strips and hung herself; out of fear of punishment, it was thought. Apparently, during the month she had been employed in the house she had filched a number of things and they were found under a floorboard in the attic room she'd shared. It was assumed that she had already sold the bracelet.

'Only Rupert Goring voiced the opinion that the explanation didn't entirely validate. Stealing small, relatively low value things and then moving on to one of her mistress's most treasured pieces of jewellery was, it seemed to him, rather unlikely.

'He soon made it known to me that he had seen me throw the bracelet into the lake. He didn't care about the poor maid. The price of keeping his silence to not incriminate me was to become his wife. Before that, I'd thought him much the same as any other consequential gentleman: rich and successful, intelligent and witty. He soon showed me in several ways that he was actually an amoral bully with sadistic inclinations. He lives to be the top man, to crush others beneath him, to see them suffer and squirm. He's a beast. He terrifies me. To become his wife would be to surely sign away my own sanity. To end up much the same as the unfortunate Jane Hartley.'

She had finished and, unable to look at Adam, she hung her head. He must think her a thousand times shallower than his earliest opinion. Her selfishness trailed far behind her spite, thievery and willingness to allow the name of a dead girl, although a thief, to be unfairly sullied.

Adam let out a long, heaving breath. To him, Rupert Goring sounded vindictive and dangerous. If he were continually rebuffed, he'd likely seek a lot more revenge than just ruining Georgette's reputation and pushing a wedge between her and Harry. 'Georgette, you must go to Harry at once and confess everything to him. In the light of all you've told me any disappointment and anger he'd feels towards you isn't important.'

'I see that now. Looking back just a few days ago and watching a pleasant young woman, Hattie Stapleton, fight to keep her sanity, and then witnessing her sister completely losing her mind, has made me see things at last in the right perspective. Thank you, Adam. It was good fortune and a blessing that you and I should meet here today.'

Adam regarded her. Georgette appeared the exact opposite of the spoiled, grasping, superior madam who he had loathed. It was something of a spiritual revelation to see someone's soul crushed and reborn for the better. 'The best person to help you is yourself, Georgette, and you have realized that. I will help you and so will all the family. I'll take you to Harry. I'll fetch him and Tobias outside of Morn O' May so no one else will wonder about your tattered dress. You are not alone in this, Georgette.' He reached out his hand to help her up.

She took it gladly. Except for Harry, she had never touched a man unless in a strictly formal manner, but now she lifted her other hand and feathered the back of her finger down his face, his face so cold and unyielding, his eyes virtually lifeless. 'Nor are you, Adam. We're not alone and never will be because we have people who love us and always will.'

Adam nodded and moved his face away. With Thea keeping faithfully by Georgette's side, they moved off, reversing the way she had come. He helped her up and down over the stile. She went along in silent contemplation and Adam had his head down, as usual. Every now and then he glanced at her.

Shortly afterwards, Harry strolled with Georgette to the quiet and peace of the graveyard for a long talk. Tobias did the rounds of the hamlet to inform the brethren that one of their own was under threat. Adam rode to Meryen – to the New Oak – to talk to Logan.

'I'm so sorry, Harry. After all you've done for me, the way you've always loved me, and you find out I've repaid you only with disillusionment,' Georgette whispered where they stood, gazing down at the graves of Harry's forbears. 'This is a very poor reward for you indeed. I've let you down, and your dear parents, and those lying at rest below us, and the Bonythons whose graves you visited in Falmouth.'

'It is not all your fault, Georgie.' Harry sigh-ed. 'Papa and Mama and I indulged you too much, leaving only Netty to discipline you, and even she pandered to you more than corrected you. We made you believe you were a fairy princess when indeed you were just a dear, precious little girl. We all did the wrong thing by you.'

'I was an orphan who was lucky not to have ended up in the workhouse. I should have been more grateful, acted more decently.' She shud-dered. 'It's frightening seeing myself for what I've become, but it's a blessing now that I do. What will happen about Goring? I thought you'd go straight to the hotel. I was fully pre-pared to go with you and face him and tell him to do his worst back at home. I'll sacrifice a high social life but it isn't as important to me. You are, Harry, and the Kivells, who are my family too. They're such good people to accept me for my faults and failings, to swear to protect me. I should have been a better sister to you, Harry, and I'm so sorry. I shouldn't have put so much importance on you seeing me only as perfect. That was shallow of me.'

Harry swept her into his arms. 'You're precious to me and always will be, Georgie. No one is perfect, and I prefer the "you" that you have become to the unimpeachable doll I was partly responsible for turning you in to.' Above her head so she could not see, Harry's features twisted with sheer animosity. 'I did not go to

312

the hotel for I and our kin have a different way of dealing with the insidious Rupert Goring. He's dangerously clever; so clever that he fooled me into believing he was a good and honourable sort, but he will find he has met his match in a far greater force. I want you to be brave, my darling girl, and face Goring tonight. He will not be allowed to sully your name and reputation in the slightest, and he will not go unpunished. Also, Deedes needs our consideration and protection, don't you agree? Do not fear, Georgie, everything will work out for the best, I promise you.

'Now, let us speak of another thing. Georgie, I have grown to love Burnt Oak, Cornwall and especially Falmouth. I feel the call of the sea in my blood and I have no wish to stray far from it. Indeed, I think I could not. I want you to come to Falmouth with me. It's such a different, fascinating way of life there. There is so much worldwide trade going on, so many influential people. Go with me with an open mind, darling, and see what effect it has on you. I want to settle there, to sell the businesses in Yorkshire and start a new life. There are Kivells at Falmouth. In fact, we couldn't go far in Cornwall without encountering kin. I feel I belong here. It is my dearest hope that you will too. What do you say?'

'It's good and kind of you, Harry, to give me a choice after all my transgressions.' She snuggled into him, tears laden on her lashes. 'There is nothing for me to return to in Yorkshire.

Adam has showed me the value of being your true self. Even though he still suffers his incurable grief he cares enough about those who love him to go on for their sakes. I want to be like these people here; to be more like Clemency. I don't think I could leave them either.'

Kissing the crown of her head, Harry said with warm emotion, 'You couldn't have made me any happier, Georgie. A new life it is for us then. Let's keep it to ourselves for a while longer and announce it tonight at Jowan's celebration.'

While Georgette and Harry had headed away from Morn O' May, Matthew had headed towards it. Troubled, he had brought a letter with him and, when he arrived, he took Clemency aside and placed it into her hands. 'I couldn't delay in bringing this to you, darling. Read it and tell me what you think.'

Clemency darted her eyes over the well-formed lettering. 'It's from Sir Julian. About Georgette. Oh! I can hardly believe that she would stoop to such wickedness, yet on the other hand I suppose I *could* imagine her performing such an act of despicable mischief.'

'It's to be taken seriously in any case. Julian left on the enigmatic remark that Georgette was poison. It has been plaguing my mind as to what he had meant. It seems he has been thinking through his sorry time spent at Poltraze and has linked mysterious facts together. Georgette needs to be challenged about this without

314

delay.'

'We'll go to her now. She's with Harry. This will be the second time today he will be faced with an unpalatable truth about his sister's character.'

Twenty-Four

Clemency took a good, long look at Georgette. Was her distant cousin a conniving, deceitful bitch or had she really turned over a new leaf?

Harry had given her the benefit of the doubt. Matthew had said he did, but had confessed to Clemency afterwards, during their goodbye embrace, that he had done so reluctantly. 'She sounded convincing but I still don't trust her.'

Faced with the damning words of Sir Julian's letter, Georgette's tears and near collapse from the shock of the accusation had *seemed* convincing. Clemency had elected to stay close to Georgette until the time of the party, in case Rupert Goring decided to act out his vindictive scheme earlier than scheduled. 'Be very careful, darling,' Matthew had said, kissing her hands on leaving. I shall stay as close to you as your shadow when I return tonight.'

He had gone, and Clemency had been left feeling empty and incomplete, already aching for the time when she would have him back with her. Harry had walked the women to the farmhouse, glancing swiftly at every bush and towards any sudden sound as if afraid that danger was imminent. He had said very little, but had acted cheerfully optimistic in a fatherly way, while swearing to Georgette his absolute protection. Clemency had seen how hard it was for him. He had returned to his tasks at Morn O' May, a downcast man.

Now, before Clemency could usher Georgette over the threshold, Georgette clutched her arm. 'You do believe me, don't you? All that I'd told you and Harry and the squire? That it wasn't me who took Hattie's baby from his cradle and hid him for a time to send her hysterical with worry? It was me who put him back, but I swear to you, Clemency, I swear on Harry's life that I found Master Freddie hidden behind the curtains in the corridor. I heard him whimpering and saw his little hand sticking out. I thought Hattie must have done it in a moment of mindlessness; who else could it have been? I wanted only to protect Hattie. I knew Freddie's reappearance would have been horribly confusing for her, but if it were thought she was a danger to her own child then Sir Julian might have ordered that Freddie be kept from her and that would have made her condition only worse. I'm guilty of a lot of things but I wouldn't have done a thing so viciously wicked, you've got to believe me, Clemency. I can't bear it that Sir Julian believes I'd do something so malicious.' Georgette wiped away fresh tears with her fingertips, sniffing between inconsolable little sobs.

Clemency was impatient with her. Then she felt sorry for the girl. Georgette had not had the advantage of growing up in an environment where the reality of life and its ups and downs were squared up to; where ills and distresses were acknowledged and overcome and duly learnt from. Easing Georgette into the shelter at the side of the porch, she took her into her arms and patted her back. Holding on to her tight Georgette cried on her shoulder. Clemency gave her two minutes. 'Better now? Now, take a deep breath and dry your eyes, Georgie. The truth is out and very soon that madman Goring will be dealt with. Then it's up to you to make it up to Harry; to show him you are a different person. I'll slip you up to my room where you can calm yourself. We'll drink a little wine while I see to your hair. Then I want you to find some fighting spirit. To learn the Kivell way, to be a part of it, to live it and breathe it. Together we stand and God help anyone who tries to steal our peace.'

'Oh, Miss Georgie, there you are at last,' Netty greeted Georgette, in Georgette's room. The maid was as excited as a small girl and she missed the simpler dressing of her mistress's hair and bedraggled gown, and that she was pink-cheeked and glowing, for she was slightly tipsy, having drunk a little too much wine with Clemency. 'Come and see what I've made. I've been busy with my basket of silk scraps. I've worked so hard on these. I've sat up half the night since we got back. They're intended for Mr Jowan's party tables. I do hope he will accept them, he and Miss Clymo, and that they'll keep them and find some use for them in their own home.'

Georgette allowed Netty to take her hand and lead her to a small table set in the light of the window. Laid out on silver tissue was a collection of small, delicate posies of intricately made rosebuds, in dusky pink and ivory. They were perfectly formed with not a stitch in sight. Netty had transformed many of Georgette's clothes with her sewing aptitude but this was the best example of her needlework that Georgette had seen.

'They are absolutely beautiful,' she said with enthusiasm. 'You are so clever. Jowan and his bride will adore them.'

Radiating pride, Netty waited for the inevitable clamour from Georgette to have similar rosebuds made for her. When it didn't come, Netty poked out her slim lips, astonished. Miss Georgette had gone out as grumpy as an old bludger but was now in a subdued, yet dizzy, sort of mood. It was very strange. Who had she been with? Netty smelled the drink on her breath and frowned, hiding her anger. It seemed the primitive Kivells had started drinking for the party already and had seduced Miss Georgette to their base ways. She urgently needed to be chaperoned tonight but Netty was keen to be there anyway. She asked insistently, 'Do you think I might make an unobtrusive presence at the party and be able to present my gift to the bride and groom myself?'

'Of course you must come. Simply everyone attends the big important celebrations here, all the way down to the lowest scullery maid. Oh, Netty dear, I beg your forgiveness. I've been completely thoughtless with my dress. I shall do just penance and repair it myself.' Georgette went to the solid-oak wardrobe and gazed at her gorgeous gown hanging ready for tonight. She had got her dressmaker to make up the peacock blue and green satin and tulle in a Parisian design she had seen in a ladies' magazine. There was barely room for an eighth of her things in the wardrobe and most still lay in the trunks. She had resented that. Now it wasn't important.

She wondered what Adam was doing. Exactly what he had said to his brother Logan. Was he on his way home? Or had he gone to the churchyard, his soulless eyes with the touch of death in them, to stand over the remains of his poor dead wife? A silent tear formed in her heart for Adam. She longed for a little warmth to worm its way into his being. Closing her eyes for a moment she asked God to do this for him.

She touched the filmy overskirt of her gown. 'This is my most gorgeous dress; almost like a bridal dress. I don't want people to think I'm trying to outshine the bride-to-be. I'll wear something simpler, Netty.'

'But, Miss Georgie, there's nothing wrong in looking your very best,' Netty uttered loudly, shock and impatience in her tone. 'You deserve to dress up after the total lack of proper social events you've endured down here. It will be good for you to be seen at your resplendent best. I want to see you wearing that gown tonight. Do this for me if not for yourself.'

Wrapped up in how she was going to cope during the occasion, Georgette missed her maid's vehemence. She studied the party dress. 'Mmm, no, I won't change my mind, Netty dear. It's the wrong thing to wear here. It's too much. I'd look and feel quite out of place. Any other of my evening gowns will do nicely. Now, I need to get out of this and take a bath and then have a little rest before I get ready for the party. Let's go ahead.'

While obeying her instructions, Netty kept tight-lipped. She couldn't figure out why her young mistress had downgraded her standards so dramatically, and to Netty it was very worrying.

From late afternoon the lanes leading to Burnt Oak were busy with traffic as Kivells from near and far, on horseback and in various wheeled conveyances, began to arrive for the party. Clemency enjoyed meeting all her relatives, in the main, large, extended families. To Georgette, who was wearing low pumps and a gown of fawn brocade with a white-flowered gauze over-dress – an understated but beautiful affair – there was a bewildering number of people, all indulging in bewilderingly strident ways of greeting. Many of the old and young alike bore some mark of the Kivells; some were black-haired, of towering height and well muscled, but their air of pride and dominion was the prominent feature. Most of these people were to stay overnight, crowding into the homes and anywhere else they cared to lay their head. The population of Burnt Oak more than trebled and the air was shrill with the voices and cries of reams of children.

'There won't be room for everyone in here,' Georgette said to Clemency, anxious about getting crushed. They were helping to place the table decorations and the unending dishes of food for the buffet. The smells of the countless varieties of hot and cold, sweet and spiced, and savouries were the most appetizing Georgette had experienced in her life. Netty was there joining in and, to her delight, had been invited by Eula Kivell, the mistress of Morn O' May, to arrange her silk rosebuds on the white-damask cloth of the table set aside for the enormous two-tier engagement cake.

'People won't try to cram in all at once, don't worry, there's plenty of room throughout the house,' Clemency laughed in reply. 'A lot of the men will haunt the barns, bedding down in them, drinking and boasting as if warriors of old. They see it as their right. It will be the women who will get life returning to normal in the morning.'

As the girls worked they both kept looking out for sign of Adam and Logan, in the hope of learning what had been said and what they planned to do. They noticed them soon enough from a window, drawing up in the court with Logan's wife Serenity, Jenny, the future bride, and Jowan. The women didn't appear in the buffet room. Clemency explained that they would have gone upstairs where Jenny, as was the custom, would be got ready for her special celebration by an array of married women. The men stayed out in the court, where they were joined by Harry, Tobias and other men. They held a short conference.

'What do you think they're saying?' Georgette whispered, her nerves jangling.

'Someone will let us know bye and bye. They'll do their part,' Clemency said confidently. 'All you need do, Georgie, is whatever you're told to.'

'Is something the matter?' Netty probed, suddenly there and trying to peer between the girls' shoulders.

'No,' Georgette said, quick-witted, not wanting Netty to fuss. 'We're just giggling over what a herd of bucks the men out there are.'

'They'll be planning challenges and prizes to vie for, from knife throwing at targets to wrestling and drinking contests,' Clemency explained. Such behaviour was an inevitable part of any Kivell gathering.

'Oh, that's all right then,' Netty said. She patted her tummy to settle the squirming inside it. It was so close. The time when Miss Georgie would accept Mr Rupert Goring's proposal, and a successful marriage would be ensured. It would nip in the bud Miss Georgette's slip into a reduced standard of conduct.

'That was a strange thing for Netty to say,' Georgette told Clemency, after Netty had moved away.

'Yes, a strange thing for her,' Clemency answered thoughtfully.

Pascoe the bellboy hesitated and pulled an anxious face outside the suite of Mr Jonathan Howard. Pulling at his thick, well-cut hair, he wished it were his afternoon off. He wished even more that he had not so eagerly offered off-the-job services to the gentleman who had just rung for room service. Mr Howard paid well but the tasks he'd asked of Pascoe were, from the start, uncomfortable to perform. 'Utmost secrecy must be kept at all times,' Mr Howard always stressed. After the first couple of times, the gentleman's order had seemed more a threat. He was asked to pass sealed notes, via a delivery man, to and from the butler at Poltraze, whom Pascoe guessed was familiar to Mr Howard from a former place of Rumford's employment. Pascoe was interrogated about the Bonythons and what he could glean was currently going on at Burnt Oak. Brains weren't needed to see Mr Howard was up to no good where the Bonythons were concerned. Pascoe was terrified what Mr Logan would do to him if he discovered he was, in effect, betraying him and his family. It wouldn't just be a case of instant dismissal.

Pascoe knew why Mr Howard had sent for

him. Not long ago Mr Logan had been joined by two of his brothers, and Mr Howard had rung the instant the brothers had left. Pascoe couldn't tarry. The hotel was prided for its swift service, and Mr Howard would be suspicious if Pascoe didn't arrive quickly. Pascoe knocked on the door: his own efficient tap-tap.

'Come,' was Mr Howard's authoritative reply.

In Pascoe went, working hard to keep his usual keen and subservient image. 'You rang for room service, sir.'

'I rang specifically for you, Pascoe.' The fake Mr Howard turned penetrating eyes on the young servant. 'You will have information for me. To the point, why did Logan Kivell receive a sudden visit from two of his brothers? I've a feeling it had to do with more than just tonight's party at Burnt Oak. The men went away empty-handed so they had not come here to collect anything. What did you glean? What sort of mood were they all in?'

As if a chamber labelled 'good idea' flicked on in Pascoe's mind he saw a way out of this without betraying Mr Logan and the Kivells. 'Well, at first they were hearty, as is usual, Mr Howard, but they soon grew serious. They stayed deep inside Mr Logan's office for some time, and kept their voices low. I did my best to listen, finding excuses to go pass the office. I'm afraid I could hardly make a thing, but –' he paused for effect, sure the next words he said would alter the other's hard and impatient facial cast – 'I did catch the name of Mr Wallace being mentioned. For some reason I'm sure they were talking about him.' There, he had given away some information – vital, he was certain – without really being a traitor.

Pascoe was next breathing all manner of relief inside his rangy frame, as it appeared to be enough to satisfy the eagle-eyed and distrustful gentleman. A hint of a twitch about his precision-barbered upper lip was the evidence. Without further show of emotion, Mr Howard flipped a guinea piece. Pascoe caught it deftly and secured it on his person so rapidly that only a magician's practised eye could have noticed. A curt nod from his underhanded benefactor and Pascoe knew he was dismissed. 'Thank you, sir.' He bowed formally. When he reached the door Howard ordered, coldly, 'If there is anything else return to me at once.'

'Of course, sir.'

Rupert Goring waited for the door to make a respectful click shut. He paced the fine Eastern carpet but he did not have to ponder over what Pascoe's information meant. His cowardly companion, although afraid of him, had evidently worked up the courage to remove the white feather in his heart and had warned the little bitch Georgette that her nemesis was waiting to pounce on her. All would have been well, and he would have soon been back now in Yorkshire with his unwilling bride, if her damnable brother hadn't taken himself off to Falmouth. The extra time spent languishing in this primitive backwater had been long enough to give 'Bertie Wallace' – the wretched Peregrine Deedes – the collywobbles. He probably saw Georgette as an innocent maiden who had made one tragic mistake and was undeserving of being punished for the rest of her life.

'She'll still get her punishment, in one form or another.' Goring swore under his breath, moving his jaw as if he was chewing glass. When he had finished tarnishing her reputation she'd not dare show her beautiful face in Society for the rest of her life. She would be forced to look far down the scale for a husband. No mansion, or giving a fashion house a hectic time again, for her. While staring into the nearest mirror he shrugged fatalistically. When the mood suited him he would have to content himself with some other lady to take as his wife.

Pouring himself a large Scotch, he sat down in an armchair at the fireplace and put his feet up on the upholstered leather stool. He lit a fat Havana cigar and puffed out a long stream of fragrant smoke. So, Harry Bonython and the pretenders to wealth and importance, the Kivells, believed he was to turn up at Burnt Oak tonight and force an acceptance from Georgette to marry him. They had laid a trap for him there – God only knows what form of retribution they would take – otherwise he'd already have been dealt with. He snickered. As soon as the Kivell rabble living in Meryen had cleared themselves out of the village tonight he would shoot off on his way with Deedes. Now, how should he punish the turncoat? He could not act yet. He inhaled a deep, satisfying lungful of cigar smoke and took pleasure in deciding what would be the best excruciatingly cruel fate to bestow on his two-faced so-called friend.

Twenty-Five

By six-thirty nearly all the guests, family and otherwise, had gathered at Burnt Oak, and the party was well under way. Music of all kinds – classical, rural and particular to the Kivells – was being played lustily. The Kivells liked to celebrate in the luxury of time. And food and spirits too, Georgette saw with awe, as she entered the music room on Harry's arm. The guests had brought their own noted delicacies and more and more had been compacted in on the tables and every other available place. The polished-wood floor threatened to give way under the weight of every conceivable meat – including a suckling pig – and pie, tart, cake, flan, sandwich, savoury and pudding, cheese and biscuit, nuts and fruits, and giant jugs of custard and cream. Bottles, flagons and barrels choked one end of the room. Glasses heaped like pyramids sparkled like chandeliers in the light of hundreds of candle flames. Georgette had been to many balls and receptions but the decor had not matched this radiating scene. She felt a sense of magic and history. She felt at home, she felt safe among this crush of people who gladly made her one of their own, and it helped to still her nerves and anxiety at what she must face before the night was done. The introductions to new faces were endless and she grew giddy trying to remember all the names and connections, but the more family she met the more her confidence grew. Soon she was kissing and hugging as readily as the flood of uncles and aunts and cousins who enveloped her in warm, eager arms.

She had never seen Harry so happy and she grew ever more thrilled for him and to be a part of this with him. To stay here in Cornwall was the right decision. It was a blessing. Once the one small interference that was the odious Rupert Goring was sent on his way, there would be no looking back, no regrets, just a happy life of belonging to look forward to. She laughed to herself at the thought that she would welcome taking a husband from among this handsome warrior breed of men.

Netty had trailed in to the party behind Mr Harry and Miss Georgette, her palms together and head bowed a little, like a small rowing boat bouncing happily on playful waves in the wake of a grand fleet. She was wearing her best dress, of dark-blue sateen, and the silvery lace shawl Georgette had given her one Christmas – both rarely seeing the light of day, and now sprayed with rose water to disguise the smell of mothballs. She had parted her brownish hair centrally – as was the fashion for all classes – but not so severely tonight, and had allowed an extra ringlet in front of her small ears.

'Why, Netty,' Georgette had declared sweetly. 'You are a singularly attractive woman. I've not given much consideration to your needs before but that will change from now on. If you made the best of yourself I don't see why you could not secure a fine husband for yourself; a cleric perhaps.'

'It's very kind of you to say so, Miss Georgie,' Netty had twittered, and had blushed coquettishly. 'But my only desire is to serve you and see you do well in life.'

'Oh, that will be assured after tonight, Netty.' Georgette had then given her an embrace steeped in affection.

'My darling girl –' Netty squeezed back for a moment – 'Indeed it will.' Netty could not be happier. The experiences of staying at Poltraze had changed Miss Georgette for the better. Netty was pleased, and she knew that Mr Goring would be pleased. He adored Miss Georgette and had come all the way down here to prove it. They would be the crème de la crème of Society, and Netty's status would ascend to the heavenly proportions of being the future Lady Goring's personal maid.

Netty positioned herself close to the table displaying the opulent engagement cake, absolutely amazed when told by an elderly Kivell woman that a young man of their blood had produced such a skilful confection. Pale-pink iced rosebuds and slightly darker iced twirling ribbons swarmed all over the two-tier beauty and its huge silver stand. The rosebud decorations Netty had made as a gift were the perfect compliment to the cake and she received praise from all quarters. The commendation she got from the vicar and his wife, and the surprisingly significant number of gentry present, meant the most to her. She hoped Mr Goring would notice her rosebuds before he swept Miss Georgie and Mr Harry off privately to gain his heart's desire. She kept her eye on her young mistress waiting for the blissful moment. Mr Goring would teach these Kivells a thing or two about romance. *Oh, happy, happy, happy*, Netty thought. *I couldn't be happier if I was to be a bride myself.*

During the party, Harry refused to move a hair's breadth from Georgette's side. He would remain her shield and protector in case of the tiniest danger to her, but he anticipated none, eager for the time to arrive when he could grab Goring by the throat, look into his malicious eyes, and hiss that if Goring as much as murmured a whisper to sully Georgette's reputation, he would personally rip his head off. He would make Goring swear to sever his malevolent hold over the more honourable Peregrine Deedes. And Goring would be told, in the most chilling terms, that he was never beyond a Kivell's reach. That their retribution to a hurt caused to one of their own was both swift and merciless. It was not entirely necessary to put Georgette through facing the swine. He, Logan, Adam and Tobias could have served him his just dues at the hotel, but while Goring was undergoing the full might of the Kivell fore-warning, it wouldn't do badly to ensure this was a way to prevent Georgette from regressing to her former spoiled ways.

Harry and Georgette were joined by Clemency, who was linked closely to Matthew's arm, both to show off their love and to protect Matthew from minor accidents due to his limited sight. They were also part of Georgette's guard. At intervals, Clemency and Matthew passed each other secret touches, both loving and sensuous. As soon as the drama was over they planned to slip away quietly to make love. 'It seems years since we were together,' Matthew had breathed against her ear on their first tender contact that night. 'I want you so much.'

'I too.' She had kissed him with all her love and passion, uncaring who saw. 'Not long now. Hopefully, Goring will want to make his triumphant entrance very soon.'

Then Jowan and Jenny entered the room to a thunder of stamping feet, clapping hands and roars of congratulation and merriment. Following an announcement by Logan, as Jenny's guardian, the couple took to the floor in a slow, romantic dance traditional to Burnt Oak from centuries back. All the presents were laid out in another room and, before they went to look at them, they gave a special thanks to Netty for her gift. Bursting with pride, Netty could hardly bear the expectation of Mr Goring's arrival.

Another dance was announced: *The Miller's*

Wheel. It was a stomping, raucous country affair that involved the men and women, and boys and girls, weaving in and out around each other, clapping hands, stamping to each side and whooping intermittently. After watching for a while to gain the movements, Harry swept Georgette into the rollicking mêleé.

Netty frowned at her mistress's laughing antics. Miss Georgette would never have lowered herself to join in such a spectacle before now. Mr Goring would, quite rightfully, put paid to any more such vulgarity. Quieter, more melodic dances saw the squire and Miss Clemency on the floor, she watchfully leading him away from possible collision with other couples. At the end of these dances Miss Georgette and Miss Clemency linked arms and went for refreshment together. What had suddenly made them inseparable? mused Netty. They had not exactly seen eye to eye until this. In fact, everyone seemed to be casting a great deal of attention at Miss Georgette. Her gown was simpler than the first choice and she was wearing her birthday diamonds. She looked stunning, but so did some of the other women, including the bride-to-be and Miss Clemency. Why should she be the centre of interest when, in fact, apart from the one dance, she was being circumspect? Netty hated all the noise and bustle. Her head began to throb and she found the air getting stuffier by the second. Any noise or a movement startled her now all seeming like flashes of whip cracks before her eyes.

Georgette, fortified by champagne, was quite enjoying the occasion, despite what was in store. She peered through the people, as active as grasshoppers, in search of Adam. He wasn't to be seen. The evening wore on. The cake was cut and the speeches were done. Georgette longed to know where Adam was. She visualized him in some dark, lonely place, not far away, thinking about his dead wife, and watching for the arrival of Rupert Goring. She knew, and believed it wholly, that Adam was carefully watching out for her safety.

Another noisy hour went by. The frolickers enjoyed some solo dancing from an elder Kivell, rather like the Morris dancing seen on a typical English green. Younger couples performed a dizzying, spinning dance that went on and on and grated on Netty's nerves. She nibbled on cake and tried to sip some punch but her insides were as choppy as a stormy sea. Her heart was thudding like a racehorse's and her nerves were getting shredded. *Hurry up, Mr Goring.* She couldn't stand this for much longer.

Gradually, the people began to thin out. The younger children were taken off to bed. Courting couples slipped away. Some of the men went out to the sheds for competitions of knife throwing, wrestling and other exclusively masculine pursuits. Empty platters were swept away and the white-linen spaces on the tables were quickly filled up by fresh hills of food. 'Everyone will return at midnight for another

335

round of singing and dancing,' Verena gaily told Netty. Netty longed to be somewhere quieter. She wanted to slip outside and see if Mr Goring were just arriving – surely he wouldn't be much longer – but she steeled herself to stay put because Georgette did. And so did Clemency and the squire, and Logan and Tobias Kivell, and a group of brawny men who, to all intents, were actually surrounding Georgette.

'Oh, at last,' Georgette suddenly gasped.

Netty's spy antenna went on full alert. Why should Miss Georgette be so thankful to see the odd and reclusive Adam Kivell? Why was he beckoning to Miss Georgette and her entire guard? Mr Harry gave Miss Georgette a wry look. What could that mean?

Netty thought she would scream with frustration when the select group followed Adam Kivell out of the room. Mr Goring, accompanied by Mr Deedes, should have been here by now. This must have something to do with them. They weren't coming. Something had gone wrong. And it had something to do with these bloody upshot Kivells!

'Are you feeling all right, Netty?' Verena inquired kindly. 'You look hot and uncomfortable. Can I get you some water?'

'Yes! No! I mean I am feeling rather overcome. Excuse me, Mrs Kivell, I need a little fresh air.' Netty's nerves finally snapped and panic surged through every last part of her. She rushed out of the room and after Georgette.

She stopped dead in her tracks. Her quarry

and her entourage were just inside the next room, a small parlour, huddled together and listening to Adam Kivell. Tobias Kivell saw Netty staring in and he shut the door, blocking her out. Netty's blood boiled in her brain with anger. How dare she be excluded from whatever vital news had been brought to Miss Georgette? Her little Georgie, whom she had served all of the girl's life, making sure they both had the very best of things. She was more important to little Georgie than Mr Harry and certainly the rest of the wretched people in that room.

'Netty.' Verena was there and nudging her arm. 'Can I take you somewhere for a quiet sit down?'

'Leave me alone,' Netty fumed between her teeth.

Verena did not appear offended by her rudeness, but neither did she go away. 'I really must insist you come away, Netty. If you're worried about Miss Georgette I can reassure that there is no need to be. She will be out soon and will tell you what is going on herself, no doubt. There's a chair near the end of the passage. Sit there. I'll ask for some brandy to be brought for you. That should see you right again. Then, after you've spoken to Miss Georgette, I'll arrange for you to be walked back to the farmhouse if you'd like.'

Netty swallowed the bile filling her throat. 'Forgive me, Mrs Kivell. I'm not really myself, you understand. You promise Miss Georgette will speak to me the instant she comes out?'

'You have my word.'

Netty seated herself on the high-back chair and the brandy was placed in her hands. Verena stayed beside her. It wasn't long before the parlour door opened and those holding the conference spilled out of it.

The instant Georgette saw Netty slumped on the chair, looking decidedly ill and feverish, she hurried to her. 'Oh, my dear Netty, what ails you?'

Netty wrung out a weak smile. 'Just a lack of air, that's all, Miss Georgie. What's going on? I was so worried to see you all go off like that.'

Georgette knelt down in front of her maid – the devoted woman who was her lifelong carer, her mentor, her foster mother – and felt guilty for keeping the cruel intentions of Rupert Goring from her. Adam had come in from out of the cold to tell them a messenger had arrived from the hotel. He, Logan, Tobias and Harry had assumed a backup plan if somehow Goring had got on to them. In the event of Goring wanting to hotfoot it out of Cornwall – and he had done so, by ordering his and his companion's bills and a carriage for their already packed luggage – only Mr Deedes, alias Mr Wallace, would be allowed to leave. A couple of strongmen would 'insist' that Goring go with them down to the hotel cellar. There he would be blindfolded, tied up and left for the entire night. Tomorrow morning he would find himself confronted by the men who had just left the Morn O' May parlour and, after many a warn-

338

ing – all to remain in force for the rest of Goring's life – he would, one way or another, agree to hand over any joint business dealings he had with Mr Deedes solely to Mr Deedes, and be warned never to bother him in the slightest manner ever again. He would be made fully aware of the Kivells' long reach and what he could expect if he offended them. It was reckoned he would understand the intention of Peregrine Deedes being rewarded and left in peace, and that he himself was getting a good bargain out of it all by being allowed to leave Meryen alive and intact.

Georgette explained to Netty her fears of Rupert Goring and her happy deliverance from him. 'And furthermore, Netty,' she went on softly. 'We are to start a new life here in Cornwall. Mr Harry is going to buy a fine property at Falmouth. Isn't it wonderful? Just think of the refreshing sea air. We'll have such happy days ahead.'

For some moments Netty sat in rigid shock, leaned over by a sea of concerned faces but not comprehending any of them.

Georgette rubbed her wrists. 'Netty, aren't you glad?'

'How could you?' Netty gasped finally, her tone full of raw venom.

'What do you mean, Netty dear?' Georgette frowned.

'After all I've done for you,' Netty screeched. 'To ensure that you wouldn't end up with your useless parents in some tiny cottage, scraping for a living, and me being let go and perhaps ending up in some lowly position or even the workhouse because, after the scandal of your father losing his wealth, no one else would see me as a worthy employee. Then you turn down the gentleman who saved you from public humiliation over your thievery and now you've got these shit-worker people here to send him away!'

Obviously shaken to the core by Netty's rage, Georgette rose and stepped back from her. 'What's got into you, Netty?'

Netty leapt up. 'How could you do this to me? I don't want to live in some insignificant place full of smelly fish and sailors.'

'But Netty, it wouldn't be like that,' Georgette pleaded. 'Falmouth is one of the most important ports in the world. We'll be living in a mansion house and entertaining lords and ladies.'

'Liar! No one will know us,' Netty cried, her face twisted in hate. 'You want to become a Kivell, to lay down with the men, to be part of this mongrel breed.'

'Shut your mouth woman!' bawled Harry furiously. 'Georgie, come away from her. She's either drunk too much or she's gone mad. She needs to be removed from here and sedated.'

'You'll do no such thing to me,' Netty shrieked. 'You're nothing but a scheming little bitch, Georgette Bonython. It's your fault your parents are dead. It was all for nothing. I burned down their house – making sure they perished in it –

and rescued you. They were going to ruin us both. My gamble paid off that some kind rich people would have sympathy for a tragically orphaned child and take you and me in. But it was all for nothing. You deserve to die too!'

In an arc of rapid movement, Netty flung the brandy over Georgette's billowing skirts. Reaching up to an iron wall-sconce she snatched out the lit candle and dashed the lighted end to the splashes of brandy. The flames ignited the alcohol and then Georgette was screaming in terror and pain as towering flames shot up from her gown towards the ceiling.

'Georgie, no!' Harry screamed.

As the others went rigid with shock and confusion, Clemency threw Georgette face down on the floor and tried to stamp out the flames raging about her. Adam yanked her out of the way, shouting, 'It's too dangerous. You'll catch alight too.'

Harry flung himself at Netty than shoved her bodily far away so she could cause no further injury. He joined Adam in pulling off his coat and throwing it over Georgette's legs and waist to suffocate the fire by beating on them with their hands but with little success.

'Get off the runner!' Adam screamed at the others. Tobias had already run to the kitchen to fetch water. Clemency dragged Matthew away to safety inside the parlour. Those spreading out from the music room, headed by Jowan and Jenny, to see what the commotion was about, pushed and shoved those coming behind them until they were all back inside the room. Adam wrenched the carpet runner out from under the oddments off furniture and, with Harry, rapidly rolled Georgette up in it then held it down to starve the fire of oxygen.

Netty suddenly lunged at the moaning, smoking lump on the floor that was Georgette. 'No, no, Miss Georgie, I didn't mean to hurt you,' she babbled, arms outstretched.

Harry turned on his knees and sent her crashing down by her legs. 'Get away from her you bitch!'

Clemency came running out of the parlour with a big vase of flowers.

'Clemmie!' Adam pointed to a smouldering place under the carpet and Clemency deftly threw the water there. Tobias came rushing with a bowl of water, maids following him from the kitchen with large pitchers and other receptacles. Adam pulled the runner off Georgette. Tobias and the maids formed a semicircle and threw their water over Georgette in one mad splash, saturating her and taking some of the heat out of her body. 'Out of my way!' Adam yelled. 'I'll take her to the water pump outside. She needs to be drenched.'

Clemency was part of the crowd of horrified onlookers in the back yard, desperate to know what they could do to help, while Adam held Georgette in his arms, moving her from side to side while Harry pumped the cold spring water to completely saturate her. Georgette shrieked with the shock of the cold drenching. It added to her pain and distress but it had to be done to stop her burns cooking into her and to lessen the likelihood of blistering. Someone guided Matthew to Clemency and she clung to him and wept.

He held her tight, unable to see more than flashes of frantic movement in the darkness, lit by the few holding up lanterns. 'Your Aunt Eula and some women are preparing a room for her. Your kinsman, the apothecary Henry Cardell, is preparing treatment for her from the medicine stock kept here. The village doctor is also standing by. After all the quick action to save her she may not be too badly burnt.'

'God, I pray not,' Clemency sobbed. 'Where's that wretched woman?'

'She became totally hysterical and screamed she wanted to die. The doctor gave her something to make her sleep for hours and she's been taken to another house, under guard. She will be charged for attempted murder as soon as she comes round.'

'Poor Georgie. If she survives the shock and danger of infection she'll be disfigured for life. She's changed greatly since leaving Poltraze. I was just getting to know her and like the new side of her. She didn't deserve this.' On a thought, she led Matthew away from the scene. 'Darling, are you all right? This must bring back terrible memories for you.'

'Don't worry about me.' He caressed her smoke-streaked face. 'What's done is done. If not for the fire that maimed me I would never have come to Poltraze and met you. You're worth any amount of suffering, Clemmie darling.'

There was a hush in the turmoil and everyone became still. Then came Jowan's firm voice. 'I want you all to make way for our cousin to be taken inside and tended to. Jenny has suggested we then all go back to the music room and hold a quiet vigil for Georgette.'

There was a lowering of heads and the party-gatherers parted in two swathes from around the pump. Harry led the solemn little procession with Georgette, now unconscious, in his arms. Adam followed, as soaked through and dripping with water as if he had been caught in a howling storm. Verena, Henry Cardell, the doctor and the vicar were waiting for them at the door.

'Poor Harry,' Clemency whispered. 'He did not expect something so terrible to happen when he came all the way down here to meet his family.'

Twenty-Six

'So this is Poltraze,' Harry said, having led his horse by the reins along the courtyard approach to the ancient house. He took in every irregular line of roof and wall, and every crazy chimney and quirky addition.

'What's your first impression?' Clemency asked, also on foot, her pony trailing dutifully behind her.

He took his time to answer, looking, angling his black head, pondering. 'I don't find anything outlandish about it; not in the gloomy sense, I mean. Every old house wouldn't be complete and intriguing without a few ghosts inside it. It has something about it. After all you've told me that had gone on in there, strange as seems, I think I rather like it. Is Matthew really going to pull it down? I know the work to demolish the old dower house has started.'

'He was seriously considering it. Matthew definitely doesn't want anyone else to live in Wellspring House.'

'I think it would be a mistake to pull down this old place.'

'It's the conclusion he reached in the end.

After what happened to Georgie he clearly saw that it's people, not bricks and stone, who make bad events happen. I agree. Clarry and Phee, so simple in their ways, have never had cause to fret about anything in the house since they've lived in it. They love it here. We'll probably be accosted by their spaniels at any moment.' She laughed.

'And you're quite happy about becoming mistress here?'

'Poltraze has never really bothered me. It belonged to me first, in a way, before Matthew took it over. I used to wander it, length and breadth, during the two years it stood empty. Matthew and I are about to start on some quite significant changes inside. We're going to open up the place more. Have part of the wall in the Long Corridor knocked down to let in more light. All the dark paintwork will be redone in lighter shades. There's a new butler now the scoundrel Rumford has been dismissed. We have a lot of plans for entertaining, beginning as soon as we get back from our honeymoon. It will only be a short honeymoon after our wedding next week, in the circumstances.' She smiled to herself. It was to be a rushed wedding for she was eight weeks pregnant. 'We plan to fill this house and gardens with children.'

'Quite so, large families are part and parcel of being a Kivell.' Harry was happy for her, and he knew that Georgette was looking forward to the baby's arrival.

The couple saw a dog bounding towards

them. It was Sandy, and Matthew came into view in the garden. 'Clemmie darling!' he called. 'I knew it was you. Sandy has a special way of changing his gait when he knows you're about. I see you've brought Harry with you. Welcome to Poltraze, Harry.'

'I'm glad to be here. Can't think why I've not ventured here before. Clemmie has been telling me about the changes you're planning to make.'

'Let's take some mead on the lawn,' Matthew said, after sharing a passionate embrace with Clemency. 'We'll tell you more about our plans. But first tell me how Georgette is faring.'

'The doctor and Henry Cardell are pleased with her progress,' Harry said, as they all ambled to the cane chairs and table that had been placed on the lawn. 'As you know, thanks to the swift action of Adam and the others, the burning was mercifully kept to a minimum. The scarring on her legs and abdomen will fade considerably in time. Her face, arms and neck were spared so she can be comfortable with her outward appearance in the world. It was the mental trauma that has given her and us the most concern. Dear Georgie has had to come to terms with the fact that Mary Nettle deliberately murdered her parents and plotted against her with Rupert Goring, although Nettle didn't know his true nature. She believed Georgie had foolishly turned down her best prospect as a husband. Then Nettie maliciously tried to kill Georgie, or maim her at least. After all the years

Nettle had been with her Georgie couldn't find it in her heart to hate Nettle or to want her punished. With Nettle's mental condition quite rightly established as insanity after this last crime, Georgie has found a little comfort knowing I had Nettle put in the same institution as your sister. Indeed, I have been informed they have been placed together and each is finding some small measure of comfort in Nettle acting as maid to Mrs Hartley.'

'I have had a letter to that effect.' Matthew nodded. 'It makes me feel better about my sister's situation. Clemmie tells me you have found a suitable residence at Falmouth, Harry.'

'Indeed I have. It's near the seafront. I could not leave Georgie until I was absolutely sure of her recovery and recuperation but I shall be moving in at the weekend. Georgie will follow when she is ready. For now she is content to stay in Aunt Verena's care at the farmhouse. She's very much under Adam's watchful eye too,' he went on softly. 'Adam feels he has a duty of care to her. And Georgie's happy to encourage his company.'

'It's one good thing that has come out of the whole dreadful business,' Clemency said, calling up touching scenes of her cousin walking as far as she felt able with Adam, and talking to him and being read to by him. 'Adam has found a new purpose in life at last. I believe he and Georgie have a need of each other.'

'I agree,' Harry said. 'In fact I fear Georgie may never join me at Falmouth, but –' he grinned – 'it is only a tiny fear. I will be happy with whatever will be will be.'

'We'll have a toast to that,' Matthew said, raising his glass of mead. After they had drunk the toast, he focussed his sight on Clemency.

The unimaginable beauty of his eyes enchanted her, as always. 'What is it, darling?' she asked.

'I've been thinking.' He smiled enigmatically.

'And?' She smiled back, leaning in close to him.

Grinning at their intimacy, Harry turned his head and feigned interest in a sparrow flitting in a camellia shrub.

'It will take us a few years to have the house bursting with children.'

'I suppose it would. Have you come up with a solution?'

'I know of some children who would benefit from being given a new, permanent home here; or at the very least they might enjoy a visit here to us.'

'The four Juleff children!' Clemency gasped with joy. 'That's a marvellous idea, Matthew. I've never forgotten them. Little Joe and Jacka will always need special care and this is the perfect place for them to flourish without critical eyes to bother them. Becky and Eddie would thrive with a careful education and I have the very teaching skills, and you, darling, can provide them with both. Yes, they must come to live with us. I can't wait to make plans for them.'

As they chattered on excitedly, Harry excused himself to happily wander about Poltraze alone, dreaming of his own happy future, and of Georgette's.